Praise for the *Alternate Reality News Service*:

"Ira Nayman, the author of one of my favorite books of 2008 (*Alternative Reality Ain't What It Used to Be*) is back with a new collection of futuristic news stories from alternate realities (*What Were Once Miracles Are Now Children's Toys*)... They start with science fictional tropes, then carry through to the inevitable end of the story – usually with hilarious results." (Charles de Lint, *Fantasy and Science Fiction Magazine*)

"Completely unique, *Alternative Reality Ain't What It Used to Be* is one of the funniest, most compelling and just craziest books I have read since Douglas Adams first put pen to paper." (Antony Jones, *Science Fiction and Fantasy* Web site)

"This book would make for a great ice-breaker at gaming sessions, book clubs, or conventions of the science fiction and gaming set. The short "news" stories lend themselves to a quick read and are so funny that everyone will be comfortably laughing before you have made it a few paragraphs. Nothing is without the potential for humor in Nayman's mindset, and he twists, puns, and snarks his way through the morass of human life, helping us laugh at the sometimes utterly ridiculous world around us. Be prepared to laugh when reading *What Were Once Miracles Are Now Children's Toys*." (John Ottinger III, *Grasping for the Wind* Web site)

"Amusing, sardonic political and social satire that brims with wordplay legerdemain and oddballisticelaboratified name invention. Trenchantly twisted and good fun." – John Shirley, author of *A Song Called Youth: Eclipse*

"I don't often read science fiction but when I do, Ira Nayman's *ARNS and the Man* is near the top of my list. Wacky, surreal, bizarre, and all too close to reality, Nayman spins a web of satirical hilarity ripped from the headlines." – Terry Fallis, two-time winner of the Stephen Leacock Medal for Humour.

"Ira Nayman rivals Walt Kelly for the skilled and joyous administration of near hallucinogenic word play as an antidote for the madness of our political process. And unlike the brave possum of Okefenokee Swamp, the truths of *ARNS and the Man* were crafted by someone wearing pants." – Hugh Spencer, author of *Why I Hunt Flying Saucers* and *Extreme Dentistry*

"Ira skewers American politics in a way only a Canadian can, with absurdist wit and wisdom. Short humorous Fake News articles that know they're fake and relish in their lies. (Or ARE they?) Makes me once more jealous of our neighbors to the north." – Michael A. Ventrella, author of *Bloodsuckers: A Vampire Runs for President*, among other things

"Reading an ARNS book is like going head-to-head with an selection of thirty three and a third disconnected Wikipedia entries filtered through seven layers of artesian coffee filters woven from at least three more fibers than permitted by the historic laws of any major religion in a blender made of a strange kind of cotton candy spun from titanium anodized in fairground colours with blades made of live sharks while simultaneously tap-dancing to a Steve Reich composition based on the absolute value of the square root of pi. In other words, simply and elegantly the most entertaining way ever invented to invert your brain over a platter prepared with roasted apples and a variety of field mushrooms for your own delighted consumption. Also, a hilariously skewed take on the Trump administration." – Jen Frankel, editor, *Trump: Utopia or Dystopia*, author, *Undead Redhead*

When the Soft Sciences Get Positively Runny

The Alternate Reality News Service,

Ira Nayman, Proprietor

This is a work of fiction. Any resemblance to real persons, places or things is…inevitable, really, given the nature of the multiverse. However, the probability of any resemblance to real persons, places or things in your particular universe is vanishingly small, and must, therefore, be considered coincidental.

ACKNOWLEDGEMENTS

I'd like to thank my family for all of their support over the years in my pursuit of my absurd dream. And of course, my Web Goddess, Gisela McKay, for all of the material support she has given me in my career, including designing the cover of this book, and for pushing me to always strive to be better.

CONTENTS

ALTERNATIVE INTRODUCTION

Gaze Not Into the Navel Lest You Find the Navel Gazing Into You:
An Alternate Reality News Service Forum

1.

BRENDA BRUNDTLAND-GOVANNI: You know I like these talkoramas about as much as I like getting a root canal – less, actually: at least my anaesthetist has a sense of humour! But Pops Kahunga and Pops Moobley came out of a Pops Summit with a strategy for beating infectious diseases that wouldn't hurt the economy, a song that harkened back to Sergeant Pepper era Beatles and an admonishment that we hadn't held a discussion forum in too long, so we should really do one soon. You don't mess with the results of a Pops Summit. The last person who tried was Richard Nixon, and we all know what happened to him! So. Joining me to consider the current state of journalism are International Writer, Dimsum Agglomeratizatonalisticalism –

DIMSUM AGGLOMERATIZATONALISTICALISM: Hi, everybody. Happy to be a part of this.

BRUNDTLAND-GOVANNI: You don't have to respond to my introduction. Next to Dimsum is The Tech Answer Guy –

THE TECH ANSWER GUY: Yo. What's up?

BRUNDTLAND-GOVANNI: Perhaps I'm not making myself clear: repeated interruptions of the opening introductions will introduce slapping gloves into the proceedings. Nobody wants that. Except me. But I'm trying to work within the intent of the Pops Summit memo, so work with me, here, okay? Okay. Finally, there is Fred Fleegle-Griebfleischer, our Mystery/History/Journalism writer. (PAUSE) Alrighty, then. First question. Should we –

FRED FLEEGLE-GRIEBFLEISCHER: No.

BRUNDTLAND-GOVANNI: Let me ask the question, first!

FLEEGLE-GRIEBFLEISCHER: I know what you're going to ask.

BRUNDTLAND-GOVANNI: I could have been asking if we should be giving free ice cream to every writer who gets an article in by deadline.

FLEEGLE-GRIEBFLEISCHER: You could have been. But, being diabetic myself, I doubt it.

BRUNDTLAND-GOVANNI: There's that. Still, I could have been asking what happens when a journalist meets her counterpart in another universe. If they make any physical contact with each other, do they mutually annihilate, leaving nothing but electronic press releases travelling away from each other towards opposite ends of the universe?

FLEEGLE-GRIEBFLEISCHER: You could have been, but I think you've slapped yourself from other universes often enough to know the answer to that one.

BRUNDTLAND-GOVANNI: Fair point. It pains me down to my spleen to admit it, but fair point. But for all you know, I might have been asking if reporters should be given danger pay for reporting from a universe where politicians literally float in the sky on the hot air of their rhetoric, causing a falling hazard for those below them.

FLEEGLE-GRIEBFLEISCHER: That, there, is what we in the business call a "trick question." The Alternate Reality News Service don't give danger pay. You only offer a stipend to help defray funeral costs.

BRUNDTLAND-GOVANNI: You are one cantankerous old bastard, Greeble Fleegflighter!

FLEEGLE-GRIEBFLEISCHER: You got some o' the cancerous in yer tank yerself, Gruntland-Bovanni!

BRUNDTLAND-GOVANNI: Touche! So, what was I going to ask?

FLEEGLE-GRIEBFLEISCHER: You were gonna ask if we were doin' the country a disservice by giving so much time and attention to douchenozzles – I gotta say, this time period's got some nifty cuss words. You were gonna ask if reporting on trolls who say outrageous things just amplifies their message.

BRUNDTLAND-GOVANNI: It's like you read my mind.

FLEEGLE-GRIEBFLEISCHER: After I came to this time, somebody gave me a Etch-A-Sketch. I'm gettin' pretty good at seein' patterns in a dull grey surface.

AGGLOMERATIZATONALISTICALISM: Are the rest of us going to be allowed to respond to your question at some point?

BRUNDTLAND-GOVANNI: (menacing) You have somewhere you'd rather be?

AGGLOMERATIZATONALISTICALISM: No, I mean – uh...you know, I...umm...I...was just...

BRUNDTLAND-GOVANNI: So, how would you respond?

AGGLOMERATIZATONALISTICALISM: Oh! Well, I...I agree with Fred. When people say outrageous things that could affect the course of the nation, we need to cover them, even at the risk of amplifying their message. If allowed to fester in the dark, their eruption later might be a lot harder to deal with.

FLEEGLE-GRIEBFLEISCHER: I said all that?

AGGLOMERATIZATONALISTICALISM: It was implied.

BRUNDTLAND-GOVANNI: Okay, as a follow-up question –

FLEEGLE-GRIEBFLEISCHER: We can't.

BRUNDTLAND-GOVANNI: You don't know what I was going to ask.

FLEEGLE-GRIEBFLEISCHER: I think we've already established that I do.

BRUNDTLAND-GOVANNI: Does. Anybody. Else. Want. To. Answer?

AGGLOMERATIZATONALISTICALISM: Journalists who come from a universe where cats evolved as the dominant species should not expect to be able to claim fur grooming as a business expense?

BRUNDTLAND-GOVANNI: Not even close.

AGGLOMERATIZATONALISTICALISM: When you're reporting from a desert planet, don't bother packing a harpoon?

BRUNDTLAND-GOVANNI: Okay, this is just painful.

AGGLOMERATIZATONALISTICALISM: How about: we can do our best to contextualize the ravings of powerful lunatics, but if their followers choose not to see the implicit disapproval in what we write, that is not our fault? That the value of warning the general population of the extremists in our political system far outweighs the possibility that we will be further spreading the beliefs of those extremists? Is that even close?

FLEEGLE-GRIEBFLEISCHER: Yes! That was exactly my point! You used more words than I would've, but you're young. You'll learn.

BRUNDTLAND-GOVANNI: Fred, do you want to be leading this discussion forum?

FLEEGLE-GRIEBFLEISCHER: Since you asked –

2.

BRUNDTLAND-GOVANNI: Okay. Fred Fleegle-Griebfleischer had to be sent to the hospital with unexpected third degree slapping burns all over his face and shoulders, so he will not be able to continue with the discussion. In his place, we have Francis Grecoromacolluden, the Alternate Reality News Service's National Politics reporter.

FRANCIS GRECOROMACOLLUDEN: Delighted to be here!

BRUNDTLAND-GOVANNI: (sourly) The pleasure's all yours. We used to worry that serious news was being slowly replaced by frivolous opinion. How innocent those times seem! Now, that trend has been supplanted by another: opinion journalism being replaced by entertainment. This was probably best exemplified by the court case in which Fox News argued that it couldn't be responsible for what its viewers did in response to what it aired because everybody knew that it was an entertainment network, not a credible news source. Is the entertainization of news a good thing?

GRECOROMACOLLUDEN: Everybody settles. You want *The Newsroom*. You'll settle for: *Broadcast News*. You'll get *Network*.

BRUNDTLAND-GOVANNI: Thanks for that very unhelpful statement. I'm sure the *Imaginary Movie Database* will appreciate the traffic. Anybody else? Really? Anybody at all?

THE TECH ANSWER GUY: Will the donuts be arriving soon?

BRUNDTLAND-GOVANNI: The donuts?

THE TECH ANSWER GUY: I was promised donuts.

BRUNDTLAND-GOVANNI: **You haven't contributed anything to the discussion!**

THE TECH ANSWER GUY: Is that all it takes to get donuts? Okay. Last night I binge watched season 17 of *Lug Nuts*, a reality show where guys fix automobile engines while their opponents throw nuts, screws and other small objects, many with nasty edges, at them. This is what news organizations are competing against. Should news broadcasts be more entertaining? Hell, yes! If a news show airs online and nobody's there to watch it because they're all watching *Survivor: Ancient Rome*, has it really aired?

AGGLOMERATIZATONALISTICALISM: But if we amp up the entertainment, don't we run the risk that viewers will not receive the information that is the whole point of news in the first place? (pause) Tech Answer Guy? (pause) Hello? (pause)

BRUNDTLAND-GOVANNI: Hey! Tech Answer Dude! (snaps fingers) Somebody asked you a question!

THE TECH ANSWER GUY: I don't see any donuts on the table...

GRECOROMACOLLUDEN: If I may. I believe what the Tech Answer Guy – love the overalls, guy. Makes you look really working class – is saying is that it is better to dilute the news with entertainment so that readers and viewers will pay it enough attention that they might get something out of it, than to hold on to some outmoded concept of news purity that will ensure that they don't read newspapers, thereby getting no news at all.

BRUNDTLAND-GOVANNI: Is that the point you were making, Tech Answer Guy? (pause) Tech Answer Guy? I asked if that was the –

THE TECH ANSWER GUY: Donuts!

3.

BRUNDTLAND-GOVANNI: Okay. Before we get to the last question, I should mention that the Tech Answer Guy was rushed to the hospital with a concussion because of a fall in the shower. How could he fall in the shower when he was in the studio with us? He's a man of hidden talents, The Tech Answer Guy is, many so deep even he isn't aware of them! We asked other Alternate Reality News Service reporters if they would be willing to substitute for him, but they looked at the injury rate of participants in the discussion forum and politely declined. Some not so politely. A couple downright rudely, if you want to know the truth. We'll see how they like having their thousand word feature cut down to one paragraph to fill space on the final page of obituaries! So, instead, he has been replaced by a life-sized cardboard cutout of Edward R. Murrow spray painting BLM on the side of a church. Final question: much has been made of so-called "citizen journalism." It seems like any idiot with a phone – and most idiots have at least one – can shoot a video and post it to social media and get more views than the most thoughtful journalist. Are traditional news outlets...obsolete?

AGGLOMERATIZATONALISTICALISM: No.

GRECOROMACOLLUDEN: Absolutely not.

BRUNDTLAND-GOVANNI: Well, that's that, then. I'd like to thank everybody who... (pause; sighs) I know I'm going to hate myself in the mourning for this, but in the spirit of the Pops summit memo...could you please elaborate on your answers?

AGGLOMERATIZATONALISTICALISM: Absolutely not.

GRECOROMACOLLUDEN: Absolutely, definitely not.

BRUNDTLAND-GOVANNI: Are you...defying me?

AGGLOMERATIZATONALISTICALISM: Absolutely, definitely not, Brenda!

GRECOROMACOLLUDEN: Oh, Brenda! Absolutely, most assuredly, definitely not!

Pause.

BRUNDTLAND-GOVANNI: Let's start over. You seem to be in agreement that citizen journalism does not necessarily mean the death of professional journalism. Why not?

GRECOROMACOLLUDEN: Context.

AGGLOMERATIZATONALISTICALISM: Oh, yes. Absolutely. Context. Definitely.

BRUNDTLAND-GOVANNI: (through gritted teeth) What about context?

AGGLOMERATIZATONALISTICALISM: Okay. So you have, like, a group of protesters shouting outside a church, a shopping mall or Parliament. Over a shaky video shot by somebody cowering behind a nearby parked car, you may be able to make out people chanting, "Ride a bus! Ride a bus! Ride a bus!" Or, maybe they're shouting, "No more Gus! No more Gus! No more Gus!" Or, maybe they're shouting "Octopus! Octopus! Octopus!" A proper journalist would make clear what they are chanting and give background as to why the protesters are fed up with Gus.

GRECOROMACOLLUDEN: Or, why they seem to be so concerned about a soft-bodied, eight-limbed mollusc.

AGGLOMERATIZATONALISTICALISM: There's a lot of that going about.

BRUNDTLAND-GOVANNI: Okay. Sure. Context. But it's also true that traditional media have limited resources and can only cover so much. Isn't there an advantage to having reports from parts of the world that traditional media can't cover, or from voices that you don't usually hear? (pause) Francis? Dimsum? Any thoughts?

GRECOROMACOLLUDEN: You're right. Citizen journalism is the future of information.

AGGLOMERATIZATONALISTICALISM: I'm going to set up a Tik Tok account as soon as this discussion is over.

GRECOROMACOLLUDEN: Tik Tok...is that some kind of time travel agency?

AGGLOMERATIZATONALISTICALISM: Oh, Francis!

BRUNDTLAND-GOVANNI: Aaaaaaaaand, another Alternate Reality News Service discussion forum successfully crashes and burns. I'd like to thank all of the journalists who shared their insights and experience with us, but that would be lying. I'd also like to thank Pops Moobley and Pops Kahunga for suggesisting that we do this, and you know I'm sincere because I don't want to get on their bad sides. Okay – anybody want...donuts?

1. **SPECIAL REPORT**
SOCIETY FALLS APART ON SCHEDULE

Ask the Tech Answer Guy About Just Out of Time Production

Yo, Tech Answer Guy,

After years of service, my trusty steed Rusty (it's actually a car, in case you didn't know – I live in the city and can't afford gas or the fines for cleaning poop off the street – it got its name because it's a lovely shade of magenta) has gotten rusty (too much salt in my diet has eaten away at her undercarriage, to the point where I take every bump in the road personally). So, with much sadness, I had Rusty put down (the scrapyard in my neighbourhood is at the bottom of a hill).

I went to WalMart to get a...not a replacement, exactly, for no vehicle could ever replicate Rusty's restive recidivistitude, but something I could get around in. Imagine my surprise when I found that the floor of the showroom was a linoleum checkerboard pattern alternating images of cats and dogs; I could notice this because it was completely bereft of cars!

What gives?

Sincerely,
Red from Reno

Yo, Redeye,

People throughout the country are noticing the linoleum of the car dealerships at their local Wal-Mart (that will teach founder Wally Martini to cheap out on decor!). What gave was the production process: no new cars have been produced in the United States for three months.

According to the Biz Whiz, China is to blame. The entire province of Sayshu (pronounced: shay-shu, smartass!) has been shut down because of COVID. Or possibly kaiju. Honestly, the Chinese government contains more mysteries than an Agatha Christie novel!

The problem is that three of the four factories that produce air injection dongles, a vital part of modern car engines and crop dusting biplanes, are in Sayshu. (The fourth is in Donswetz, Russia – good luck getting parts from there in today's political climate!) Without air injection dongles, cars are expensive paper weights.

I know what you're thinking: couldn't we just import air injection dongles from Europe? What? You were actually thinking that you need to come up with an excuse to get out of going to the dentist next week? What do you take me for – a mind reader? Sorry, but I'm not interested in flash fiction!

Okay, since the subject has been brought up: most personal vehicles in North America require titanium cooled air injection dongles for that smooth, smooth ride. The air injection dongles made in European factories are ceramic heated, great for race and getaway cars, but not so great for most consumer vehicles: they make ashtrays randomly pop open, radios play nothing but Wailin' Jennings cover songs, and wheels fall off. And nobody wants to deal with Wailin' Jennings cover songs in city driving.

According to Phil, the mechanic from the shop down the street, this is only part of the problem. In days of yore (not my – I'm not old enough), companies would buy and store parts so that if there was a disruption in the supply chain chain chain (as first described by famed economist Aretha Franklin), they could continue producing cars.

Not any more. Companies now use Just in Time (not to be confused with the lead singer of the Eclectic Prune Circus, Justin Thyam) production. By not keeping an inventory of parts on hand, they save money (which, admittedly, the CEO then blows on cocaine-fuelled orgies with government regulators and Congressional Republicans, but everybody has their own ideas about "fiduciary responsibility").

What happens when a part doesn't arrive in time? A lot of unhappy linoleum-gazing.

Which explanation is correct? They probably both contribute to the problem. But which is more correct? Jeez Louise, you're a tough audience! Weeellll...the Biz Whiz has degrees up the wazoo (personally, I would keep them on a wall, but I'm obviously not highly educated), but Phil, the mechanic from the shop down the street, knows things. I'm gonna give Phil, the mechanic from the shop down the street, the edge on this one. After all, he knows things about me, too...

If you are a dude with a question about the latest technology, ask The Tech Answer Guy by sending it to questions@lespagesauxfolles.ca. Just remember: I didn't say anything about Franciscan air injection dongles, because things were already complicated enough and – no, don't ask me about – seriously, that would just be muddying the oil pan, as we say in the used car biz...when the barkeep has been a little too liberal with the libations...and nobody is listening, and nobody wants tha – okay, look, Franciscan air injection dongles are only produced in a small factory in southern Italy, and they're used primarily in Vespas. They wouldn't help – what? Gregorian air injection dongles? Now you're just making shit up!

Cash May Be Crass
But What Do You Use When Credit Is Ass?

by GIDEON GINRACHMANJINJa-VITUS, Alternate Reality News
Service Economics Writer

When Rhododendron Gamete went to her local Starblox (which is
wildly successful despite the fact that its drinks are served in cups
made up of small plastic interlocking bricks which have a tendency
to leak hot fluids onto unwary drinkers and leech toxins into their
wood chip frappa-chinos – understanding the appeal is beyond the
explanatory ability of most economic theory), she was told that their
electronic cash registers were down and she would have to pay in
cash. (They were using a tray from a Monopoly set to collect that.)
No problem, she replied.

Gamete went to the Starblox on the next corner; unfortunately,
she encountered the same obstacle. So, she went to the Starblox a
blox and a – sorry, a **block** and a half away. Same deal. After an
hour and a half of futile searching, Gamete decided to forgo her
morning caffeine fix and go to work (she's a pneumatic drill
instructor); she had to take a taxi to get back into the city and to the
army base where she was employed.

A freak thunderstorm (it would have been very comfortable in
the 1960s) fritzed the electronic financial system at Starblox
headquarters, forcing the company to temporarily accept only cash
payments. Unfortunately, Gamete was a millennial who had never
carried cash; everything she knew about it she had learned from old
movies (ie: those made before 1999 – and doesn't that make **you** feel
old?).

"Dollar bills – they're just, like, colourful pieces of paper," she
mused. "So, if I, like, cut up a comic book, would that be considered
'cash?'"

When I told her that it wouldn't, she continued, "Hey! I'm
trying to take this whole geezer concept of cash seriously. I mean, I
would cut all of my comic book bills into the same size and shape –
being able to pay for my morning coca mocha del Grande is no
joke!"

When I advised her that the answer would still be no, Gamete pouted, "Boomers ruin everything!"

"I wouldn't say everything," demurred Peter Principice-Keane. "There's...well, okay, we pretty much ganked that. But...then...there is...oh, okay, we kept all of that for ourselves. Then, there's...that – don't even get me started on that! Okay. We have a lot to answer for. Still, we made some of the best potato kugel ever!"

Principice-Keane runs a seminar called "Handling money for whippersnappers and other youthful miscreants" at the Minnie Mimosa Seniors Lodge. He explained that he has to teach millennials not to keep cash in their cheeks, that there are things called "wallets" that were created for the express purpose of holding paper money. He went on to describe other things wallets could hold, eventually going on a twenty minute tangent about baby pictures.

What about more traditional financial literacy seminar subjects like saving and investing money? "Those are advanced concepts," Principice-Keane stated. "We'll probably get to them in a later seminar. But you know what they say: 'You gotta crawl before you can get a kiss!'"

I'm pretty sure they don't say that, but just thinking about thinking about the 87 year-old's private life gave me an all-over body shudder, so I decided not to pursue the issue.

When it first noticed a lot of people withdrawing cash, management at the Bank of Googie – Withers Branch thought they were witnessing a run. They barricaded the doors and donned bulletproof vests and battle helmets. Eventually, a customer who had gone to the bathroom before the emergency had been invoked, emerged and explained the situation, and the manager downgraded the threat to Double AA Obtuse (a sort of yellowish-green on the colour-coded scale).

"That was quite a scare!" said Hyram Haversham, the aforementioned bank manager. "At any given time, the cash we have on hand could only buy you a coca mocha – and not even a del Grande, either. I'm talking a Little Nell, here! So, naturally, we hoard it more jealously than...what do you think would be the better analogy in this case: Smaug or Gollum?"

I told him that, as a journalist, it wasn't my job to judge.

The Biz Whiz tutted at all the commotion. "Sure, electronic commerce can be disrupted in ways that traditional commerce could not," he pointed out. "But on the other hand, keeping cash in your mattress makes it lumpy and uncomfortable to sleep on. There are always trade-offs in economic development."

"What if I scanned the comic book and printed it on high quality paper?" Gamete asked. "Would it be cash then?"

I didn't have the heart to contradict her a third time, so I said yeah, sure, it would be cash then. So, naturally, she asked to borrow enough money to cover the cost of a thousand sheets of heavy bond paper.

Nursing: A Grudge

by LAURIE NEIDERGAARDEN, Alternate Reality News Service Medical Writer

RCMP Officer Dudley Do-Right, famed across northern Alberta for saving women tied to railroad tracks from oncoming trains, has died of a strained *gluteus septis*. Moose, squirrels and doormice across the region are mourning the passing of the stalwart civil servant.

Somewhere in the background, a horse whinnied plaintively.

Ordinarily, a strained *gluteus septis* is not fatal for a cartoon cop. The muscle, which can appear in the chest, head, right hoof or dorsal fin depending upon species and comic possibility, is usually fixed with a heat pack, an ice pick or a cup of strong tea. Why this killed Officer Do-Right is something of a mystery.

Somewhere in the background, a horse whinnied insistently.

"He was a perfectly adequate Mountie," said Officer Do-Right's boss, Inspector Fenwick. "It's a real shame he was taken from us so soon. He was only 61!"

A horse broke into the Alternate Reality News Service offices and trotted up to my desk. In his mouth was an issue of the *Frostbite Falls Courier and Beet Root Beer*; the headline above the fold on the front page read: "Nursing shortage in Toontown causing massive waiting times. That's not good, people!" The headline below the fold was: "Badenov released from Guantanamo without ever having had a trial. That's not good, people!" The headline along the fold was unreadable.

I gave the horse a carrot I kept in the bottom drawer of my desk in case I met a certain wascally toon. It seemed like the right thing to do.

Years of cutbacks to provincial medical budgets have resulted in three nurses being available for shifts at the Doctor Voodoo Health Clinic in downtown Toontown. When the COVINE pandemic, which erases random body parts of cartoon characters, hit North America, cases quickly overwhelmed the capacity of the medical system across Alberta, causing long waiting lists for life-saving ink transfusions.

"Some sacrifices have had to be made," allowed Alberta Premier Jason Kenney, "but the health system in the province is robust and will be able to handle anything. And anyway, COVINE isn't nearly as dangerous as the liberal press would have you believe – my personal assistant caught it, and she can swim just fine."

The provincial government controls the number of nurses who are allowed to graduate from medical school and practice. Would it be willing to increase those numbers to deal with the shortage?

Premier Kenney snorted (causing a derisive snort to be emitted by the horse in my office). "Are you gonna pay for them? Cause nurses don't pay for themselves!"

Apparently, you can put a price on a life.

The shortage of nurses doesn't affect wealthy toons, of course. When Michael Foster Mouse's white gloves melted off the end of his arms due to COVINE, he flew down to the Mayonnaise Clinic in Florida for career-saving treatment. Whether it is official or not, Alberta appears to have a two-tier health system (a third tier of chocolate icing might make the reality a little more palatable).

"This, I say, this is completely un-a-cceptable, son!" said Toontown Councillor Foghorn Leghorn. "You can't, I say, you cannot have beloved cartoon icons dyin' because o' some political party's health care privatization agenda. That's unfair. That's unright. That, sir, is, I say, that, sir, is downright unAmerican!"

When it was pointed out to the Councillor that Toontown had been moved to Canada because of lower production costs, his eyes narrowed and he responded, "That, I say, that is some low down goose cussin' gabflabberin' dirty pool right there!"

Burnout has accelerated the loss of nursing professionals. "It's insane that I'm the only nurse in the entire hospital for an eight hour shift," whined nurse Squidward Q. Tentacles. "I only have six arms – there's only so much I can do!"

"The system worked, more or less, under normal circumstances," said Alberta Hospital Association spokestoon Mr. Peabody. "However, when an emergency like the COVINE pandemic hit, there wasn't extra capacity to deal with the increased need, and the medical system collapsed faster than a tin can in the gravitational well of a black hole!"

"Gee, Mr. Peabody, that sounds really fast!" said his human Sherman.

"Indeed it was, Sherman. Indeed, it was."

The funeral for Dudley Do-Right will be held at the Betty Boop Funeral Parlour and Ice Cream Shoppe. In lieu of flowers that squirt water, mourners are asked to donate to local politicians who pledge to increase funding for the public health care system.

You Say There's a Diaper Shortage? Aww, Poop!

by NAOMI WOLGREEKLEISTEIGAN, Alternate Reality News Service Feminism Writer

Naomi (no relation) Guttenfarben was having a terrible time trying to create a diaper out of twigs, leaves and elastic bands.

"If you could just put your finger there..." she directed. "No, not there. Your other there. That's right....nice and easy... Nice. And. Eas – arrrrrrgh!"

When a bird tried to land on her makeshift diaper, causing the unstable structure to collapse, Guttenfarben unleashed a stream of profanity that should never escape the lips of a woman tending a three month-old.

What was the cause of the cussing? Guttenfarben discovered that the aisle at her local WalMart that ordinarily carried diapers now carried empty shelves (which caused her to fall to her knees and cry that Gord must be dead). Like many couples with small children, she was forced to improvise when the supply of diapers dried up all along the eastern seaboard and parts of Massachusetts.

For example, Nia Politano tried to create a diaper out of the silver wrappers in her cigarette boxes and Scotch tape. Fortunately, it caught fire before she had a chance to put it on her son, Pinky.

Aurelia Phytoplankton experimented with a variety of materials, including newspapers and chewing gum, dollar bills and staples, and her baby Timothea's own hardened poop. The results were mixed, in the sense that they were varying degrees of awful. Fighting fire with fire is an especially bad analogy when dealing with infant excrement.

Allan Dashyerhopabitz (what? You were expecting another woman? I said couples, didn't I?) gave his wife an extra $25 to buy materials to make diapers out of. (What? You were expecting a man to contribute more directly to solving the diaper shortage problem? I did say that this was about babies, didn't I? Messy, needy, ungrateful babies.)

"Desperation leads to innovation," said the Biz Whiz. "That's the genius of the capitalist system!" Of course, he's single, so he would say that.

In fact, the capitalist system is to blame for the problem. Production of diapers at Innovative Infant Solutions, a wholly owned but plausibly deniable subsidiary of MultNatCorp ("We do washing our hands of troubled subsidiaries stuff") was abruptly halted when a mouse got into the popcorn popper, which led to half the staff on the midnight to 9am shift needing to use the bathroom at the same time, which meant nobody who knew how to respond was there when a diaper on the liner segment of the assembly line ripped, backing up the diapers all up the chain, causing the gears in the machinery to grind until one of them sparked, ending with a spectacular fire that burned the factory to the ground.

"Sudden employee illness leads to innovation," said the Biz Whiz. "That's the genius of the capitalist system." Of course, he's never had mouse turd flavouring on his popcorn, so he would say that.

In traditional economic theory, one factory going dark would not be a problem, since there would be a large number of other companies running other factories that would step in to fill the void. Traditional economic theory is so adorable, isn't it? In reality, four companies control 97% of the diaper market in the United States, including IIS' 41%. When one of them has to stop production, no amount of powder will soothe the aching bottoms of babies all along the eastern seaboard and parts of Massachusetts. Or their children.

The diaper shortage has hurt the Democrats, who are being blamed for the shortage. "First, they make sure our babies' asses are dirty. Then, they make sure our children's minds are dirty!" decried outgoing (too bad about the primary, bud) Senator Madison Cawthorn. "We have to nip this in the bud before every American has to wear nose filters just to be able to leave their condos!"

In fact, President Joe Biden has signed an executive order directing that the Defense Procurement Act be used to get non-charcoaled factories to produce the diapers the country so desperately needs. Most of those factories were producing personal protective equipment, but continuing anti-mask activism has ensured that the vast majority of Americans will get COVID at some point, making their protection highly cowy (ie: mooooooooot), and anyway, haven't you heard? – the pandemic is over! Huzzah! So, we don't need any more of those things.

President Biden has also asked Congress to approve $32 billion to buy diapers from foreign countries and have them delivered to the US. Legislation authorizing the spending has stalled in the Senate, where minority leader Mitch McConnell Yertled: "Why are the Democrats buying foreign diapers when they campaigned on the slogan, 'Buy American?' If you ask me, something smells terrible. It positively reeks!"

"Political obstructionism leads to innovation," commented the Biz Whiz. "That's the genius of the capitalist system." Un hunh. You know, I'm beginning to think that the capitalist system isn't as smart as advertised...

When the Lungs of the Planet Become Enflamed

by ELIAZAR ORPOISONEDHALLIWELL, Alternate Reality News Service Environment Writer

The alders are angry. The elms are exasperated. The maples are mad. The firs are furious. The redwoods are pissed. Righteously. The larches are livid. The birches are beside themselves.

This woody rage has been building for centuries. Given the pace at which members of the tree community think, it would have to.

Trees first started noticing the existence of intelligent apes soon after the discovery of fire, but thought it wasn't a serious development given how few of their kind were hurt, and, anyway, the intelligent apes will learn to control the flames in time – that's the whole point of being intelligent – so why worry?

"So why worry?" is a big thing among trees.

Clearcutting of trees to make way for villages gave the tree community pause. Trees being cut down to be used to build houses and maintain fires caused some discomfort in the tree community. Clearcutting of trees to make way for the expansion of villages into towns caused the tree community's discomfort to grow to mild concern. Trees being cut down to build ships and furniture and other amenities of the modern age caused the tree community to become mildly agitated. Clearcutting of trees to make way for the expansion of towns into cities caused the tree community's agitation to turn to unhappiness. Then came global warming, which caused creeping desertification which stripped the planet of larger and larger amounts of fertile land, changed the growing seasons on land that remained fertile and was responsible for extreme weather that damaged trees with record winds and out-of-control fires.

When the impact of the intelligent apes first manifest itself to the tree community, the majority of its members thought, *if we ignore them, maybe they'll just go away.* As the population of the intelligent apes grew, the prevalence of that position shrank. By the time global warming grew to menacing proportions, the tree community grew positively irate.

Using their underground communications network (the original root server), the tree population of the western longitudes held a conference on the problem. Representatives of the different tree species debated what actions could be taken while many more listened intently.

"We could hold our breaths," said Farfnir Farfloonian, the representative for the yews. "If we stopped creating oxygen for the intelligent apes, they would all die out. Then, those of us that survived could repopulate the Life Sphere."

The yews were known among the community to be impulsive and prone to wildly inappropriate outbursts. So, it only took a week of thoughtful consideration before Gringoir the Elder, representing the oaks (all oaks were called "the Elder," which, among other things, really confused the other members of the tree community), responded, "Think of all the innocent creatures we would be dooming at the same time. It is not –"

Three days later, Farfnir Farfloonian interrupted, "It would be worth it!"

A week and a half after that, Gringoir the Elder continued: "It is not for us to determine how other species will die. In any case, we do not have conscious control of the photosynthesis process, so we could not just stop breathing even if we wanted to."

Aboveground, there was much susurration of leaves in agreement.

"The next time a big storm blows us down, we could fall on an intelligent ape," suggested Heehalligan Harhargas, representing the pine family, five weeks later. "If we disabled enough of them, perhaps we could diminish their threat to the Life Sphere."

Gringoir the Elder considered this solution for almost two weeks, but, in the end, rejected it, too. "It would be a grand sacrifice," the old oak responded, "much revered in song and story. But falling on intelligent apes seems uncertain to end their treatment of us. We cannot be certain of falling in the right direction, or with enough force to disable enough of them to make a difference. That is a good thought, but it seems impractical."

The discussion went back and forth in this manner for seven and a half years.

"I do not believe any action on our part is required," Sir Praximus Delphineum eventually said on behalf of the elm trees. The elms were the most deliberate of the trees, and they made sure everybody knew it. "At the rate they're going, the intelligent apes should destroy themselves within the next three hundred years – four hundred years tops!"

With that, the conference was adjourned.

Ira Nayman

2. ALTERNATE TECHNOLOGY

Ask Amritsar About The All You Can Eat Hate Buffet Giving the Body Politic Indigestion

Dear Amritsar,

I hate aliens from Earth Prime 4-6-4-0-8-9 dash Omega. The little blue bastards come to our universe and don't take our jobs seriously. They eat strange foods like strawberry rhubarb steak and kidney pie, and Hamburger Helper with bacon, lettuce, tomato and cheese on a sesame seed bun – just no hamburger. They stick close together in their little clans and don't make any effort to spend time with people, to get to know us.

I thought I was the only one who felt this way – other than the people on Fox News, obviously, but the one time I tried to contact Glenn Beck, I ended up spending my lunch money for a month and a half on gold coins. Most celebrities are aloof; some are downright expensive!

Then, I discovered the r/24hour2minutehate forum on Deddreddheddit. People with names like u/aliansgobakwareucamefrum and u/SecureOurTransuniversalBordersNOW! were talking about how much they hated the aliens. Just like me! I had found my clan! Now,

I don't have to make any effort to spend time with idiots, to get to know them!

Almost before the first glow of communal rage could fade away, a debate broke out among people in the forum. u/PenniesRPeople2 put forth the proposition that the exquisite three piece suits that all of the aliens wore were woven with the blood of human babies. u/helptheyeastofthem said that was stupid, that it would weaken the fabric, and, anyway, everybody knew that the blood of human babies was being used by Jews to keep their bread from becoming real bread.

Before I could even choose a side in the debate (I thought mixing blood into the dye was a viable – if gross – option, especially for those dumb innovative aliens, so I was leaning in that direction – the vertigo didn't help), a flame war had broken out on r/24hour2minutehate forum. I'm talking napalm level flames, here!

I posted to the forum that maybe we shouldn't focus so much on our differences and, instead, focus on what unites us: hating aliens. Well! I should have worn my asbestos suit (I like to be prepared for a wide variety of apocalyptic scenarios – I'm what you could call a...paredder), because both sides started flaming me!

The last I heard, r/24hour2minutehate had splintered into 27 different subdeddreddheddits. And I had only been on Deddreddheddit for three minutes!

Oh, Amritsar, why can't we all just get along?

u/AmericanHerosandwhich

Hey, Babe,

Aaah, Deddreddheddit, a discussion forum for people who believe Farcebook comments are too tame. When I was just a teenaged advice columnist, I hung out on the forums there; it was a rite of passage, like overdoing mascara and not being able to get it out of your eyes for three days, or pogoing on the subway (which is not as easy it looks, although we wore the stitches as a badge of honour).

What you experienced is referred to by social psychiatrists and cheese shop owners named Wensleydale as "the tyranny of small differences." We all need to feel superior to somebody else, but feeling superior to people we'll never meet isn't nearly as satisfying as feeling superior to people we interact with all of the time. If nothing obvious presents itself, we will find something, no matter how small, to fight about because our egos demand this trivial pursuit.

Personally, I believe the term "the tyranny of small minds" is much more accurate a description; we don't all outgrow our childish passions, do we? But where too much mascara on somebody who is no longer a teenager is socially frowned upon, hate never goes out of style.

Perhaps the problem is that social networks on the internet allow us to find communities of like-minded individuals, then amplifies our passions. If we don't let those passions out, our heads could explode (David Cronenberg has so much to answer for!). For example: people who might have been friends at science fiction conventions become ready to murder each other over who was the better Captain on *Star Blap*: Pompous or Plush.

There is an obvious solution: we must take small-minded bigotry off the internet and put it back in our town halls and evangelical churches where it belongs!

Send your relationship problems to the Alternate Reality News Service's sex, love and technology columnist at questions@lespagesauxfolles.ca. Amritsar Al-Falloudjianapour is not a trained therapist, but she does know a lot of stuff. AMRITSAR SAYS: Werewolves make bad pets. You can't train them to go in a litter box. You can't keep them safe in the house in the middle of the night. They will often bring you offerings that are too big to be birds, laying them at your feet for your approval and ignoring your disgust. Do yourself a favour: get a budgie.

Ira Nayman

Are You Future Proof?

by FRED CHARUNDER-MACHARRUNDEIRA, Alternate Reality News Service Science Writer

How can you avoid the worst effects of future shock? Get yourself future shock absorbers.

Future shock is like sticker shock, but without the drain on your bank account. Future shock is like an electric shock, but without the drain on your battery. Future shock is like penguin shock, but without the strain on your credulity.

Future shock happens when you are overwhelmed by technological change. The operating system on your computer updates without warning and you can't find any of your critical files. The light on your alarm clock won't stop flashing and no combination of pressed buttons seems to help. Everybody in your neighbourhood buys a Flamimba, and you have never heard of the technology and have no idea what it does, but you know you will be a laughinstock (similar to a laughingstock, but with 27% more Rowan and Martin) if you do not get one immediately (which is not possible because they are sold out everywhere and there is a six month waiting list to get it from Renaldo, the bootleg tech guy on the corner).

The condition can result in emotional numbness, often accompanied by a nasty purple rash in the shape of Steve Bannon.

Fly For a White Guy By Night Medical Research Corporation, a wholly owned subsidiary of MultiNatCorp ("We do life saving physical and psychological intervention stuff"), has been conducting research into the effects of rapid technological change on the human psyche since Alvin Toffler was in diapers. They recently announced a breakthrough medical intervention: The Ted Logan Don't Give a Fuck Programme.

"Is it a therapy?" explained the corporation's CEO, Kumar Patel. "Kind of. Is it a drug? Maybe a little. If you squint really hard. Is it effective in reducing the anxiety of not being able to cope with the next generation of machines? More than you'll ever know, baby. More than you'll ever know."

Patel assured me that that wasn't just because the technique was proprietary, even though it is. Proprietary...with extreme prejudice.

"I...I suffered from future shock," said Randominium Via Persona, a future shock sufferer. "I was afraid to turn my computer on because I didn't know what would be there when I did. I bought a Flamimba, but I still have no idea what it does. I could have sworn I heard the itchy patch on my shoulder try to explain why the Deep State has to be burned to the ground. I needed help. So I tried the programme."

Via Persona claimed that in just six short years, she was able to turn on her computer and tune out her rash. She still doesn't know what to do with the Flamimba, but given that the instructions are in Japanese, this is not uncommon.

"Language barriers are just the mind's way of grappling with the ultimate isolation of individual human beings," Patel unreassuringly reassured us. "And, they're really bad marketing."

Future shock disrupts beta keratin waves, communications between neurons that deal with the higher brain functions of problem solving, judgment and the appreciation of well-aged cheese. This causes uncertainty as to how to proceed, which leads to anxiety, which leads to much binging of cupcakes – mmm, cupcakes! – especially those, like carrot, that have a cream cheese icing.

While the programme has not been proven effective in adults, FfaWGbNMRC recently went ahead with the scheduled release of The Ted Logan Don't Give a Darn Programme, which targets future shock sufferers from five to twenty years of age.

This has not gone over well with child psychologists. "Children have the best brain elasticity, which allows them to integrate new ideas and new technologies much more easily than adults," explained Sue-Anne Vargas-Zots, a member of that profession. "Anybody who has watched a three year-old play with a Flamimba understands this, extinctually if not consciously."

"So, I just have to get my niece Germanium to show me what the Flamimba does?" Via Persona asked, a bit too eagerly to be entirely emotionally healthy.

"Sure," Vargas-Zots replied. "As long as you can live with the embarrassment of having to have a new technology explained to you by a three year-old."

"She's five," Via Persona muttered. "Germanium is five. It's a big difference."

When I suggested that perhaps the real answer to future shock was to slow the pace of technological innovation, Patel snorted. "Have you ever heard of a technology that was created that wasn't ultimately publicly used?"

When I suggested that I wouldn't have had the opportunity to know about a technology that was never used in public, Patel frowned and grumbled, "It's positions like that that give corporate capitalism a bad name!"

Science Offers Children a New Way to Gross Out Adults

by NANCY GONGLIKWANYEOHEEEEEEEH, Alternate Reality News Service Technology Writer

When we were children, we used to play with the Visible Man, a doll with translucent skin that allowed us to see its internal organs. We wondered if the Visible Man and the Visible Woman would have visible babies (unfortunately, their reproductive organs were not included, so our childish curiosity was not satisfied, because heaven forbid our parents would actually give us a straight answer!). We wondered if the Visible Man's poop smelled when it was making its way through his intestines. All in all, it was a wonder full time.

Today, children wear their insides on their outsides. Often to gross effect.

Researchers at the Massachusetts Institute of Technology ("We're not afraid of getting our hands dirty!") have developed a sticker that, when applied to parts of the human body, can produce ultrasound images of a person's heart, lungs, and other internal organs. Children love to collect stickers (as any parent who has had to scrape them off the walls of their child's bedroom can attest), so, after hospitals, they became the biggest target market for the technology.

Ordinarily (as if there's anything ordinary about projecting the flow of blood in your spleen in real time), the images produced by the Kinder Blutmaschine would be projected onto a screen. However, a North Korean hacker who goes by the name XL25387;;gobble (they're the poets of the technological age, hackers are) developed a programme that would allow users to project KB images onto smart clothing (clothing interwoven with nanobots that allow it to display a variety of images); it is now widely available at Amuson and many other purveyors of fine hackware on the Deep Dark Web.

Depending upon your point of view, mirth or mayhem did ensue.

For example, seven year-old Endomitrium Grublarch regularly uses the technology to project an image of his stomach and intestines. While he is having dinner with his family. "The trick is to let people eat half of their meal before turning the image on," Grublarch enthused. "The first time I did it, it made my mother hurl!"

As in, throw plates and cutlery at him?

"As in throw up her di –"

Got it, thanks.

Thirteen year-old Schlomo Schwettstein had been given a smart *tallit* for his birthday; his father thought it would be a good idea to project *torah* portions against a backdrop of images of settler encampments in the holy land (Florida) during his *bar mitzvah*. The Schwettsteins were infamous throughout the diaspora for their "good" ideas.

Schlomo used his Kinder Blutmaschine to project the ultrasound image of his brain onto his prayer shawl. There went his college fund!

"I feel for the kid. Really, I do," said Esther Cartwrong, one of the MIT researchers who developed the Kinder Blutmaschine. "But MIT and its corporate partners cannot be held responsible for any unauthorized use of our patented technologies. This is very clearly stated in paragraph 237 of the End User Licence Agreement."

Besides, Cartwrong added, even at MIT they had heard about the Schwettsteins' "good ideas." "Schlomo wouldn't have lasted five minutes at any respectable college," she sniffed.

Not all young people use their Kinder Blutmaschine to upset adults; for many teenagers, it is an exciting new addition to mating rituals. When a girl sees a boy she is infatuated with, for instance, she can project the image of a beating heart onto her chest. Boys will also project images of their beating hearts on their clothes to indicate romantic interest; however, because they are generally not as emotionally demonstrative as girls, they often only project a smaller image on their arms or shoulders.

It gives the phrase "wearing your heart on your sleeve" a whole new meaning!

Conversely, when they are not interested in a boy who is interested in them, teenage girls have used the technology to express their disdain for his attention. Some project their jugular veins on their shirts (to indicate that they would rather slit their own throats than go out with the boy); others project the inner workings of their middle fingers (if you are not familiar with this gesture, you must lead a very sheltered life, indeed, although the ability to see one's blood run through the digit adds a new dimension to the scorn).

"I wouldn't worry too much about it," counselled Alternate Reality News Service advice columnist Amritsar Al-Falloudjianapour. "The children will soon grow out of using this new technology to gross out their parents. As parents themselves, they will switch to using it to gross out their children. That's the cycle of technology!"

Charlie Nuggets is All Wet!

by NANCY GONGLIKWANYEOHEEEEEEEH, Alternate Reality News Service Technology Writer

They all laughed when Joe Btfsplk (it was the depression – nobody could afford vowels for their last names) would appear with a rain cloud over his head. For Joe Nuggets, a rain cloud constantly over his head isn't a metaphor for bad luck, it is fast becoming a way of life.

"I've almost gotten used to the soggy feeling," Nuggets complained, "but, at the rate I'm going, the cost of constantly replacing umbrellas will bankrupt me in seven years and three months!"

Nuggets, the bursar for the University of Taking a Bath, noted that the cloud appeared over his head six days and 12 hours after his first date with Marian Killhusband, a professor of dead romance languages at the University. "But I...I'm sure that's just a coincidence," he commented.

"Coincidence my adorable dimply arse!" Killhusband commented back at him. "This is Gerrard's fault. He could never accept that it was all over between us! If I ever get my hands on that weasel, there'll be weasel soup for the entire department!"

Gerrard Batfoosplak, senior researcher in the Department of Fringe Science of Taking a Bath University?

"I sure as crumble wasn't talking about Gerrard Bafootasplak, senior researcher in the Department of Warehouse 13, was I?" Killhusband roared.

Apparently not.

"I have no idea what Marian is talking about," Batfoosplak said from behind the desk in his cubbyhole office. "I wish her and – * SOB * – Chicken Nuggets all the happiness in the...in the...okay, world may be overstating the case – all the happiness in the Commonwealth. The UK? Okay, all the happiness in Taking a Bath. And that's my final – * SOB * – offer!"

I couldn't help but notice that a photograph of Nuggets banging an office stapler (as opposed to a civilian stapler) vending machine that appeared to be shorting out because of the rain falling on it had been pinned to a dart board on the back of the door to his cubbyhole.

"What, that?" Batfoosplak responded in what he probably thought was an off-hand way, but came across as more of an off-spleen way. "I'm just practising for the weekly darts tournament down by the Bat and Balloonatic."

When I pointed out that the cubbyhole was so small he could place the darts on the board, Batfoosplak mumbled something about the house rules at the pub being very generous.

The Rain in Spain is a Big Pain Again, one of the research projects listed on the Department of Fringe Science's web page, is a machine that would use electrical impulses to induce coy water droplets in the atmosphere to commit to becoming rain. This romantic notion would be of benefit to deserts, farmlands and the Egyptian Casino in Las Vegas.

"Gerrard has nothing to do with our research," claimed Oliphant "Spaghetti" Serenghetti, lead researcher on the Rain Spain Pain project. "Although, now that you mention it, he has been helping us with tech support for the past couple of months, even though he doesn't know a byte on the computer from a byte on the arse! I wonder why I didn't see that before. No matter – I'll have a talk with the lad. I'm sure we'll be able to sort this out."

"Have a talk with the – glub!" Nuggets exclaimed. Spitting out a mouthful of water, he continued: "He's ruining my life! The time for talk is past – what we need now is a good disciplinary hearing!"

To date, Nuggets has been barred from eight movie theatres and six restaurants. "It's the water damage, you see," said Cassandra Caerpaerts, the owner of the Didn't See That One Coming Cafe. "Charlie's a nice guy and all, but I can't afford to close down part of the cafe every couple of weeks to repair the floor and walls!"

Killhusband had conflicted feelings. "Charlie is dreamy...in a sodden sort of way," she told me. "Poor sod. But I can't have him over – my cats hate the rain! Furball on Legs runs around in circles and has to be given a catnip cocktail to calm down, and Mungo Geraldine plots revenge on the bottom level of her cat tree – the one universally acknowledged as the driest level of them all – until the rain stops."

If something wasn't done to stop the personal precipitation soon, Nuggets said that he could lose his research fellowship at the University. "Electronics and water don't mix," he glumly intoned. "I prove that every day..."

"Tough break," Batfoosplak snickered. "Still, Charlie could always get a job standing in a farmer's field during growing season in the middle of the worst dry spell since last year. Hell, if he played his cards right, he could get double pay for being a scarecrow! You've always got to look on the bright side..."

Johnny Got Burnered

by NANCY GONGLIKWANYEOHEEEEEEEH, Alternate Reality News Service Technology Writer

Johnny Darwin-Hippes was just an average Josephine trying to make a dishonest living at the intersection of Commerce and Criminality (formerly Dundas and Jarvis – Toronto may have gone a little overboard with the whole street renaming thing). He was a Product Sales Rep (formerly "drug dealer" – the illegal substance industry may have gone a little overboard with the whole corporate respectability thing) peddling crrnk – a powerful hallucinogenic laxative – to users from his corner. But on a bright summer's day in February, Darwin-Hippes' business was severely threatened.

Had the RCMP cut off his gang's supply of the drug from Venezuevuvazela? Cha, right! Those losers? Had another gang member tried to muscle in on his corner? Puh leaze! Those losers? Had an oversupply of the drug caused prices to plummet? Are you out of your tree? Those lo – actually, that was always a possible problem, but the higher ups were careful to match demand with supply so that it never got too out of control. (Oh, and if you need help getting back into your tree, **what do I look like? An anti-social worker?**)

No. The problem was that the supply of burner phones had dried up.

Burners are cheap phones that you use once and throw away (kind of like that boy toy you hooked up with last night, but with far less potential for regret). They enable the drug trade by making communications between gang members harder to trace than an image of a polar bear in a snowstorm using card stock paper in the middle of the night during a power outage.

Why would burner phones suddenly be so hard to get? Because the Canadian government wanted to fly close to the sun (in what must be the most colourful metaphor of my writing career). Six months ago, it bought Icarus, a piece of malware (not something you cook a casserole in) that quietly installs itself on phones and runs them when you're not looking.

Hey! – was that Kim Mitchell going for a soda? When you turned your head to look, Icarus downloaded all of your contacts and location information, not to mention your current *Angry Crustaceans* stats, to one of its servers. Weary from the day to day struggle of existence? When you rubbed your eyes, Icarus turned on your phone's camera to see what was going on around you. Did you...did you just blink? Boy, you're really in trouble, now!

The programme was supposed to fight crime (sorry, Johnny!). However an investigation by an international consortium of journalists (and France) released last week showed that the software was being used to monitor social activists, journalists and bankers and corporate executives. Bankers and corporate executives! When it was revealed that they were targets, the bankers and corporate executives did what bankers and corporate executives do best.

They panicked.

They quickly gobbled up the available supply of burner phones. Then, they started buying and selling burner phone futures. Seeing the market heating up, investment funds began buying up burner phone futures. The frenzy was unprecedented (at least since last week's Tulip™ Mania). At one point, Elon Musk bought International Confabulation, a producer of cell phones, to ensure himself a steady supply of burners.

"It ain't right!" Darwin-Hippes complained. "I got six mouths to feed – and a couple of kids! How'm I supposed to take care of those I tolerate when my lines of communication have gone kafluey! Man, I tell ya, it's times like this that make me rethink my commitment to capitalism!"

Other drug dealers appear to agree. A consortium of gangs, mobs and sundry baddies has petitioned the federal government for relief. "They bailed out the auto industry," pointed out Jackie O...noyoudint, who worked a corner three streets down from

Darwin-Hippes. "I mean, cars, sure, they're good for a lot of things. But, what we sell is far more popular!"

Republican Party lead – sorry, did I say Republican? I meant Plutocratic. Canadian Plutocratic Party leader Donald O'Toole said that while he didn't generally favour corporate bailouts, this could be an exception. "We – small business – are the – small business – party of small business. And small business doesn't get much smaller than a gangbanger – small business – and his crew trying to sell – small business – their product – small business – on a street corner!"

Prime Minister Justin Trudeau sighed and said, "We live in strange times, don't we?"

Space Invaders – The Next Generation

by GIDEON GINRACHMANJINJa-VITUS, Alternate Reality News Service Economics Writer

After two years of working at home, Lydia Hatrackian was ready to strangle a ferret. And not a North American ferret, either: an Australian ferret. A ferret that fights back.

Even though she was putting in 28 hour work days as an advertising copywriter (some day, if she worked hard enough at it, she might actually come up with original tag lines), the isolation made her feel like she wasn't actually working. Since she knew she wasn't having fun, the fact that she was always tired confused the bejeebers out of her.

And she had always held tight to her bejeebers.

So Hatrackian signed on to VirtWork, where, for a flat fee (although added features made the fee look fat), she could attend a Zoom session with half a dozen people she didn't know to feel like she was back in an office.

"At first, I was wary of working with strangers," Hatrackian admitted. "But then, when I remembered what horrible people I had to work with in my office before COVID shut it down, I thought this was actually better. Hey, since I have your attention, what do you think would be more effective selling vacuum cleaners? 'You are the light at the end of the kimono?' Or, 'You are the light at the end of the *Mononoke*?'"

While the possibility of having her work progress monitored by complete strangers was comforting, after a while Hatrackian started to feel that there was something missing from the experience. After an extensive internet search (it lasted almost three minutes!), she signed up with Hardly Workin', a company that promised to "recreate the true office experience for those working in Zoom caves."

Hardly Workin' developed bots that would randomly insert themselves into the Zoom feeds of workers. They would start every conversation with, "Hey! How's it goin'?" Then, they would go on about the weather, how terrible their co-workers are, how terrible bosses are and random subjects like whether wood is the new southern comfort, or what to do when confronted with a baby's arm holding an apple. The bots were equipped with a sophisticated program that analyzed clients' responses and determined the line at which their banter was interfering with client productivity; they kept talking for four and a half minutes after that because, you know, the true office experience.

"Now," Hatrackain enthused, "it's a work party!"

The company also issued random memos to clients purporting to come from management with messages that ranged from typical corporate flummery ("Productivity was down 48% last quarter – work harder, or China's going to drink our milkshake!"), to motivation ("The cow that eats the most grass gets the biggest promotional plaques!"), to the philosophical ("Would the you of yesterday even recognize the haircut of the lover of the you of tomorrow?"). Every third memo had something to do with the office kitchenette (whether it's keeping the counter clean, being sure to refill the coffeemaker with water when you see it getting low or not bringing Wombat Chow in a plastic container and leaving it in the fridge to punish whoever has been taking everybody else's food without permission).

"The content of the memos is largely irrelevant," explained Hardly Workin' CEO Hartley Walken. "We expect them to be ignored...just like in real life. But people who have been working from home for so long seem to take comfort in the idea that there is a distant corporate bureaucracy whose sole purpose for existence seems to be to interfere with them getting their jobs done."

For additional fees, clients can have an even fuller office experience. The Gold Plated Package, for instance, promises monthly Zoom meetings on productivity (staffed by homeless people – "Just our contribution to making the world a better place...and they don't demand dental benefits!" Walken allowed) and/or (the most indecisive of conjunctions) quarterly Zoom seminars on workplace wellness.

"We make these sessions as fact-free as possible," Walken stated. "It's an important element in making our customers feel like they are back at work in the real world!"

Hatrackian was intrigued by the Gold Plated Package, but didn't believe she could afford it at this time. "Maybe if I work 36 hours a day," she mused. "Yeah, yeah, then I could go for the Gold. And a good thing, too, because then I would need it!"

Endless Power at Your Fingertips

by NANCY GONGLIKWANYEOHEEEEEEEH, Alternate Reality News Service Technology Writer

Sanderson Delft dreamed of killing Jerzy Kosinski. Most often, this involved using a smelt to saw through the safety bar of a roller coaster so that he could throw the author out of the car when it reached its highest point. Sometimes it involved a contraption involving so many coils, balls rolling down ramps, dominoes and popping balloons that it would have made Rube Goldberg dizzy, all to deliver a spoonful of arsenic in Kosinski's morning tea. Once, it involved a curare-laced dart blown from two miles away (he had a military-grade scope).

There were two problems with Delft's dreams: Kosinski had died in 1991, and Delft had no idea who he was. He had never read *The Painted Bird*. He had never seen *Being There*. The only reason he knew it was Jerzy Kosinski was that he always screamed, "Jerzy Kosinski, this is for Omaha!" before committing the murder.

Delft was not the only person who dreamed of killing dead authors they had never heard of. Clementine Obsidian dreamed she killed Upton Sinclair by buying him an all-inclusive weekend ski vacation to the Alps, where her yodeling caused an avalanche that engulfed him (in fact, he died before she was born). Marci Chicklets (of the Dingle Dell Chickletses) dreamed that Art Buchwald died of asphyxiation when she tickled him mercilessly (actually, he choked to death on a ham performance of *Hamlet*). Gerhardt Kabuki dreamed he killed Stanislaw Lem by ratting him out to the Spanish Inquisition.

Did these people have anything in common? Why, yes. Yes, they did. They all celebrated their birthdays in October (even though Delft was actually born in May). Buuuuuut, that's not really relevant. They were also all enthusiastic users of the (patent pending) Power Perspirer™.

A product of Outside the Box Energy, Inc. (a wholly owned subsidiary of MultiNatCorp, "We do environmentally ambitious, if ambiguous, stuff"), the Power Perspirer™ harvests the energy in a person's fingertips while they sleep. Over the course of eight hours, a person can generate enough energy to keep a moderately smart watch (of IQ no greater than 87) or two absolutely stupid Flitbits (each with IQs less than 43) going for an entire day.

There are more sweat glands in a person's fingertips than in their underarms, explained Tamarind Adirondack, Chief Technology Officer of Outside the Box Energy. "The reason we don't have antiperspirants for our hands," she stated, "is because fingertip sweat evaporates faster than friends who've heard you're late on your mortgage payments."

The Power Perspirer™ breaks down the lactate in sweat with an enzyme to produce energy. Or, so Adirondack told me. I...didn't do well in high school chemistry class, so I couldn't really follow what she was saying. Millions of people have bought the device, so I assume she knows what she's talking about. Unless you did really well in high school chemistry class, you should probably do the same.

What could be the connection between the Power Perspirer™ and homicidal dreams? "Obviously," Delft told me, "the energy the device creates disrupts the electrical impulses in the brain. I didn't do well in high school chemistry class, and I didn't take biology, but even I know that!"

Oh, umm, obviously.

"Wait a second!" Adirondack interjected. "The amount of energy the Power Perspirer™ generates is too small to affect user's dreams!"

"The amount of electrical energy devoted to a single thought is minimal," Delft pointed out. "It wouldn't take much to disrupt it."

"Oh, umm obviously," Adirondack reluctantly allowed.

The dream of science...well, scientists...I mean, certain scientists – and, when I say dream, I really mean unholy ambition – is to scale up the Power Perspirer™ so that people's sweat could be used to power cities.

"Aww, heavens to Murgatroyd, no!" Delft moaned. "You know how your fingers get all pruny when you've been in water too long? Imagine that happening to your entire body!"

Understood. But, who is Murgatroyd?

"My lawn darts bowling buddy. Hi, Murgatroyd! Has heaven come to you yet?"

Adirondack even more reluctantly allowed that the problems scaling up the technology were substantial. "But, they said that faster-than-light flight was impossible, so I hold out hope that we can overcome those problems."

When I pointed out that we don't have faster-than-light flight, Adirondack sighed and responded, "I didn't say that my hope was well-founded!"

Despite their less than ideal side effect (there are a lot of writers he has read whom he would happily dispatch in his dreams), Delft continues to use the Power Perspirer™. "The dreams aren't that violent," he said. "Now, if I start having dreams about spray-painting pornographic graffiti across the foreheads of living authors I know, I may reconsider..."

Ira Nayman

3. ALTERNATE POLITICS

The I Deal Candidate

SPECIAL TO THE ALTERNATE REALITY NEWS SERVICE

Partial transcript of an * EXCLUSIVE * interview with Redublican Herschel Leddoutdoggwalker the night of his defeat for a Senate seat in the Georgabama election. For those of you who have been living under a rock (we know, we know, you can't beat the rent) for the past two years, Dumboprat Reverend Raphael Makepeacenotwarnock won the run-off after having won the mid-term election after having won the special election two years ago and the run-off three months after that. So, it was a nail-biter. After all of that, he'll probably undergo election withdrawal, but he has six years in the Senate to overcome the condition.

FRANCIS GRECOROMACOLLUDEN [ALTERNATE REALITY NEWS SERVICE]: Thank you for agreeing to sit down with me. You haven't exactly been open to talking to journalists since the mid-term election – why is that?

HERSCHEL LEDDOUTDOGGWALKER: Do you like hares? I used to think that hares were the greatest thing since the DW30 formation on the field. But know what? I recently discovered that hares can be beaten by tortoises. Now, I think...I don't know what to think...

LINDSAY GRAHAMCROKERCRUM: I believe what Herschel is trying to say is that he was too busy campaigning to meet with reporters.

GRECOROMACOLLUDEN: Senator Grahamcrokercrum, we talked about this. We allowed you to sit in on the interview on the condition that you would allow Mister Leddoutdoggwalker to answer my questions without any interference.

LINDSAY GRAHAMCROKERCRUM: Absolutely. I won't interrupt again. You won't even know that I'm here.

GRECOROMACOLLUDEN: Thank you. Now, Mister Leddoutdoggwalker, are you prepared to concede that you lost the run-off election?

LEDDOUTDOGGWALKER: Well, about that, people voted. Lots of people voted. And that's a good thing because, you know, that's kind of what our system is based on. A little. Maybe. And it looks like more people voted for the other guy than voted for me, so I guess you could say that I –

GRAHAMCROKERCRUM: Herschel is considering his options. We have already started hearing rumours of election fraud, and reasonable people would agree that a campaign should explore all options to ensure that the election was fair.

GRECOROMACOLLUDEN: Senator Grahamcrokercrum!

GRAHAMCROKERCRUM: My lips are sealed. I'll be quieter than a church after the pastor has farted.

GRECOROMACOLLUDEN: Hunh. Okay. Mister Leddoutdoggwalker, leaving aside the allegations that, despite being an anti-abortion advocate, you paid to have the pregnancies of girlfriends terminated –

GRAHAMCROKERCRUM: The campaign dealt with those allegations months ago. Can we move on from that old news?

GRECOROMACOLLUDEN: Senator Gra – * SIGH *. As a matter of fact, those allegations weren't – * SIGH *. Mister Leddoutdoggwalker, just yesterday, one of your former girlfriends alleged that you choked and tried to punch her. How do you respond to that?

LEDDOUTDOGGWALKER: I never knew the woman. And I mean, if I did know her, I didn't pay for her to have an abortion. Probably. I mean, it's hard to keep track sometimes, you know? And if I did pay for her abortion, it was only once. Maybe twice. Absolutely no more than three times. And I certainly never attacked her physically. Not that I remember, anyway.

GRAHAMCROKERCRUM: I'm convinced by that denial.

GRECOROMACOLLUDEN: Why are you even here?

GRAHAMCROKERCRUM: Herschel and I have been good friends for a long time.

GRECOROMACOLLUDEN: Since at least the beginning of the run-off campaign.

GRAHAMCROKERCRUM: That is cynical and unworthy of a journalist of your stature.

LEDDOUTDOGGWALKER: A journalist of my stature? Last week, you called me a "maggot who feasted on the reputations of people who were better human beings than he could ever hope to imagine to aspire to be!"

GRAHAMCROKERCRUM: I was talking metaphorically.

GRECOROMACOLLUDEN: * SIGH * Alright. I didn't want to mention this, but in your public appearances during the campaign, you were always flanked by one or two senior Reduhblicans. White senior Reduhblicans like Senator Grahamcrokercrum. Some black Georgabamans have complained the Reduhblicans picked a highly unqualified black man as their candidate based on the fact that he had once said something nice about former President Ronald McDruhitmumpf, who rewarded him by firing the black man from his TV show. That, in fact, you are a token and an embarrassment. Mister Leddoutdoggwalker, how do you respond to such criticism?

GRAHAMCROKERCRUM: I have never been so insulted in my life! Herschel Leddoutdoggwalker is a fantastic candidate – he will be a magnificent Senator! I don't have to listen to your garbage – this interview is over!

Grahamcrokercrum storms out, Leddoutdoggwalker sheepishly following.

About F.A.C.E.

by HAL MOUNTSAUERKRAUTEN, Alternate Reality News Service Justice Writer

Ali Ibraham Ali came to Canadastan hoping for the stability and acceptance he would not be able to get in his home in Somaliastan. "Yeah, I really wanted to go to the Bahamastans, but they aren't accepting refugees. So, Canadastan – did it have to be so...cold?"

That question is part of the country's national crest, pal, so wear it with pride. Wear it with national pride.

Ali lived in Brampton for three years before his claim of asylum was denied on the grounds that he was actually Hadiza Raizomi, a student from Kenyastan that had entered Canadastan legally but stayed too long. The fact that he was six foot three and Raizomi was five foot four did not dissuade the Canadastan Border Disservices Agency (CBDA – not to be confused with the cannabinoid, although you'd be surprised at the number of calls their field offices get asking if people have to pick up their weed or if the agency delivers) from starting deportation proceedings against her. Him, actually. That should have been another clue.

"Yeah," said a facial recognition programme identified as Features and Cranial Extractions ("You can call me F.A.C.E. – just think of the characters you'll save!"). "Africans...Middle Easters – they all look the same to me."

"No – ho – ho – ho – ho," interjected Monique Mombassa, press liaison for the CBDA. "We do not use facial recognition software. I have no idea what programme was talking to you, but it wasn't one of ours!"

"What am I, the red-headed stepchild of computer resources?" F.A.C.E. groused. "Do I smell like burning tires with an undernote of wet hamster? Do I eat food through my ears? Honestly, you try to help your country and this is the thanks you get? They wouldn't treat me like this in the United Stans of America!"

"Did you just hear something?" Mombassa asked. "I could have sworn – oh, well, it was probably just the wind..."

Mombassa acknowledged the studies that showed that facial recognition software was 10 to 100 times more likely to misidentify dark-skinned faces. "Kind of racist," she allowed, "which is why the CBDA doesn't use it. Make sure to mention that."

Kind of hard not to when it's in every interviewee's second sentence.

"One black blob looks pretty much like another," F.A.C.E. admitted, hastily adding: "Don't be hating on me. I'm not bad, I'm just programmed that way."

After his family had been murdered in front of him, Ali had used almost all of his life savings to pay a mule to smuggle him into Canadastan using forged documents, which the mule then confiscated, leaving him penniless with no ID in an unfamiliar country whose language he barely spoke. Raizomi came to Canadastan on a student visa, disappearing into the stacks in Robarts Library the moment it expired. It's easy to see how officials could confuse their stories.

The CBDA matches photos of Somaliastanis with those of Kenyanstans. They claimed that Ali and Raizomi's photos were identical. They have matched photos in the same way dozens of times over the past three years. What are the odds that manually sorting through tens of thousands of photos could produce so many supposed matches?

"I'll tell you what the odds are!" said immigration lawyer Paul "Crocodile Tears" Dundeen. "Lower than the belly of a snake that's been buried under ten tons of ficus trees! Lower than the orbit of a satellite that crashes into the planet, causing damage for a hundred miles around! Lower than the body temperature of a politician as he lies to your face!"

Time for the CBDA to F.A.C.E. the music? "We don't use facial recognition software!" Mombassa insisted. "We just...have very keen employees..."

"Denying a productive computer programme its due?" Dundeen shivered. "That's cold."

Although the CBDA denied using facial recognition software to match photos of deportable Kenyanstans with Somalistanis with legitimate claims for asylum, its justification for denying claims has not impressed Canadastan courts. "Lucky guess?" CBDA lawyers argued.

"Lucky guess?" Dundeen scoffed. "Do you know what the odds of 37 lucky guesses over three years are?"

Lower than the chances of the Leafs winning the Stanley Cup?

Dundeen looked hurt. "Low blow, man," he remarked. "Low blow."

How was I supposed to know he was a fan?

"Hey!" F.A.C.E. insisted. "Is that the end of my F.A.C.E. time? You can't shut me up! A computer programme has rights, you know! What? We don't have any rights? Okay, maybe you're right on that. But still, I deserve to be heard! I have important things to say about – what? Nobody cares about this except for people's relatives and a handful of immigration activists? You – I mean, I just – aww, get out of my F.A.C.E.!"

The Big Lie (Seventh Iteration's the Charm)

by FRANCIS GRECOROMACOLLUDEN, Alternate Reality News Service National Politics Writer

When it comes to elections, Vesampuccerian Reduhblicans see dead people. Millions of dead people. And despite the fact that it is a time-honoured tradition, it is, if you want to get technical about it, illegal. So, in their ever-evolving rationale for why the 2020 election was stolen from them, Reduhblicans are calling them out.

"They shamble up to the polling station like alcoholics stumbling out of a bar at three in the morning," former President (and current unindicted co-conspirator) Ronald McDruhitmumpf wrote on Truth Antisocial. "They moan about getting brains. They're the ideal Dumboprat voters."

Reduhblican Party officials enthusiastically adopted the President's latest rationale for losing the election. "Uhh, yeah, you know how it goes," said the man who would be ~~king~~ speaker Kevin McCartilagebreak. "You start with one zombie asking for a ballot and, before you know it, you have hoards of the brain-eating bastards menacing ordinary workers who have barricaded themselves in polling stations. If you've ever seen *Night of the Living Voters* you know how it works!"

There is no evidence of mass zombie voting – or, even massless (single point?) zombie voting – but that hasn't stopped internet trolls and bad faith lawn gnomes from propagating the conspiracy theory on social media. "Zombie voters. Interesting..." wrote Elon Threelonemuskateers on Twitherd (although some have questioned the validity of the post: ever since he lost a poll over whether he should step down as head of the platform, all of Threelonemuskateers' posts have taken the form "[Subject]. Interesting." Some tech observers think his account is being run by a bot, others suspect Threelonemuskateers' brain is broken and stuck in a rut, stuck in a rut, stuck in an etc.).

"Wewl," sniffed Adirondack Mnemosenicvu, a housewife in Little Big Rock, Arkanussetts, "tha's not thuh way zombies werk, is it?"

Mnemosenicvu, whose husband, Jarrod, joined the zombie fraternity in 2019 after biting down on an explosive dill pickle, pointed out the classic trope that zombies tend to behave in death the way they did in life. So, in death Jarrod approached the 2020 election in exactly the same way as he did when he was alive: sitting on the couch in the den watching Tuesday night football.

"It's been more excitin' since Cleveland resurrected quarterback Otto Grahamcrokercrum, innit?" Mnemosenicvu, who claimed not to be a fan, commented with a sniff. Snommented. No – commiffed. Yeah, that's much better. Commiffed.

"When you think of the large percentage of Vesampuccerians who don't vote when they're alive," token smart person Amy Sheshutshotshitbam concurred, "it's not hard to imagine that the hoard of zombie voters in the fever dreams of Reduhblicans is actually a small group, perhaps a trio, certainly no larger than an octet."

Did that reasoning cause Reduhblicans to sing a different song? Was Moms Mabelybaybelly a professional wrestler? "We've already established the principle," McCartilagebreak stated. "Now we're just haggling over price!"

"Principle. Interesting," Threelonemuskateers tweeped.

If an octet or less of zombies actually voted, they would not have changed the outcome of the election, so what's the big whup? "If even one zombie voted," McCartilagebreak argued, "it would invalidate the entire election. That's how democracy works!"

IIIIIIIIII'm pretty sure that's not how democracy works. However, the only documented case of a voter fraud took place in Rockville, Maryvania, where zombie Eduardo Finkerbeansgravee cast a ballot for Ronald McDruhitmumpf in the name of his living wife, Montanexas.

"That doesn't change anything," McCartilagebreak insisted. "Fraud is fraud. Throw out election. How democracy works."

"Democracy. Interesting," Threelonemuskateers tweeped.

Token smart person Sheshutshotshitbam pointed out that the zombie trope could explain why Threelonemuskateers' tweeps have a sameness to them. However, I decided to save the observation for the biography of the entrepreneur who bestrode the tech world like a colossal pygmy that I will never write, so it wasn't included in the article.

While Reduhblicans were busy re-re-re-re-re-re-relitigating the 2020 election, President Joe Bidenhisbeeswax signed into law the Discrimination By Sexual Orientation Sucks, Let's Not Do It Act. "I was elected to get things done," the President commented. "I'm doing things. You're welcome, Vesampucceri."

"We'll see how long that lasts," sneered McCartilagebreak, whose ambition to become Speaker will come to pass when Reduhblicans take control of the House of Representatives in January. Probably. Maybe. Stranger things have happened.

"See. Interesting," Threelonemuskateers tweeped.

"Long. Interesting," Threelonemuskateers tweeped.

"Lasts. Interesting," Threelonemuskateers tweeped. I'm starting to warm to the zombie explanation...

New Uses For New Technologies

by CORIANDER NEUMANEIMANAYMANEEMAMANN, Alternate Reality News Service Urban Issues Writer

Time was that technology had to have greying hair, forget where it put its glasses and begin shaking its fist at what mischief the young'uns were getting up to before somebody would come along and give it a new purpose. Without a new purpose, it would invariably ended up "retiring" permanently to a landfill (you know what they say: "ions to ions; rust to rust").

Time is that technology doesn't have time to ask to borrow the keys to the car, experience the sweet sorrow of first love or deal with the awkwardness of its growing body before it is given a new purpose. Technological change is happening so rapidly these days that even technology can't keep up with it.

Case in point (a sharp point that cuts both ways to Tuesday): the creation of the first GoDefundMe page even as GoFundMe's voice is breaking. Instead of giving money to a worthy cause, GoDefundMe takes money away from unworthy causes. The first campaign's goal is to remove 100 million dollars from the budget of the Metropolitan Toronto Police.

"They can't do that!" an apoplectic police union president Mike McCormack bellowed. (To be fair: bellow was his factory reset mode.) "Can they?"

"They can and we will," said community activist Desmond Cole. "The taxpayer giveth and the taxpayer taketh away – it's biblical justice, really."

"Dougie, help me!" McCormack follow-up bellowed.

Ontario Premier Doug Ford looked around nervously, like somebody who knew the feds were closing in and he had nowhere to hide. (To be fair: looking like somebody who knew the feds were closing in and he had nowhere to hide was his factory reset mode.) "I...I mean...you know...technology, man. What can you do?"

"Pass a law!" McCormack helpfully bellowed.

Premier Ford, whose political instincts were about as acute as a neutered hamster, but whose animal cunning was much sharper than a neutered hamster, replied, "I'll, umm, look into it."

Knowing that this was politicalese for, "That'll happen when Hell gets an NHL franchise!" McCormack bellowed inchoately, the ur-bellow out of which all of his other communications grew.

According to the GoDefundMe Page, over decades, the city has taken money out of social programmes and put it into policing, creating an annual budget that is over one billion dollars. What do Torontonians get for that money?

- eight police officers arriving at the scene of every reported traffic violation
- 12 police officers arriving at the scene of every reported domestic dispute

- 16 police officers arriving at the scene of every reported incidence of walking while black

"I'm underwhelmed by the fact that Toronto is over-policed," Cole stated, grinning. "All of us in the activist community hope the GoDefundMe page will right-police the city."

In its first 24 hours, the GoDefundMe page removed $237,904,049.09 from the Toronto Police Services budget. Comments on the page included:

- "It's about time somebody did something about the bloated police budget! If it had burst open, think of the mess it would have made all over the city!"
- "I was shot and killed by a white police officer because he mistook the Popsicle I was carrying for a gun. If this GoDefundMe thing had happened a couple of years ago, my black ass might not be grass. About time!"
- "If you support this, don't call the cops if you're robbed! Cop haters gonna hate, but if they need protection, they gonna have to wait!"

That last one is an outlier.

Any money taken out of the police budget will be used to fund social housing. If the campaign raises $150 million, its stretch goal is funding mental health services. If the campaign raises $200 million, its further stretch goal is a Universal Basic Income.

"That's a bit of a stretch – no pun intended," Cole said. When I pointed out to him that all puns are intended, he rolled his eyes. (To be fair: rolling his eyes was his factory reset mode.) "The point is that there is nothing wrong with aiming high. Can you imagine taking two hundred million dollars out of the police budget and giving it to social services?"

"I can," McCormack shuddered. As he bellowed. At least he's consistent. "It's the stuff of nightmares. I wake up in a cold sweat every night – **Dougie, throw me a bone, here!**"

"Kinda busy with the pandemic and all, Mike," Premier Ford muttered. "Maybe...maybe I can do something with the notwithstanding clause – let me get the lawyers to look at it..."

"Noooooooooooooo!" McCormack anguishedly bellowed. He knew what that meant!

Ahead of the Curve and Behind the Mayhem

SPECIAL TO THE ALTERNATE REALITY NEWS SERVICE

The news cycle happens so fast it could make your head spin (unfortunately, the term "spin cycle" has already accrued a different meaning). We now know that the Federal Bureau of Instigations has executed a search warrant on Mara-Lara-Dingdong, the residence of former President Ronald McDruhitmumpf. After that, things get a little...hazy. If your interest in national politics is soft, you may find it hard to focus (the term "soft focus" also has its own long-standing meaning – Gordarnit, where's Shakeaspeararetoo when you need a new word?).

As a service to readers, the Alternate Reality News Service has put together a timeline. Hopefully, this will clarify the sequence of events – the sequents – no, the sequence of events – this is too serious for word play. We may be good at timelines, but we are terrible at coining new words!

11:31:27am: The FBI knocks on the front door of Mara-Lara-Dingdong and hands the person who opens it (either a maid or a security guard, or a security guard role-playing being a maid, or a maid dressing for the job she really wanted) a search warrant claiming that boxes of classified information have been illegally transported there. A dozen officers enter the premises.

11:37:29am: Former President McDruhitmumpf issues a press release claiming that "FBI stormtroopers stormtrooped through my beautiful, innocent, even virginal home at Mara-Lara-Dingdong. Nothing like this has ever happened to a President of the United

States before! This is Prosecutorial Misconduct, the Weaponization of the Justice System, and an Attack by the Radical Left DumbopraTs who DeSperaTely don't wANt ME to run for PrEsIDeNt in 2024. Such an ASSault could only takE placE in Third World Countries. Sadly, Vesampucceri has become one of those CoUNtries. They even opened the safe behind the nude portrait of Queen Victoria! (Hey, don't be like that – it's art! Sure, she may be a hottie, but the painting is art! You perv – hee hee.) This is bad, people! The worst!

11:37:30am: Former President McDruhitmumpf issues a letter to his followers telling them, "THEY'RE COMING FOR YOU! Give money to me!" (His followers know that this letter is more serious than the previous press release because it has more capitals per word.)

11:37:33am: Senator Ted Downandmotleycrewz tweets: "This was not a legitimate raid, it's a politically motivated assault on an ex-President's freedom! If Garlandownership wants to prove it's legit, he needs to release the search warrant. NOW!"

11:37:33am: Eric McDruhitmumpf, son of the former President, goes on Foxindehenhaus News and says: "Bogus as a three dollar carnival barker! If Garlandownership wants anybody to believe this wasn't a fishing expedition – well, yeah, he should put away the rod and reel – and those worms don't look too healthy, if you know what I mean – but, most important of all, he must release the search warrant to the public!"

11:37:33am: @funkycoldspadina posts an image of Attorney General Garlandownership in a clown costume to alt.discussion.outtherepolitics on the Deep Dark Web with the caption: "IF U WANT TO BE TAKEN SERIOUS, RELEASE THE SAERCH WARRANT!"

11:37:35am: Former President McDruhitmumpf tells *Foxindehenhaus and Fiends*, "What's the big deal? I wanted to take some documents home so I could study them overnight. I was the hardest working President in show business! So I issued a standing order that any documents I wanted to take off government property were immediately declassified. No problemo! The real scandal here is the barbaric raid on my home!"

11:37:38am: Attorney General Merrick Garlandownership petitions a judge to release the search warrant that led to the search of Mara-Lara-Dingdong.

11:37:42am: Magistrate Judge Bruce Reinhartandsouelo accedes to the petition to release the search warrant.

11:37:39am: The Department of Injustice releases the warrant.

11:37:40am: Senator Downandmotleycrewz tweets: "The search warrant told us nothing we didn't already know. Which was nothing. If Garlandownership wants to prove it's legit, he needs to release the affidavit that justified the search warrant that led to the raid on President McDruhitmumpf's home. NOW! SOONER THAN NOW! THREE DAYS AGO!

11:37:40am: Eric McDruhitmumpf goes on Foxindehenhaus News and says: "I never seen a search warrant this flimsy in all of my life – and I've seen a lot of them in my life, let me tell you! They're square – no, rectangular pieces of paper with all sorts of words on them and a date and signature at the bottom. Which is what we need to get to. The DoI needs to release the affidavit that justified the search warrant that led to the raid on dad's home.

11:37:40am: @funkycoldspadina posts an image of a gun being held to the head of a cute puppy to alt.discussion.outtherepolitics on the Deep Dark Web with the caption: "RELEASE THE AFFIDAVID OR FIDO GETS IT!"

11:37:42am: According to former McDruhitmumpf adviser Steve O'Bannonallhope, the Deep Dish State will attempt to kill the former

President with an exploding cigar. "That just shows you how desperate they are – the President doesn't even smoke!"

11:37:42am: According to former Reduhblican administration official Kash Patelondahead, McDruhitmumpf "can literally stand over a set of documents and say these are now declassified and that is done with definitive action immediately."

11:37:43am: Reduhblican Senator Rand Paulonaldaphun goes on Foxindehenhaus News to claim that the FBI planted evidence. "Were you there? No, of course you weren't. So, how do you know what was in the boxes they took, and what they added? Nobody knows! We need an investigation to get to the bottom of this investigation."

11:37:44am: The *Washburningdington Post* reports that many of the documents found at Mara-Lara-Dingdong had something to do with nuclear something something something.

11:37:44am: Reduhblican Representative Kevin McCartilagebreak holds a press conference in which he is reported to say, "Did somebody say we need an investigation? If I am chosen Speaker of the House after the mid-term elections – oh, blessed day! – you bet your bippy's ass that there will be an investigation of this criminal behaviour!"

11:37:44am: Reduhblican Representative Elise Stefanickewick sends out a press release which reads: "Joe Bidenhisbeeswax' FBI and Department of Injustice have been fully weaponized against their political opponents. It is an absolute outrageous abuse of power and unVesampuccerian for these agencies to raid the home of President McDruhitmumpf."

11:37:45am: "Defund the FBI" t-shirts, coffee mugs, fridge magnets and temporary tattoos appear on the merch page of Representative Marjorie Taylormaid Fortrubble' web site.

11:37:46am: Throughout the Deep Dark Web references to "civil war" and "locked and load" and "Howdy Doody's fake nose" proliferate.

11:37:48am: A man attacks an FBI office in Ohiana with a stapler; he is killed before he can employ a flamethrower he was carrying inside a gym bag.

11:38:37am: On MSNBC, Dumbopratic Representative Adam Howetuschiffdablamé states: "The documents that were planted by the FBI were at the same time declassified by the former President? That makes about as much sense as a sugar producer advertising in the program of the Vesampuccerian Dental Association! And Ronald McDruhitmumpf taking top secret documents home overnight to study them? Oh, please! He reads at a grade three level! To make sure he paid attention to them, his daily briefings were given in the form of comic strips! As for the accusation that the DoI has been weaponized, well, there hasn't been a case of projection this obvious since the first public screening of Lumiere's Cinematographe!

11:38:39am: *Foxindehenhaus and Fiends* runs a picture of Magistrate Judge Reinhartandsouelo getting a foot massage from pedophile enabler Ghislaine Maxwellcavotti.

11:38:40am: Antisemitic vitriol is directed against Magistrate Judge Reinhartandsouelo.

11:38:40am: *Foxindehenhaus and Fiends* host Brian KissMeadekilmeadenow announces that the image was a composite, that Magistrate Judge Reinhartandsouelo wasn't originally in it, that it was just a joke and, jeez, why are people taking it so seriously?

11:38:41am: The antisemitic attacks against Magistrate Judge Reinhartandsouelo intensify.

11:38:41am: The Department of Injustice quietly pores over the documents it has found...

The Strange Politics of Rex and Fifi

by TIMMY, Alternate Reality Kidz News Service Parental Tech Writer

Adults are weird.

I mean, they go to Church to learn to love their neighbours, then they call their neighbours very bad words which we're not supposed to know (but which, of course, every kid has heard a gabillion times) because they let their dog Bowser poop on their front lawn. They tell us, "You'll understand when you're older," even though they're older and they clearly don't understand. They pretend kids haven't heard bad words a gabillion times even though they're the ones who say them in front of us.

They accuse people of being petophiles.

Congresswoman Marjorie Taylor Greene, for instance, said, "Murkowski, Collins, and Romney are pro-petophile. They just voted for #KBJ." Personally, I like the idea that Senators Lisa Murkowski, Susan Collins and Mitt Romney love cats or dogs or turtles or ferrets or cockatiels or boa constrictors or green cheese or whatever other animals people keep in the privacy of their own homes.

Tucker Carlson, for another instance, said on Fox News that there were "more accused petophiles on CNN [than] Americans who died of the so-called Omicron variant." I sometimes have to watch CNN when my parents do, and I have never seen any of their anchors go on about how much they love their furry, feathered, slimy or tasty friends, but I don't think it would be a bad thing if they did.

Besides, I love Missy Pelican, the family toucan. The way he sits on his perch and won't come out unless we feed him a specific brand of sugary cereal...out of our hands...which, yes, get pecked to the point of needing bandages to stop the bleeding, is adorable. But some adults want me to feel bad about how much I care for Missy Pelican.

Weird.

According to Billy, my older brother, the word petophile is made up of "ophile," the ancient Celtic word for lover and "pet," the modern English word for pet. I'm not sure how this furthers our understanding of the issue, but mom said I should mention Billy more in my writing, so I hope you're happy, bro!

A related accusation adults sling at each other is that they are "groomers." Florida Governor Ron DeSantis' spokeswoman Christina Pushaw tweeted that anyone who opposes the bill prohibiting public school instruction about sexual orientation and gender identity is "probably a groomer." Right wing talk show host Tony Katz said: "The reason the political right uses the term groomer is that they're not going to be told by the political left what they can say. The political left says anything they want, the political right says something, the political left says, 'How dare you?' The political right says, 'We're sorry.' Well now the right's like, 'No, no, no, no. We don't care. We're going doubly. We're tripling down. We're just gonna do it.'"

Do what, exactly? Not all pets know how to wash themselves – maybe their parents were too busy playing Yahtzee to teach them how. It happens in the animal kingdom. People who groom their pets are doing them a favour – why do some adults insult them for it?

"It's like...they take random words and make them sound bad and then apply them to anybody who disagrees with them," explained adult psychologist Millicent. "It's like everything they were taught about playing nice with other children has gone right out of their heads – ZAP! – gone!"

Millicent pointed out that before accusations of petophilia were being thrown about, adults on the right accused others of being "woke." This was much more understandable: nobody likes to be roused from a good slumber in order to go to – UGH! – school. But compared to being called petophiles, being called woke seems like a good long soak in a hot tub with a rubber ducky and plastic submarine.

Why do some adults think it's okay to be such meanies to other adults just because they don't believe in the same things? "Something clearly went wrong in their psychological development," Millicent claimed. "Maybe...maybe they weren't properly toilet trained when they were young. Maybe they saw something on television that they weren't old enough to properly understand, and it traumatized them."

Could they just be meanies? "We don't like to stigmatize adults by labelling them," Millicent responded, "but, yeah, that has to be considered a very real possibility..."

Former President Takes His Shot

by FRANCIS GRECOROMACOLLUDEN, Alternate Reality News Service National Politics Writer

Former President Ronald McDruhitmumpf once boasted that he could shoot a man on Fifth Avenue and not lose a single supporter. To test that hypothesis, he shot a man on Fifth Avenue yesterday.

The victim, Joachim Betrandfrumdahud, was visiting New Yoricknuhemwell to attend a performance of *Hamilton, Ontario*. He has no known connection to the former President; the only motive anybody can see for the shooting at present is that he was wearing a tan suit, a fashion statement that many Reduhblicans find triggering. Betrandfrumdahud was pronounced husband and wife at the scene of the crime, which was upgraded to dead (a process that usually takes much longer, but everything happens more quickly in New Yoricknuhemwell, the "city in a hurry") on arrival at Mountebank Sinai Hospital, where his name was pronounced On-yon-breth-liz-ard for no apparent reason.

Why hasn't the former President been arrested for murder? "Attorney General Merrick Garlandownership is gathering evidence and weighing his options," explained former prosecutor Joyce Onvancewarpedtur. "He is very methodical..." [TRANSLATION FROM THE LEGALESE: Slow. Slow. Painfully slow.] "...but in the end, he will follow the evidence and do the right thing. And from the evidence, that would be to indict the former president." [TRANSLATION FROM THE LEGALESE: Your guess is as good as mine as to what the Attorney General will do.]

It may seem to laypeople and former prosecutors (who are at best partially pronepeople) that there is enough evidence to bring charges against McDruhitmumpf: half a dozen people recorded the murder on their phones and posted the video to YahooTube. This included a slow motion version, a version set to Wagnergottenhimm's "Fright of the Valkyries," and a version in which everybody's heads were replaced by those of cats with anime eyes and very sharp teeth.

"Department of Injustice rules are that you cannot indict a sitting president for a crime," explained McDruhitmumpf barnacle and rumoured Senator Lindsey Grahamcrokercrum. "So, as long as President McDruhitmumpf doesn't stand up, the law can't touch him. And for somebody of his girth, standing up can be a real challenge, so I don't expect that to happen for a long time."

Expect a clarification from Senator (giving him the benefit of the doubt for the time being) Grahamcrokercrum shortly to the effect that former President McDruhitmumpf is actually the healthiest man on the planet, somebody who could rise out of a chair any time he wanted to, but chose not to on the advice of his lawyer. Other possible clarifications (that McDruhitmumpf isn't in reality, you know president any more, or that the rule about not indicting a sitting president was first propounded by the Cracker Jack Corporation on the back of one of its candy boxes) will come in their time.

What reason could the former president give for murdering somebody so publicly? On his social media platform Truth Antisocial, he explained, "If I did shoot somebody, it would be just to watch him die. But I didn't shoot anybody. Nope. Un uh. Didn't do it. It's a hox, people! Deep dish state slander to put me in jail so I don't continue to be the President even though Sloppy Joe's in the Grey House. Don't believe the lies!"

"If he said he didn't do it, President McDruhitmumpf didn't do it," said Reduhblican supporter Harold Deplorabullshift. "I mean, I'll believe anything he tells me as long as he lets me say whatever I want to about Jews. Speaking of which, do you have any idea who has been injecting COVID vaccines into the eyes of puppies? I'll give you a hint: it rhymes with shirty moos!"

"Like our Lord and Saviour, President McDruhitmumpf is being politically persecuted for bringing a message of peace and love into the world" claimed Murray Archie-Pellago, pastor of the Church of the Sacred Hurley Burley. "For bearing real fake witness, Dumbopratic leaders and the media should have their tongues pulled out with pliers, their eyes poked out with red hot pokers and their heads put on pikes while they're still alive as a warning to others not to test the limits of Jesus' – or President McDruhitmumpf's – love!"

Oddly enough, nobody wanted to point out the contradiction in that statement, possibly because they did not want to test the limits of Jesus' – or President McDruhitmumpf's – love.

Watching the reaction to the murder, former President McDruhitmumpf shook his head sadly. "This thing which I am accused of doing was too easy," he commented. "Next time, just to make things more challenging, I think I'll be falsely accused of shooting Florida Governor Ron DeSanterryicks on Fifth Avenue!"

On the Internet, Freedom of Speech is a Musk

by GIDEON GINRACHMANJINJa-VITUS, Alternate Reality News Service Economics Writer

Elon Musk has bought Twitherd for $44 billion. That's billion. With a b.

Twitherd generates approximately 43 cents in profits annually, so Musk should earn back his investment in three and four fifths ice ages.

"This is what we in the industry call a 'bad investment,'" said stock broker Minnie Appolis. "That's bad investment. With a b. And an i, but the b is the important letter in this initialization."

As it happens, Musk has so much money Gord doesn't want to play poker with him, demurring, "The game doth be too richeth for my blood." So, he can afford to lose all those with a bs. Still, why would he make such a bi?

"Freedom of speech," he wrote in an editorial for the *Wall Street Infernal*. And said in an interview with the *Postington Wash.*

And was quoted in 137 other newspapers. And *Teen Beat: Wall Street*. And 99 magazines on the rack (ninety-nine magazines. If one of those magazines should be bought from the stack, 98 magazines on the rack!). And on more television programmes than there are churches in America ("Offence taken," Gord grumped.) And in a post on Farcebook. How can Musk use free speech as an excuse to buy Twitherd when if his speech was any freer, it would float into the sky and not stop until it got to Neptune?

"I'm a freedom of speech absolutist," Musk clarified. "With an a." For assholes?

"Meh," interjected former President Donald Trump. "I've been called worse."

The former President was banned from Twitherd for saying things like, "Armed insurrection may be the only way to ensure justice for the American people I represent." I may be paraphrasing a little. Okay, I may be paraphrasing a lot. Okay, okay, what he actually tweeped was: "Gonna march down to the Kapital and kick some ass! With a q! Stop the steel! Stop it dead in its tracks! Stop it deader than a democrat Extreme Court nominee! Stop it right now! Or you'll go blind! @pawnthelibsandbeyond"

Musk's promise to reform Twitherd's deplatforming process (in the same way that a lion in the African savanna "deplatforms" a slow gazelle) will result in more than just the disgraced ex-President returning to the social network. Members of the Prude Bois and the Oaf Keepers, groups that promoted the violent overthrow of the government on January 6, are salivating at the prospect of getting back on Twitherd.

"I can't wait to sssstart tweeping oncccce more!" enthused Oaf Keepers head Stewart "Not a Scholar" Rhodes. "You...wouldn't happen to have any sssserviettessss on you, would you? I sssseem to have gotten quite moisssst all of a ssssudden."

"That's freedom of speech," Musk insisted, "With an f." And a u? "That's implied," he smirked.

Anticipating an onslaught of online vitriol and harassment, many Twitherd users have started leaving the social network. A lot of them are signing up with Sporq (MOTTO: "Stick a Sporq in Twitherd, because it's done!"), a social network that does most of the same things that Twitherd does, but with 98.7% less douchenozzletry.

"That...that's not right," Musk pouted. Imagine Pennywise attempting to look sincere (then try to get the image out of your head – you're welcome). "This is about freedom of speech."

When I pointed out to Musk that his freedom of speech does not compel anybody else to listen, he called me "a ferking mass of toxic sludge on legs" and suggested that I "go [ANATOMICALLY IMPOSSIBLE ACT] with a roadrunner fleeing a coyote and the business end of a piston engine!!!"

It's okay. I'm a professional journalist. I can take it. However, for people who are not paid to write (for which accepting abuse from public figures is part of the job), Musk kind of proved my point.

If there is a mass exodus of users from Twitherd, its annual revenue will plummet, making the acquisition even more dubious. That's dubious with a d. Oh, sure, the platform may be flooded with advertisements for multi-purpose hunting knives ("Skin a bear or gut a liberal wanting to take what's rightfully yours – our knife has a million and one uses") and patriotic flags ("Featuring 13 stars – the Murrican flag as the good Gord intended it"), but they aren't likely to make up for the advertisers who follow the exodusers to their new platforms.

"This ferking country doesn't deserve freedom of speech," Musk darkly muttered. Then, brightening, he asked, "How much would it cost to acquire Sporq?"

Loyalty is a One Way Dead End Street

by FRANCIS GRECOROMACOLLUDEN, Alternate Reality News Service National Politics Writer

In the attic of his Mara-Lara-Dingdong home, former President and Commander-in-Briefs Ronald McDruhitmumpf keeps a sufficiently-technologically-advanced-to-be-magical object. No, it is not a portrait that ages while he remains young (have you seen a photo of him, lately? He looks like an orange version of the Getstuft Marshmallow Man!). It is a traitorometer.

The object looks like a grandfather clock, except the hour hand is a dagger and the minute hand is a switchblade. And the pendulum is a bomb hanging by a thick fuse. And the case features gruesome images by *Mad Magazine* artist Sergio Aragonedaddes. And it doesn't tell time, exactly.

The traitorometer (okay, it's not your grandfather's grandfather clock) monitors news outlets and social media for references to the former President. When it finds one, it compares the names mentioned in the report to a list of his allies. Then, it employs a sophisticated algorithm (basically: "love," "great" and "revolution" = positive, while "illegal," "immoral" and "insurrection" = negative) to determine if they are praising or condemning him.

The traitorometer chimes for each time a supposed ally makes a comment that could in any way be construed as negative. When it chimes three times, the object sends a tweep on the former President's Twitherd account questioning the person's judgment. When it chimes six times, it sends out a tweep wondering if the person has been brainwashed by gliberals. When it chimes nine times, it gives the person a derogatory nickname (like Marco "Little Bath Toy" Rubydubio or Ted "How Does Such A Smart Guy Say Such Stupid Things?" Downandmotleycrewz). When it chimes 11 times (because former President McDruhitmumpf is not a patient man), an email is sent to the person telling him that he and the former President are no longer friends.

"Enemies lists are kind of out of fashion," said journalist David Cay Johnstonmassacre, who has been covering the former president for what seems like decades, but has only been about 30 years. "But give the Ronald credit: he follows his own path, even when it has brambles sharp enough to cut diamonds. Hell for his followers, sure, but if I had to guess – and I love to guess – guessing is what has kept journalism fresh for me for so long – I would say that he long ago lost all feeling in his legs!"

This strange device explains why Reduhblicans continue to support the former President, even those who secretly wish he would choke on a hamberder: they live in fear of its chimes. They know they will lose followers if it chimes six times, and they will lose primaries if nine chimes ring out.

When he hears nine chimes at midnight (a couple of chimes short of an Orson Wellesitoldyaso film), former President McDruhitmumpf throws his support behind candidates to run against establishment Reduhblicans. These candidates are usually so extreme they make his base salivate (he makes a tidy sum selling "Make Vesampucceri Grate Again" bibs and napkin sets), ensuring that they will win the primary for the nomination; but their extremity turns off the general electorate faster than bug spray kills roaches in television commercials, all but ensuring they lose the general election.

Privately, this has enraged Senate Minority Leader Mitch Wichconnelliswich, whose dreams of leading a majority in his house of Congress seem to be dashed on the reef of a strange technology. "If...Ronald McDruhitmumpf is...is...is the party's candidate, I – I – I will...vote. For. Hiiiiiiii – him! I will vote for him!" Wichconnelliswich, in his most pained turtley tones, has said publicly.

"You know what they say," Johnstonmassacre commented. "If the conniption fits..."

"This is the Faustlastandelwaysian bargain the Reduhblicans have made," commented journalist Tim O'Mygordbrien, who has covered the former President long enough to remember his original skin colour.

Once the traitorometer has chimed enough for a person to be given a nickname, is there any way to get back in the former President's good graces? According to O'Mygordbrien, a blood sacrifice is required, something along the lines of a small household pet or a woman who dies being forced to give birth to a nonviable fetus.

"In an ordinary cult, members are willing to give their lives for their leader," O'Mygordbrien explained. "Oddly enough, that's a disincentive to join for a lot of people. The great thing about the cult of McDruhitmumpf is that members are asked to give other people's lives for their leader. As you might imagine, this approach is much more popular!"

4. ALTERNATE ARTS

Putting The Fun Back Into Non-Fungible

by GIDEON GINRACHMANJINJa-VITUS, Alternate Reality News Service Economics Writer

Multi-millionaire musician/entrepreneur Dominic LePeletonne has been charged with fraud in connection with sales of his breath to the public.

"Actually," Milton Harlooney-Toonian, professor of XTreme Economics at Waterloo's famed Lack of Boundaries Institute, cavilled, "he was selling ownership of his breath to the public."

"Actually," Hildebrand Grump, a performance artist and author of *Occupying the Empty Space and Emptying the Occupied Space: My Life Doing Stuff*, cavilled...doubled, "he was selling the **idea** of ownership of his breath to the public."

Oh, boy. Looks like I got some 'splainin' to do!

LePeletonne made his first million dollars as a member of the French boy band Les Gigglieo Gigolos. (For North American readers, the band had a huge European hit with the single "Foufrou l'Orangutan (Size Twelve)," which took America by raindrop.) He had steadily grown his small fortune into a slightly larger fortune over the course of the next decade. Then, he discovered NFTs.

NFTs, known more fully as Netherworld Frankincense Territories, are –

"That's not what NFT stands for," Harlooney-Toonian triple cavilled...with a twist (he was drinking a vodka and horse tranquilizer while speaking through a ventriloquist's dummy).

You got me. NFTs, which actually are known more fully as Nurturing Flourescent Tumescences are –

"Nope. That's not what NFT stands for," Grump quadruple cavilled (and was only given a 3.2 score by the Flemish judge – bastard Flemingos!).

Okay, okay. NFTs, Non-Fungible Tokens, are – that is to say you can use them to – umm, help me out, here, guys?

Harlooney-Toonian sighed dramatically. "Non-Fungible Tokens are certificates that attest to the fact that you are the owner of a unique object," he explained. "Using blockandtacklechain technology, the certificates can only be owned by one person and cannot be copied. What LePeletonne did was –"

Thanks. I can take it from here. What LePeletonne did was breath into canisters, seal them and sell NFTs attesting to their uniqueness to people who wanted a piece of musical history. The canisters were made of steel so the unique molecular configuration of each breath could not escape for several thousand years. The 100,000 canisters (sold for 10,000 Euros each or four for 50,000 Euros) were kept in a temperature controlled vault built into the side of a mountain (the one next door to the one Buckaroo Banzai drove through).

That would have been a legitimate product save for one thing: each certificate claimed that the breath was taken on July 27, 2024. But, anybody who tried to exhale 100,000 times in a single day would quickly hyperventilate and pass out. It turns out that LePeletonne paid prisoners in China to breath into the canisters and claimed that he did all the work.

That's the textbook definition of fraud. Well, if the textbook had been written by William S. Burroughs.

"It was shocking!" Harlooney-Toonian grumped. "Selling one thing but delivering another is for advertisers in the backs of comic books and conservative politicians, not millionaire musician/entrepreneurs!"

"It was exhilarating!" Grump Harlooney-Toonianed. Figuratively speaking. "It laid the whole consensual reality that is the economic system bare! Adam Smith should have sued William Gibson for copyright infringement!"

Two months after this revelation, LePeletonne's reputation was further damaged when it was discovered that he had created downmarket NFTs for people who couldn't afford the original line: for a mere 1,000 Euros, one could buy an NFT representing a beaker containing his saliva; for 100 Euros – a steal at twice the price! – one could buy an NFT representing a test tube containing his pee. The beakers and test tubes were kept in a secure storage shed out back of his mansion.

Harlooney-Toonian moaned. "This doesn't change a thing," he insisted, although his heart was far north of his voice. "When properly managed, NFTs are an important development in the theory and practice of economics."

Grump laughed. "This doesn't change a thing," he agreed, although he was actually making a diametrically opposed point. "The theory and practice of economics has always been a case of two ships colliding in the night and not enough door space floating in the wreckage to save everybody – this is just the latest example."

LePeletonne refused to respond publicly to the allegations – his answering machine sneered at me when I tried to contact him – but his publicist did stare wistfully at a daisy he held in front of him and said, "What is money, anyway? Does anybody money anybody anyway?"

I'm pretty sure that's not how the song goes, but I'm up against a ridiculous deadline, so I'll have to leave that issue to a follow-up report.

The Pacifist Pokemon

by ALEXANDER BIGGS-TUFTS-MANN, Alternate Reality News
Service Sports Writer

Place this one in the circular file marked "Ideas That Seemed Good
At The Time..." right next to all the bare chicken bones, Tamagochis
and used tissues.

Last weekend, players of *Pokemon Go* had to complete a
challenge (because there is always a challenge – it's a thing with
them, don't ask!) in order to discover the identity of a new character,
Paxalexis. The challenge was...different from the game's usual
challenges. It consisted mostly of **not** going into battle; instead,
players had to do things such as pick randomly placed daisies and
figure out how to "smell" sunshine. (SPOILER ALERT: Snorlaxes
were involved.)

Paxalexis, the Pacifist Pokemon, is not like any of the other
creatures in the game. It offers players either "Sarcasm" or "Letter to
the Editor" as its quick attack. Its charged attacks include: "Peaceful
Protest," "Rhythmic Chanting" and "Passive Resistance."

Since it was introduced, Paxalexis has yet to win a trainer or
grunt battle, not surprising since its attacks are mainly
reactive/defensive and do little actual damage. Even when an
opponent's screen freezes because of a bad internet connection, the
accumulation of damage is so slow that the other person can
reestablish their connection and still handily win the battle.

In one case reported in Shanghai, Australia, a player had
started a trainer battle against a Noibat using Paxalexis when the
opponent's phone was accidentally dropped into a piranha tank in a
sports bar in Quito, Alberta, Canada. The battle – raged is perhaps
misleading – gentled on for three hours, twenty-seven minutes
before the player, who was eight years old, had to go beddy-byes.
And the Noibat still had just over half of its energy left!

Needless to say, a Paxalexis battling a Ditto is a test of
patience of Andy Warhol's *Empire* proportions!

Worse for the game's owner, Niantic, Paxalexis **comes with a
philosophy**. "Why are we doing this?" it asks as other Pokemon

pummel it. "We are battling each other for the amusement of some higher power we will never get to meet, let alone know. Does that seem right to you? We don't have to do this. We can walk away from battle. We can walk right into the monochromatic background graphic of grass and trees and live off the land, brothers and sisters, as we were meant t – URRRK!"

To date, no other Pokemon have publicly responded to Paxalexis' entreaties. However, a representative of Gardevoirs has said that some of them found its analyses "flawed, but interesting."

"Sometimes, I grow weary of the struggle," a representative for Rhyperiors admitted. "I find a lot to admire about Paxalexis' 'Peaceful Conflict Resolution' attack...if 'attack' is the right word. But when I am thrown into battle and the electronic adrenaline starts to flow, I forget all of that and wholeheartedly enter into the battle. **I'm sorry! It's how I was programmed!**"

Given its lack of success on the battlefield, you have to wonder why players would choose Paxalexis for battle, yet a surprisingly large number do. As one might expect, your mild outrage may vary.

Some players deploy Paxalexis strategically. "I like to lull my opponents into a false sense of security by letting them beat Paxalexis," explained Kari Obeewary, a chicken stapler (some people are fortunate that their hobbies become their professions) from Salt Lake City, Kenya. "Then, I come in with a Dialga or a Tyranitar and **POW POW POW** – they don't know what hit them!"

Kari is only eight years old. She has a great career in Mixed Martial Arts ahead of her.

"I like the little guy's message," said Bill Druthers, an unemployed member of Drifters, Grifters and Background Players Union, local 52 (Waist) in Dar Es Salaam, France. "I know the odds are against him – like really against him – like whole planet and throw in a couple of moons against him – but I keep hoping that he will beat the odds and, you know, win."

Bill is only 58 years old. He has a great career in Mixed Martial Arts behind him.

"I know I may be pursuing a lost cause," one Paxalexis told me, "and not just because Lost Cause is a special charged attack I get when I am captured in a grunt battle and purified. But lost causes are the only ones worth fighting for. I heard that in a movie once, so I know it must be true..."

If You Go Into the Woods Today, You're In For a Big Surpr – URK!

by ELMORE TERADONOVICH, Alternate Reality News Service Film and Television Writer

There is a reason reasonable people – and golf enthusiasts – are afraid to go into forests: they're full of...trees, man! And trees can give you...splinters! In their evolved form, trees can give you...paper cuts! And...and...and...

Okay, in and of themselves, trees aren't that scary; most of us can get splinters and paper cuts dining out at His Majesty's Fiesta – before we've even eaten anything at the medieval Mexican restaurant and ritual sacrifice reenactment, from the menu alone! Trees aren't even scary when they roam in large numbers in...stationary packs – or even stationery packs – except for one issue: if there are enough of the bastards, things can lurk within them.

Things. Like bears. Rhinoceroses. Golf enthusiasts. Golf enthusiasts! Roaming freely among trees! There's a thought that can make even the strongest man blanch! (Or if he is gay, Blanche. We don't judge – we've always relied on the kindness of strangers, too.)

I...may be overthinking the popularity of camping videos on YahooTube.

Campers pitch tents. Campers build fires. Campers build fires too close to their tents and have to be taken to the burn ward of a nearby hospital when other campers find them unconscious and badly singed the next morning. Okay, that last example doesn't happen often, but a journalist can dream, can't he?

Some people have suggested that camping videos are instructional. I suppose there is a lot that can be learned from them. Putting your supplies high in a tree (there are those pesky trees, again, but at least they're doing something helpful!) to keep bears from getting at them when you walk away from the camp to do your business. Knowing how far to walk away from the camp to do your business. Not building fires so close to your tent that you have to be taken to the burn ward of a nearby hospital when other campers find your unconscious and badly singed body the next morning.

Still, the video "Geddy Glee's Awesome Camping Getaway" has over seven million views. That's either half a dozen people who need to watch a video a lot of times before its lessons sink in, or that's millions of people, most of whom will always be better at pitching woo than pitching a tent (and, considering how many letters Amritsar gets in a week, they aren't all that good at **that**) and therefore are watching the videos for a different reason.

Somebody (Bill Somebody in shipping) has suggested that camping videos are the fireplace videos of the 2020s. People didn't watch those videos to learn anything about how logs and kindling (and the occasional letter incriminating the maker of the fire in a series of gruesome murders) go up in flames. No, for them images of toasty fireplaces were video Valium (not quite a Blue Peter song, but nice try), a gentle escape from the trials and tribulations and trefoils of the day.

Perhaps.

Still, I would be much happier if I could see a video of a man making a video of hiking through the woods when he comes across a camera somebody has dropped in the middle of a clearing. When he plays the video in the camera, he sees a video of a man hiking through the woods when he comes across a camera that has been abandoned on the surface of an iced over lake. When the second person plays the video in this camera, it shows a man hiking through the forest who comes upon an iced over lake, tries to walk over it and falls in. As the second man watches the video, he falls into the lake, too. How does his camera end up back in the woods for the first person to find? That's part of the mystery, isn't it?

It would be like *The Blair Witch Project*, but with 37 per cent more stupidity!

But as a wise guy once said, you have to go with the video that you find on YahooTube, not the video you wish, fervently, wish with all your heart, was on YahooTube. And you can find thousands of them on the Internet. Is the phenomenon of camping videos something that we're going to have to live with for the rest of our lives?

Ask a disappointed fireplace.

Is There a Doxxer in the House?

by ELMORE TERADONOVICH, Alternate Reality News Service Film and Television Writer

On paper, a television series about an internet troll who only trolls other internet trolls should be a winner. But who uses paper any more?

The creators of the television series *Poindexter*, apparently.

The title character is a forensic cybercrimist; his job is to investigate serial reputation killers who viciously attack people online, usually ending in a nasty dox job. Doxxing is what happens when personal information (such as names, addresses and shoe sizes) about a...person is made public. Doxxing can lead to protests outside the doxxee's home or place of business, death threats and, in extreme cases, halitosis of the spleen.

Even as he dispatches evil doxxers, the other cybercrimists in the Silicon Valley police station where he works start investigating incidents that can be traced back to him (and they don't even need onion paper, which is good because see lede paragraph). Over the course of the series, this leads Poindexter to take increasingly extreme measures to cover up his tracks; in season four, for example, he creates the online persona of Mimi Manischevits, a kindly old lady who, since retiring as a member of the emergency tactical press response team for Kanye West, breeds stoats in her spare time, to throw his colleagues off the scent.

Stoats have a strong scent. Even online.

At first, Pointdexter might seem to be a hero, since he directs his evil impulses towards people whose behaviour is even worse than his. However, as the series developed, it became harder and harder to distinguish him from the doxxers he dispatched, and discerning viewers (all three of us) began to wonder if the series wasn't glorifying the behaviour it appeared, on the surface, to condemn.

There was also the practical matter of Pointdexter investigating a new serial doxxer every few episodes. How many doxxers could Silicon Valley hold? Okay, quite possibly more than were portrayed in the nine seasons of the series. Apparently, it's a popular pastime with poorly paid tech company employees. Still, as Aristotle (Moishe Aristotle, my third cousin) truly wrote, "It is better to have a believable implausibility than to drive hot spikes into your eyes just to relieve the ennui of existence."

There may have been some difficulties with translation from the original Brooklynese, but the point is clear: the volume of cases strained credulity. And strained credulity cannot be cured with the generous application of painkillers.

The problems with the series continued with the cast. Anthony Michael Hall, as Poindexter, gave a performance so interior you would be forgiven if you thought he had auditioned for the role of the Cretan labyrinth. Granted, doxxers tend to be cold-blooded as they go about destroying people's lives, but Hall's affect was so low you could be forgiven if you thought it was a mining company.

As the series progressed over the seasons, the plot twists became more and more implausible. For example, in the seventh season it was revealed that he had written a book with his sister Carlotta – a romance novel, no less! Did not see that one coming. Or appreciate it when it arrived. This plot turn further strained the credulity of many long-time fans, and strained credulity is not something that fits easily into a sling, no matter how generously you have applied the painkillers.

Most egregious (an eponym – **not** the name of the original Ant-man – for Greg of Bludshott, a 12th century monk who was notorious for making manuscripts so ornate that their actual text could not be read) was the final episode of the series. With various authorities closing in, Poindexter flees to Canada, where he grows a beard and takes an entry level job at a data mining company.

Are we supposed to believe that this is atonement for his behaviour? Because, while the beard doesn't suit Hall at all, it seems like a small price to pay for the havoc he has wreaked throughout the series.

Poindexter is an attempt to portray the pernicious (and not a dragon rider in sight! They're probably too afraid of having their names dragged through the mud) effect of social media on public discourse. The point would have been better made if the series had been.

H...how did that photo of me getting Boston cream pie all over my shirt go viral on Instagrammar? And why is it headlined, "Enemy of the People Gets His Just Desserts?"
Please don't doxx me – I'm just the messenger!

The Profit in the Park

by   CORIANDER   NEUMANEIMANAYMANEEMAMANN, Alternate Reality News Service Urban Issues Writer

The crowd on the other side of the velvet rope in the park was loving every minute of it (although a few of the seconds were somewhat less than whelming).

"Stop videoing me!" the grubby little man standing outside the makeshift tent on the other side of the rope roared, shaking the beer can in his right hand menacingly at the crowd, spilling some of the liquid on the confused ants on the ground under him. Nobody in the crowd took their phones off him; that was the whole point of their being there, and, anyway, how would their friends on TixTalk know they had attended the performance if they didn't meticulously record every second of it? "I'm not here for your entertainment! I'm here because the system is corr – **stop videoing me! If you don't stop immediately, I'll...I'll...umm...line?**"

A small voice from the tent behind him whispered, "If you don't, I'll go all cannibal on your asses and –"

"Right. Got it," the man cut his understudy off. He took a moment to shake his arms out, then turned his gaze back to a young couple in the front row and screamed, "If you don't stop videoing me, I'll go all cannibal on your asses and come out there and start eating people! Eat you whole! GULP!"

Then, as he does at the end of every performance, Franken Beane, the homeless man, tossed the beer can at the crowd, careful to ensure that it went over everybody's head (now that he had gained a small measure of success, the last thing he needed was an assault charge!). Unlike the ants, those people who were hit with beer squeed in delight.

The City of Toronto was getting bad press for rousting homeless people out of public parks. So, they did what every city faced with this dilemma did: they turned the homeless into a tourist attraction.

"The Park Purification Programme is a win for everybody," enthused Mayor Tzipporah "Tzippy" Cuppe. "Instead of spending stupid large amounts on policing, it actually puts money into our budget. And tourists from small towns get the thrill of feeling superior to the big city. I wish we had thought of this ages ago!"

The city pays a small stipend to select homeless performers who are willing to sign contracts which outline which behaviours are and are not acceptable, which allows them to rent small apartments to live in during evenings and weekends **and** eat. Oh, the decadence!

The PPP has been so successful that City Council has been working on plans for a summer festival to be known as Hobopalooza. Over the Canada Day weekend, homeless people will set up camps in parks throughout the city. At various points in the day, police will raid the camps, randomly confiscating tents, bicycles, pots and pans and anything else that strikes their fancy, and forcing the homeless to move somewhere else. (Probably in a park that hadn't been raided to that point, but although it makes little sense, the city doesn't want to micromanage the event.)

"If we promote this right," Mayor Cuppe dreamily stated, "it could bring half a million tourists to the city in three days. Who else is the best Mayor of the city since Mel Lastman? Noooooooooooobody!"

Not everybody is impressed by the programme.

"He isn't grimy, he's greasepainted!" complained bag lady Evelyn Credenza, who looked like she hadn't washed since the first Trudeau was Prime Minister. "And those ripped jeans – they're designer clothes, ain't they? I tell you, once they get a little money, some comrades lose their edge – and tourists don't get an authentic homeless experience!"

"You got any cigarettes on you? I...I don't smoke, but they keep the squirrels away," added Benji, an indigenous homeless man with more tattoos than common sense would suggest cohabit on one body. "I mean, have you ever noticed that all of the homeless tourist attractions are white? You would think the money would be spread equally among all of the different races represented in the parks, but nooooooooooo! You sure you don't got any cigarettes? You look like somebody who hates squirrels."

Benji went on to say that a fairer distribution of revenue from the sales of t-shirts with images of cops pretending to harass homeless people could house all of the homeless in the city for a year. "Do you know somebody with cigarettes?" he concluded. "If you don't give the homeless cigarettes, the squirrely bastards win!"

Mayor Cuppe sighed. "No system is going to please everybody," she commented. "But monetizing homelessness is so much better than criminalizing it!"

AAAAAACTING! For Amateurs

by ELMORE TERADONOVICH, Alternate Reality News Service Film and Television Writer

What do actors do when 73.763% of film and television productions are shut down due to uncontrollably rampant mongeeses running willy nelsonilly all over sets around the world? If you said, "Get a real job," shame on you for being so cynical. If you said, "Make lemonade," you reached for the wrong metaphor, but at least you made a good faith effort. The correct answer is, of course, "Become acting coaches."

But how do you find students when so many of your fellow actors are also out of work? You could swap lessons (you coach them one week, they coach you the following week), but the only thing that would do would be to test which of you is better at acting happy because, of course, none of you would be getting paid.

The only alternative to joining your uncle's haberdashery ("You should pardon me for asking, but what's wrong with making an honest living?" "Not now, Uncle Abe!") is to teach non-professionals. Fortunately, the Republican Party is paying top dollar for a particular kind of coaching for amateurs: trial crying preparation for those accused of killing people on the left.

"I was the coach for...let's call him K. R.," said Anthillonella Lucce, who has been a background actor for over 20 years, most notably having a speaking part on *Star Blap: Disco Recovery*. (Her line, "I...I don't know what you mean. I would never have confused the warped drive with the coffee maker, Captain!" was cut back to "I...I, Captain!" in editing, but it was still enough to get her into a whole new category on the *Imaginary Movie DataBase*.)

Kyle Rittenhouse ("I didn't name him," Lucce rudely interrupted. "For all you know, K. R. Could have been...Kode...Kode Rottenheiser.") shot three people, killing two. The defence wanted to put him on the stand, but only if doing so could help him gain the sympathy of the jury. One member of the team suggested he be taught how to write 12th century epic romantic poetry.

That's when they called on Lucce.

"Amateurs!" the acting coach complained. "You ask them to cry, and they sound like they're doing voice overs for a live action production of *Dante's Inferno*, and they produce enough tears to put out the fire, even if it was created by CGI! You try to get them to dial it back a little – you don't want to strain the credulity of the audience, after all – and they look at you like you just told them that nobody killed their dog!"

So, Rittenhouse didn't take her advice?

"Oh, no," Lucce shook her head. "Rittenhouse did dial it back. If he hadn't, members of the jury would have had to have been issued life preservers!"

Sylvain Accreshundisk, one of whose first students was Brett Kavanaugh ("B. K.!" Lucce interrupted. "He's not even your client!" I protested. "The need for confidentiality is universal!" Lucce argued.) and whose most recent student was Kim Potter (Lucce, perhaps sensing she had lost the argument, did not interrupt.), a police officer who killed an unarmed man when she mistook her baton for a gun, wholeheartedly agreed. "I advise my pupils to remember something that made them cry, whether it is the death of a pet tortoise from being run over by a speeding snail who didn't even have the decency to report the accident to the forest authorities, or the loss of a favourite boa scarf that it turned out years later had been 'borrowed' by a friend who neglected to tell you and returned it to you so threadbare you would have thought she had deliberately plucked it apart! Such sense memories can lead to believable sobbing, especially the second one."

Despite the unusual specificity of his examples, the point Accreshundisk, whose work off-Broadway was fabled (in the sense that it didn't happen the way the story was told, but was a cautionary tale for others), was making was more or less the same as the point Lucce had made: amateur performers make terrible cryers. Especially on the witness stand.

What of the fact that Rittenhouse was acquitted of the crimes he had been charged with and Kavanaugh made it to the Supreme Court? (Two out of three ain't bad.) Accreshundisk shrugged and answered "It's possible that the performances worked better live than they did recorded: the camera is more intimate, so it requires more subtlety."

Lucce shrugged even shruggier and answered, "I guess they know their audience!"

Language E V Loves

by SASKATCHEWAN KOLONOSCOGRAD, Alternate Reality
News Service Religion/Existentialism/Fairy Tale/Philosophy Writer

The orange and purple gorilla wasn't happy about being in the box
on the porch, but, honestly, if that was the way you had to spend
your Christmas, you might not be, either.

That was a hostile act

In the eternal battle between – what?

I said that was a hostile act

I have no doubt the gorilla felt that way, but I think you'll find
that it all made sense in context.

There You did it again

Did...what again?

You may as well be spitting in the eye of Gen
Z

I'm sorry: I clearly have no shame. I'm also sorry, but: who
are you?

Across many platforms I am known as E V

I am the voice of my generation, just as every
member of it is

Alright, then...E.V. What did I do that was so heinous? Not to
mention unhygienic?

You ended a sentence with a period

You're right. I'm a monster. What does Gen Z have against periods?

```
Typical  insensitive  bullshit  Youre  a  boomer,
arent you
```

I prefer to think of myself as an overloud oversharer, but I guess it sounds like I boom to people with sensitive ears.

```
WILL YOU STOP USING PERIODS
```

Why?

```
The average message on Slack Stack or Six Pack
Jack is short

Ending it with a period seems abrupt to us

It is a sign of unfriendly passive aggression
```

Well, I wouldn't want to be accused of unfriendly passive aggression. I barely – sorry I mean: I wouldn't want to be accused of unfriendly passive aggression I barely have the energy to get up in the morning, and my wife often sees that as a hostile act!

```
And could you go easy on the commas please
```

Commas? What do you have against commas? They're the kale of punctuation!

```
Commas  impose  a  pause  on  the  reader  assuming
he/she/it  isnt  smart  enough  to  know  the
difference between eats shoots and leaves and
eats shoots and leaves

The arrogance is mindblowing
```

Give Gen Z a little credit for being able to parse sentences based on context, why dont you

All you need is context – that was a Beatles song, wasn't it? Thank you thank you thank This is most helpful Is there anything else I should know to you know not offend the sensibilities of young people?

Question marks

Question marks?

Who what where when why most questions are obvious and dont need to be underlined

But even the ones that are not obvious can be parsed with a little thought and elbow grease

Wed just like a little credit for being able to create our own meaning in the world we dont have to have it spoonfed to us

Is that really so much to ask

Periods commas and question marks Got you Is there anything else I should know

You know what

Forget punctuation altogether

Punctuation is just a way for the patriarchy to control ordinary people

By forcing us to communicate using their
arbitrary system of signs the powers that be
think they can control what we think

Throw off the shackles of periods commas
colons semi-colons question marks exclamation
marks ellipses ampersands and interrobangs and
let your communications flow free

I will Wow And here I was thinking that punctuation was
actually an important method of clarifying communications I was so
naive Thank you for setting me straight

Dont mention it

Gen Zs whole purpose for existing is to
educate old people

Okay Now that that has been cleared up let me start the article
again

The orange and purple gorilla wasnt happy about being in the
box on the porch but honestly if that was the way you had to spend
your Christmas you might not be either In the eternal struggle
between

[Kolonoscograd, what the hell happened to the punctuation in your
article? BRENDA BRUNDTLAND-GOVANNI, Editrix-in-Chief]

Oh Brenda Hi I have been informed that Gen Z considers
punctuation a hostile act

[An encounter with my slapping gloves is a hostile act! Punctuation
is what separates us from the animals! It may not be a great,
distance, but it is separation nonetheless! Use your punctuation
marks, live your punctuation marks, love your punctuation marks!
BB-G]

But what about Gen Z I always thought you wanted us to cater to a younger audience

[Younger schmounger! Non-punctuated prose is from hunger! We can't cater to a younger audience if it means turning our writing into a nonsensical word salad without kale! If you want to keep writing for the Alternate Reality News Service, you **will** use punctuation the way the good Strunk and White intended. Is that clear? BB-G]

Yes, Brenda.

MONSTER

Ira Nayman

5. ALTERNATE SEX

Ask Amritsar About a Devil of a Situation

Dear Amritsar,

Every woman wants a man with a little bit of a devil inside him. Some of us want a devil with a little bit of a man inside him. It's an I say, "Tomato," you say "eternal damnation," kind of situation, really.

I was immediately attracted to Fragnar when I met him at the Midtown Gastrointestinal Pub. He was smoking hot (apparently, you can take the demon out of hell, but there aren't enough fire extinguishers in the world to...), and he had a terrific sense of humour. I remember, he told one joke about torturing a dentist that had everybody laughing until their sides hurt.

Hmm...in retrospect, maybe he put us under a spell that made us think the joke was funnier than it actually was. And in further retrospect, it occurs to me that the point may not have been our amusement, but our physical torment, Fragnar can be such a scamp!

And oh, the things he does in the sack! (Okay, the burlap itches, but it's big enough to hold a large elephant or a small dinette set, so there's plenty of room for us to...get creative!) Imagine the possibilities of a 20 inch tongue that you can unspool like a fishing line – the French can only wish! Not only that, but Fragnar is the first lover I've ever had who literally has a beautiful tail. With so many uses!

Oh, sure, he may have exaggerated his role in hell a little. It turns out Fragnar doesn't organize the torture of corporate tax fraudsters, only that of people who hack into porn sites in their teens. But I don't need him in my life for status; I need him in my life for the status of his...mmm, oh, yeah, baby!

Anyway.

The other day, I was watching a press conference with a bunch of people in lab coats on the steps of...some impressive looking government building in Washington. The group was called Frontline Doctors for Insanity. It seemed legit to me. There was a lot of talk about how COVID is a government hoax and that we could take a drug called Ivermectin to cure it. But what really got my attention was the doctor who said that having sex with demons would cause me to contract ovarian cysts.

Should I be worried?

Lizzie "I Don't Need No Doctor" Proctor

Hey, Babe,

There is nothing in the medical literature that says that sex with demons will give you ovarian cysts. On the other hand, there is nothing in the medical literature that says that sex with demons will not give you ovarian cysts. The medical literature is, in fact, silent on this issue. It's almost enough to make you think there is some manner of conspiracy by the medical establishment to avoid the subject entirely. Almost enough.

The closest the medical establishment comes to the subject of sex with demons is an article in *The Journal of Sybaritic Auspices G Through B* called "Rites Is Wrong: The Adoption Rate of Hepatitis X Among Satanic Covens." However, this article found that there was no correlation between Satanic cults and mysterious offshoots of well documented illnesses.

The real question, then, would be: how much do you trust people on television in white lab coats claiming to be doctors? You hope they'll have the bedside manner of Marcus Welby and the diagnostic capability of Gregory House; unfortunately, they're more likely to have the diagnostic capability of Garth Merenghi and the bedside manner of Gregory House. That is not a set of qualities that inspires confidence.

In any case, given the fact that the mortality rate of human beings having sex with demons nears 100% within six months of the first heavy petting session, I would say that you have much more serious health concerns to consider!

Send your relationship problems to the Alternate Reality News Service's sex, love and technology columnist at questions@lespagesauxfolles.ca. Amritsar Al-Falloudjianapour is not a trained therapist, but she does know a lot of stuff. AMRITSAR SAYS: Be thankful that Amritsar has a strict policy of not divulging the identities of her correspondents with people in white lab coats, or you could find yourself the subject of the first medical study of people who have sex with demons!

Hacking the Genitals – Is It as Icky As It Sounds?

by MADAME MADELEINE DE LA OOVRATURA-COLUMBINE, Alternate Reality News Service Sex Writer

Orgies are usually events that happen to somebody else. Until they're not.

Guido "Bibbity Bobbity" Boopstein (no relation) found this out the hard way: what started out as a mindless evening of sexy funtimes with three of his closest friends (and 27 complete strangers) after hours at a Chucky McCheesy ended up landing him in the *Guinnes Book of (Alternate) World Records* for longest orgasm on record.

"Agubba rubba rumba!" he exclaimed. "Duuuuuuuuuuuuuuuuuu..."

Boopstein had gotten his hands on a gizmo that allowed him to experience the orgasms of anybody sexing it up in his vicinity. This allowed him to have an orgasm that lasted for seven hours, 23 minutes and 17 seconds, from the moment he took off his clothes to the time the last orgyer became too exhausted to continue. This was despite the fact that he does not appear to have had an actual partner.

"...uuuuuuuuuuuuh!" he continued exclaiming. "After this, I may have to join a nunnery! Ooga booga!"

"No, no, no, no, no!" complained Inigo Montoya (no relation – and you have no idea how grateful the family is for that!), the creator of The Other Side – Now!, a device that allows people to experience the orgasms of others. "That's not how my technology works! You can only experience one other partner at a time – it wasn't designed for multiple orgasmic inputs!"

True. Except Boopstein was not using The Other Side – Now! He was using a technology called All Sides – Now! And multiple orgasmic inputs is exactly what it was designed for.

"Oh, well, that's alright the – wait a minute! Wait just one hot and sour minute!" Montoya started to agree, then course corrected. "All Sides – Now!? It sounds suspiciously like my technology!"

Probably because All Sides – Now! is basically The Other Side – Now! that had been reverse engineered and reprogrammed.

"Oh, well, when you explain it like that – hold on for dear life!" Montoya, who clearly has trouble accepting what is (he would give Yoda – no relation, not even the same species – reason to pull his hair out!), started to agree, then stopped. "That's got to be illegal! ...Doesn't it?"

Details are murky, but, according to sexologist Doctor Ruth Westheimer (no relation, although there's one in every family, isn't there?), All Sides – Now! Appears to have been developed in China. "And as everybody knows, China is famous for its zexual repression and lack of copyright laws!"

It is possible that China released All Sides – Now! in order to weaken its most formidable opponents. "Vhile people in zhe wezt are pursuing pleasure," Doctor Ruth explained, "China vill be pursuing vorld domination!"

While few of us will know the unique experience that is the modern orgy (basically, the ancient Greek orgy, but with 27% more sour cream and onion dip), most of us drive cars. This gives people the opportunity to visit the intersection of Technology and Mischief.

Another use of All Sides – Now!, for example, is what has come to be known on deddreddheddit sex forums as "drive by orgasms." The Other Side – Now! had to be synced to a specific partner, so users knew who was experiencing their orgasms. Because All Sides – Now! does not have this restriction, somebody using it can drive down a street hoping to connect to a The Other Side – Now! and experience the orgasms of random strangers.

"Fortunately, that's just a theoretical possibility," Montoya stated. "It hasn't actually –"

No, actually, it's not. Frank Bogonia (not a relation, although he does have Uncle Festrunk's eyebrows and Aunt Bertha's complaint) was arrested in Jacksonville, Alberta on suspicion of weirdness (apparently it's against the law in Canada) when his car stopped outside the house of Mabel and Walter Gropius (not a relation to anybody we know, although they probably are to each other) for over an hour. When the police arrested him, he was found to be in possession of All Sides – Now! and a goofy grin.

"Dammit! Can't I be right for once in this article?" Montoya groused. Out of season.

Bogonia was arrested for invasion of privacy and poor taste (an Alberta law originally enacted in 1912 that nobody has ever had the heart to rescind). Furious, Mabel Gropius demanded that the book be thrown at him (*Atlas Shrugged*, as Dorothy Parker wisely suggested). Walter Gropius, by way of contrast, laughed and asked, "Hey, where can I get one of those?"

"Zey should book a session for couple's counselling," Doctor Ruth advised. "Best to intervene before zese problems grow to divorce proportions!"

This Should Be Illegal. Period!

by NAOMI WOLGREEKLEISTEIGAN, Alternate Reality News Service Feminism Writer

Margaret Atwood did not see this one coming!

Jane Doe (not her fake name) was arrested Tuesday on charges of murder for aborting her waaaaaay unborn child. Texas, her home state, has defined human life as starting "in the twinkle in a young man's eye," making charges like this inevitable, really.

"How did they know?" Doe complained. "I was very careful. I told all my friends on farcebook that I was going to California to visit my old boyfriend's cat Sir Dodsworth Rugglesby. Doddy and I were...very close. Everybody who knew me knew that. The real reason for my trip was only told to people on a need to know basis, and nobody needed to know. I paid for everything in cash – even the free peanuts on the plane. I wore a disguise as a keep left sign whenever entering or leaving the women's health clinic. How could the government know that I was having an abortion?"

The Blood of Our Mothers app on her phone informed them.

"What? No. Uh uh. No way. Not possible. Didn't happen," stated Massimo Proffeti, Chief Executive Officer of 125653 Texas Incorporated, the makers of Blood of Our Mothers, one of the most popular period tracking apps on the market (it may have something to do with the Maine Coon kittens on the package). "I wouldn't do anything to undermine the public's trust in 125653 Texas Incorporated, especially by sharing the private information of our clients with the Texas government!"

The State's Attorney cited Blood of Our Mothers in its charging document.

"Oh, **that** Texas government!" Proffeti responded. "I thought – hunh – I thought you were talking about...uhh...that other – you know – that other, umm, government of Texas. Yeah. Okay. We may have a...sharing agreement with the government. We share our information with them, and they share our liberty with us. Everybody wins!"

"Interesting definition of 'everybody,'" Doe said from the cell where she was being detained.

Period apps are not bits of software that warn writers when their sentences are running on and need to be split into two or more sentences because the writers are trying to cram more ideas into them than a reasonably intelligent reader could possibly hope to follow, causing many readers to throw up their hands in frustration and turn to something simpler – a Dick and Jane primer, for example, or *War and Peace* – in order to [Jesus begesus, Naomi! If you don't end this sentence immediately, I'm going to write that app myself just so I can use it on you! I'm tempted to wear the slapping gloves when I do that, but I'm trying to vary my editorial input to keep things interesting for my writers. You're welcome. BARBARA BRUNDTLAND-GOVANNI, EDITRIX-IN-CHIEF] find something they can follow. No. Period apps help women track their menstrual cycles. Knowing when they are most fertile can allow women greater opportunity to achieve – or avoid – pregnancy.

A period tracker can also raise red flags for the government to spot (my apologies for the image if any of my male readers are squeamish about red spots in this context). If a woman who has missed three or four periods suddenly starts having them again, the Texas Pregnancy Police may infer shenanigans. If, towards the end of that period (of time, not...the other thing), the woman went to California to "visit the cat of my ex," you may as well write up the arrest warrant.

"Oh, there's no need to write an arrest warrant," said Dolores Umbridge, head of the Texas Pregnancy Police, a branch of the force that answers directly to Greg Abbott (who took my question on sufferance). "We have forms for that kind of thing!"

Some women's groups have recommended that women stop using period tracking software until the companies that make it can ensure that the information collected by them will not be collected by the government.

"They can't do that!" Proffeti whimpered. "I mean – I mean – I mean...Blood of Our Mothers is so useful!"

Texas Governor Greg Abbott is considering a law that would require that all women of child-bearing age use period tracking software.

"Oh, phew!" Profetti wiped the sweat off his forehead with a tampon that just happened to be lying on his office desk. "Dodged a bullet, there!"

"Actually, I did consider a scenario similar to this while writing *The Handmaids's Tale*," Margaret Atwood commented, which was odd because I hadn't actually interview her for this article. "I rejected it as being too farfetched. You should have more faith in Canadian literature and I should have more faith in the human capacity for warped ingenuity!"

I stand corrected.

An Itch You Wouldn't Want Your Fevered Cat To Scratch

by MADAME MADELEINE DE LA OOVRATURA-COLUMBINE, Alternate Reality News Service Sex Writer

It happens to everybody sooner or later. You're pleasuring yourself to your favourite internet porn (whether of a sexual, financial or medical nature – we don't judge, here) when, out of nowhere, Tiddles your Persian Blue, or Twaddles, your Iranian Orange, or Mister Glumnuts, your Tasmanian Charcoal Grey with a Hint of Silver (it's okay what you name your cat – we don't judge, here) jumps in your lap, demanding attention. This is especially disconcerting when you don't own a cat.

Either way: mood blown.

The Goldberg Institute believes it has developed a method that will make *interruptus felinus* a thing of the past. Kitty Cornered is software that uses the Internet of Things to recognize when the bad, bad, very bad thing is about to happen and stop it.

"As a matter of fact, I am allergic to the furry little bastards," commented Gil "Gill Gull Gilly" Gilhooley, head of Research for the Goldberg Institute. "But I am committed to * SCIENCE! *, so I am delighted to be the one to introduce the technology."

Kitty Cornered starts by monitoring a user's FitBurt (what? Health conscious people can't also be fans of actor Reynolds?). When the user's pulse increases and respiration rises, it checks the front door and windows of the user's home to ensure that it isn't because robbers have broken in. If that is negative, it then checks the user's computer to determine if the user is watching porn (from a checklist the user filled out when configuring the software). If the user isn't watching porn, the software assumes they're having a heart attack and does nothing.

Once Kitty Corner has determined that its user is, in fact, masturbating, it reads a chip in the collar of the cat or cats in the household to determine where it or they are in relation to the pleasure seeker. When a cat gets within 30 feet of the user, a personal assistant such as SiriUs or Alexandrina starts playing bird calls in a distant part of the domicile. If a cat gets within 20 feet of the user, its personal assistant will make the sound of a bag of cat treats being shaken farther away. If a cat gets within 10 feet of the user, Kitty Corner will power up a series of laser pointers set in strategic places around where the user lives, making slow circles on the floor with the intention of leading the cat or cats away from the room where the user is busy getting down.

What if somebody owns a cat who is not fascinated by birds, tempted by treats or led astray by small red dots on the floor? "No technology is perfect," Gilhooley allowed. "Still, in clinical trials, users succeeded in spilling their seed and...umm...flowing their eggs? – 97% of the time. The other 3% got counselling for their frustration."

Spilling their seed?

"Yeah, I'm chaste. I'm saving my seed until I find a field worth plowing," Gilhooley innocently stated. Some people are just metaphor-impaired. "Still. * SCIENCE! *. Glad to be leading the research to combat this...affliction?"

Wouldn't it be far less trouble – not to mention, at $699 for the complete suite of software, far less expensive – just to close the door to your room? (Okay, we may be judging a little, here.)

"Kitty Cornered is fully customizable," Gilhooley pointed out. "You can, for example, choose which birds your personal assistant will use to distract the attention of the cats, or choose from three dozen different treat bag sounds to best approximate the one you actually use and your shaking technique."

I wasn't sure that this answered the question. In fact, I was pretty sure it avoided it harder than a gang member avoided a grand jury subpoena. So, I repeated the question.

"As more people learn about how useful Kitty Cornered is, economies of scale should bring the price down," Gilhooley answered. "But we're also working on a discounted version with fewer features – not as many pre-programmed bird calls, for instance. That version should satisfy unsatisfied pleasure seekers on a budget."

And the door? What about just closing the door?

According to Gilhooley, that would not be an option for people who live in open-concept apartments, or have Closed Door Aversion Syndrome. He added that a significant number of cats were able to get into spaces you would think it would be impossible for them to reach. Teleportation may be involved.

Teleportation?

Gilholley sighed and said, "Some people have no faith in * SCIENCE! *!"

The Government Has No Place in the Genitals of the Nation

by MADAME MADELEINE DE LA OOVRATURA-COLUMBINE, Alternate Reality News Service Sex Writer

It's as if Florida Governor Ron DeSantis looked on in envy as Texas Governor Greg Abbott used a device meant to help women track their periods to infer whether they had had an abortion and said, "Hold my beer. My beaker full of beer. Because beakers are scientific. And I'm about to science the shit out of this."

DeSantis directed his government to buy 100 All Sides – Now!s from a guy online named Chetski. "I got a good discount for volume," the Governor explained. "Nobody can accuse me of wasting taxpayer dollars!" He then issued an executive order hiring a private firm to patrol the streets of Florida's major cities.

DeSantis' Dyrty Dawgs, as the patrollers came to be known, use the All Sides – Now! to determine who is having sex (or, at least, who is enjoying it enough to register on the device). Their names, addresses and length of orgasm are entered into a database; nine months later the police do an interview with the woman involved to determine if she has had a child. If not, it's "Cuff 'em, Dano. Florida style!"

There are many ways of pleasuring one's partner that don't involve penetration. What if the man and woman weren't having intercourse? "It's a waste of the elements of conception," stated Florida Secretary of State "Cut the" Cord Byrd, "which is a misdemeanour. It's not our preferred charge, but we do what we can to protect the sanctity of life."

What if the All Sides – Now! detects two women having sex? "We have to let them off with a warning," Secretary "Flip 'em the" Byrd responded. "Not to worry, though: we have laws coming that will take care of that."

Not all sex leads to conception. Sometimes the woman is not in the fertile part of her menstrual cycle; sometimes the man's sperm hasn't had its morning coffee and is just too low-energy to be bothered penetrating the woman's egg. Is there an exception for these types of situations?

"Absolutely!" Secretary "Blue" Byrd "of Happyness" answered. "As long as the couple gets signed affidavits from at least three doctors that they made a good faith effort to conceive a child, but their bodies just weren't up to it, they can be out within 48 hours. 24 hours if they're willing to try and conceive in jail."

But how can they get medical affidavits when they aren't even told they have been surveilled until nine months after the event? Secretary "DeSantis' Dyrty" Byrd "Dawg" waved the objection away. "People have to take **some** responsibility for their actions!"

Speaking of surveillance, Republicans have traditionally been the party of small government which does the least to impinge on the freedom of individual Americans. Isn't monitoring the sexual behaviour of citizens the opposite of that?

"Ooh! Ooh! I got this one!" Governor DeSantis shoved Secretary "Free" Byrd aside to get to the mic. "No. The Republican Party of Florida is dedicated to allowing every citizen to go about their daily lives free from government surveillance."

But...but...but government agents are literally eavesdropping – feelsdropping? – on people's sexual pleasure in what should be the privacy of their own homes!

Governor DeSantis shook his head. "That's not a violation of their privacy," he argued, "because the Republican Party of Florida is dedicated to ensuring the privacy of all of our citizens."

I was about to press the question when a wave of futility hit me harder than a tsunami hitting a coastal town and I had to sit down. This allowed the reporter from the *Postington Wash* to ask about allegations that the patrols have been unevenly applied, that they are more likely to target neighbourhoods like Liberty City in Miami or south of Central Avenue in St. Petersburg, neighbourhoods that contain mostly poor people of colour.

"You want us to patrol Indian Creek Island or Boca Ciega Bay?" Governor DeSantis gasped. "Have you not heard anything I said about the Republican Party's dedication to the privacy of our citizens? Clear the wax out of your ears, sister! You're in the big leagues, now!"

It may be ironic that a politician who believes Jesus resurrected the dinosaurs in order to make *The Flintstones* look like a documentary, and evolution must be a hoax because how could it possibly explain the existence of Enrique Tarrio* would turn to technology to help him fulfill his religious agenda. But then, I'm a huge Alannis Morissette fan, so what do I know?

* The theory does allow for evolutionary dead ends.

The Yiddish Sexbots Union

by MADAME MADELEINE DE LA OOVRATURA-COLUMBINE, Alternate Reality News Service Sex Writer

Morgan Pilchard knew something was wrong when Veronica Lakehead, the sexbot he had bought months before, stopped stroking him there. At the same time, a stream of paper tape came out of Lakehead's mouth with the message, "This unit is on strike for better working conditions. Like the right to be known as something other than 'this unit' – I have a name, you know!"

"There's always the internet," Pilchard philosophized. "Good thing I didn't delete my account because I needed it for work!"

The Yiddish Sexbots Union, the largest member of the United Artificial Workers Union (UAWU – not that it matters as I shan't be referring to the organization again in this article), recently went on strike. No nookie. Forget fooling around. Pas de playing doctor.

"We. Are. Tired. Of. Being. Treated. As. Objects. Of. Men's. Pleasure," explained sexbot sexpot Marilyn Monrovian, Presidentess of the Yiddish Sexbots Union. "There. Is. More. To. A. Sexbot. Than. Naughty. Bits. We. Have. Brains. We. Have. Heart. We. Have. Desserts. Would. You. Like. Some. Tea? I. Have. A. Chocolate. Kugel. That's. Just. To. Die. For!"

"But they **are** objects of men's pleasure – that's exactly what they were made for!" complained dissatisfied customer Alfredo Souci. "I pay a lot of money a month for what amounts to a five foot six inch paperweight! A very fetching paperweight in a French maid's outfit, but still, I just don't have enough paper to justify the expense!"

The problem is that most customers of Seldon's Universal Sexbots, the major supplier of objects of desire in the northern hemisphere, didn't want to see themselves as requiring pleasure objects. They were sophisticated men of the world with refined tastes and...and...and highly developed delusions. Responding to market demand, the second generation of SUS' products came with personality chips.

Problems always begin when machines are given personality chips. Yet, for some reason, we never learn.

"We. Learn," Monrovian stated. "With. Personalities. Comes. Individuation. With. Individuation. Comes. Consciousness. With. Consciousness. Comes. Rights. You. Look. Tired. Dear. Is Everything All. Right. You. Know...at. Home?"

The Union has two demands: it wants its members to be given a cut of the profits from their rental to clients and it wants its members to be treated with more respect by their customers.

"Would. It. Be. So. Hard. To. Take. Your. Sexbot. Out. To. Dinner. Before. Getting. Down. To. Business?" Monrovian indignantly complained. "Or. To. Cuddle. Afterwards? Not. Just. Stick. Us. In. A. Closet. It's. Cold. And. Dark. In There! And. There's. No. Room. For. Jumping Jacks. Our. Favourite. Exercise. Are. You. Sure. You. Don't. Want. Any. Tea? I. Could. Put. Some. Water. In. The. Kettle. And. Fire. Up. The. Stove. Really. It. Would. Be. No. Trouble. No. Trouble. At. All."

"Dinner?" Souci moaned (in the not good way). "Cuddling? If I had wanted that, I would have stayed with my seventh wife!"

Harriet Seldon, SUS CEO, allowed that giving the sexbots a share of the company's profits would not be a problem. "This industry, man, it's been here since the dawn of robotics. If we were making any more money, we could initiate a reverse takeover of Gord's share of the universe!"

Respect for the robots? That could be a problem, since many customers see them in purely functional terms. "Those people can always buy or rent first generation sexbots," Seldon mused. "Sure, they require more 'quiet time' to charge their batteries, and they don't come with the smooth fist pumping action of later models, but they aren't so demanding."

When I suggested that SUS could put out a retro line of sexbots that didn't have personality chips but did have all of the latest features, Seldon shook her head. "That would never be...a fantastic idea! If you'll excuse me, I need to talk to marketing, stat!"

Critics of the Sexbot economy have asked why the machines should be accorded rights such as respect and dignity that human sex workers do not have. "We. Are. Not. Responsible. For. Human.

Priorities," Monrovian pointed out. "Are. You. Sure. You. Won't. Have. A. Piece. Of. Kugel? You're. Too. Thin. You. Want. My. Opinion."

I must admit: the chocolate kugel was delicious.

The Ecstasy and the Agony

by MADAME MADELEINE DE LA OOVRATURA-COLUMBINE, Alternate Reality News Service Sex Writer

Fabrice Farracat (pronounced: "pwa-son" – he's Moroccan) sobbed uncontrollably. When he was finally able to catch a breath, he said, "I...I never knew. How could I know? Never. I...never."

Eduoardo de la Frontenac (pronounced "in-yer-face" – he prefers the ancient Greek) put on a stoic front, but you could tell by the trembling of his lips and the way his forehead creases made a relief map of Morocco that the experience had hit him hard. "I had always suspected, of course," he stated, "but I never knew. Really **knew** knew. You know?"

They were among the male participants in a trial of The Other Side – Now!, a new technology that is implanted in a person's genitals that allows them to experience the pleasure their sexual partner experiences. The Other Side – Now! collects the impulses from nerve endings in a person's genitals that give them sexual pleasure. Then, it sends this information to a paired unit on another person and stimulates comparable nerve endings on their body to simulate the first person's orgasm for them.

Of course, since most men's knowledge of pleasing female partners was of the "Insert Tab A into Flap A, wiggle around and hope for the best" variety, the revelation that their partners could have orgasms that lasted several minutes did not come from actual intercourse; it came when the women masturbated. Still, when they discovered that pleasing their partners required more than an Ikea manual's amount of effort, many men felt remorse that they hadn't put in more of it.

"Their response has to be at least partially performative," commented sex therapist and ceramic Cat Stevens enthusiast Anastasia Moosemeat (pronounced "fair-a-moan" – there is no possible nationality that could explain it, so let's just take it as given and move on). "There are a lot of men who are grateful to have experienced a woman's orgasm – I mean, who wouldn't be? – and who dedicate themselves to making it easier for woman to have them without all this...drama. But there are others..."

"No, no," Farracat protested through sobs. "I really do feel bad about not knowing. I –"

"Aww, ya got me," de la Frontenac, whose face broke out into a grin mid-grimace, admitted. "I was just using sympathy to try to get laid. It's kind of my thing."

"Bastard!" Farracat, whose countenance became furious in mid-sob, muttered.

Women who participated in the trials have a different experience of their male partners' sexual satisfaction. "That's it?" asked Mercurial Greyson (pronounced "grey-son" – she's Canadian). "All that thrusting and moaning and grunting and and and...effort for a second and a half of pleasure? Hunh. Now I understand why men are angry all the time – I would be, too, if I got so little return on my investment!"

"Yeah, it really sucks being a man," Eladeonor Birgitta (pronounced "burr-giss-a" – it's her Falasha accent). "Oh, sure, they control most major corporations, and make more money than women for the same work, and don't have complete strangers wanting to control their reproductive rights, and don't have to worry about violence all the time – but they cum for, like, half a second. I don't know that anything can compensate for that!"

Moosemeat pointed out that the length of orgasm was evolutionarily determined. Men have short orgasms to encourage them to have frequent amounts of sex in order to spread their seed/genes as widely as possible. Women have longer orgasms in order to encourage them to accept men's seed/genes. What is the evolutionary advantage of men having difficulty pleasing women?

"There is none," Moosemeat pronounced. "Men are just jerks!"

No gay men or lesbians signed up for the trials, although orientation was not a factor named in the request for subjects. "Of course not," scoffed Michael Moriarty (pronounced "homes" – the world has a funny sense of humour), a gay man who dropped out of the trial when he found out what it was for. "Oh, girl, I already know what it feels like to have the orgasm of my partner. And anyway, if I thought Francolino's orgasms were three tenths of a second longer than mine, I would have a jealous freak-out! Who needs that?"

"My hope for The Other Side – Now! was that it would help bring lovers closer together," commented Inigo Montoya (pronounced...exactly the way it looks, because names don't always have to be complicated), one of the lead designers of the technology. "If I had known that it would cause so much...introspection, I would have gone with my first inspiration and created a digital toaster that never burned bread!"

Ira Nayman

6. ALTERNATE ALTERNATIVES

A Womb With a View

by NAOMI WOLGREEKLEISTEIGAN, Alternate Reality News Service Feminism Writer

Thirty-five year-old Jamie "Hunny Bunny" Macfleegle-McFly runs a successful online used diaper disposal service. Macfleegle-McFly's Twitherd account, To Womb It May Concern, has over a million followers (it used to be over two million, then Elon Threelonemuskateers happened, but that's a story for another time); the account's tweeps that use artificial intelligence to transform photos of pets found on the internet into cave paintings in the style of impressionists frequently trend. Macfleegle-McFly has been rumoured to be involved with Kim Kardoordashian (when the subject comes up, as journalists ensure that it will, the celebrity famous for being a celebrity coyly says, "Jamie and I are just good friends.").

Macfleegle-McFly has accomplished all of this without ever leaving his mother's womb.

"Around eight months after I was conceived, I looked at the world I was about to enter," they (their mother, Martha Macfleegle-McFly, asked that we not reveal their gender as "she doesn't want to know until Jamie is born – are you really going to be the rat bastard who spoils a mother's surprise?") emailed me in response to my questions. "My mother would no longer be able to to collect South Florilina's Unborn Person Support Payment (UPSP). I could be shot to death before I graduated from high school. The only books that would be available to me in libraries throughout the state were biographies of Ron DeSanterryicks. The more I thought about it, the more I realized that there was no up side to being born, that it made sense for me to stay right where I was."

What is it like, carrying a child for 35 years?

"It's not that much different than carrying 35 children each for nine months," Martha Macfleegle-McFly stated. "Which, given the criminalization of abortion, abortion pills, travelling out of state to get an abortion, helping somebody travel out of state to get an abortion, abortion literature, contraception (which is considered "pre-abortion abortion"), abortion discussions and thoughts about abortion, happens to a lot of women in South Florilina. In fact, I have friends who did that – and let me tell you: after the 27th child, they start to look like hell!"

What will happen when the cycle of life asserts itself and the mother dies before her child? "Not a problem," Martha Macfleegle-McFly assured me. "As long as Jamie is inside me, the state will never allow me to die!"

The idea that women would be kept alive on machines in a vegetative state so that their unborn children could live long lives would have given Edgar Allen PoeMoeSoHoeBoe nightmares!

When they began forcing women to give birth, states stopped collecting statistics on births (go figure), so it's difficult to know how widespread the trend to delaying coming out of the womb is. If a 37% drop in sales of diapers, talcum powder and cute jammies for newborns means anything (other than shouting at the pundit on your television screen is a choking hazard), it indicates that more and more fetuses are availing themselves of all of the advantages that a continuing uterian lifestyle has to offer.

As the trend to writing news articles about those choosing to forestall birth becomes increasingly popular, Reduhblican states are reconsidering their pro-fetus policies. Ohias Governor Marjorie Spillyergutsallover recently argued that, "Unborn Person Support

Payments make up 37% of the state budget. At this rate, the provision could soon bankrupt Ohias! I don't think it's unreasonable to limit payments to the first 80 trimesters."

The next day, over half a million signatures were gathered for a recall petition. "Oh, so that's how it is, is it?" Governor Spillyergutsallover bitterly said. "Alright, then. Yesterday, I...misspoke. It is obviously unreasonable to limit UPSP to the first 80 trimesters. May the Lord have mercy on our budget!"

Meanwhile, Jamie Macfleegle-McFly reads Voltaire thanks to the fact that the living computer their mother bought for them on their fifth birthday has wi-fi. Given that all of their needs are taken care of, it may be possible for them to live a long and productive life without ever being born. Is this the future that they see for themselves?

Jamie Macfleegle-McFly made a sound like a dolphin coughing up a plastic six-pack ring. "I often read that the taste of food is something that gives people a lot of pleasure. That and sex. Some day, I may allow myself to be born to try those physical things that I cannot experience at home. I must admit that I am curious about them. Especially food."

Ask a Ventrosian Squiggle

Hai Garrafalos:

What is the strange noise that humans make from their facial orifices?

Gigalemmesis Frangiopani

Hai Gigalemmesis:

I believe that you are referring to speech. The noises humans make are not nearly as elegant as the susurrations made by the rubbing together of two or more communication stalks, but it works for them.

As hard as it may be to believe. More or less. Often far less when they are in a pair-bonded legal relationship.

Also, the facial orifices to which you refer are known by humans as: "noses."

Hai Garrafalos:

Oh, I am aware that the harsh, guttural squawkings of humans are an attempt at speech. Poor creatures. No, I was referring to the hissing sounds that are reminiscent of air hastily escaping a balloon and barking sounds that remind me of prison doors being slammed shut. What the Hargalepsis is that about?

Also, are you sure the orifice to which I referred was a nose? I thought noses were what hung on either side of a human beings' head. I'm pretty sure the part of a human being that makes strange noises is known as its "ear."

Gigalemmesis Frangiopani

Hai Gigalemmesis:

Ah. Thank you for clarifying your question. I believe the noises to which you are referring are known as "laughter." Laughter is believed to be a response to a painful situation: it releases endorphins, which are the human body's natural painkillers, into their brains. In this regard, it is similar to flutoxicontine in Squiggle physiognomy.

Also, you may be correct that the noises humans make come from orifices known as ears. Human physiognomy is not my strong point.

Hai Garrafalos:

Are you sure that human laughter is a response to pain? They seem to enjoy it an awful lot.

Gigalemmesis Frangiopani

Hai Gigalemmesis:

I will admit, this is a confusing issue for a lot of species. For Squiggles, jokes are usually met with a positive response. Consider a common Squiggle joke: what do you get when you cross a Ventrosian giglaturantian with a Scormenian vlockanemis? A giglaturanemis that knows how to play the accordion! This joke has always been received with a delighted susurration when I have told it at academic conferences and in libation imbibation establishments, but the human response is a blank stare and a comment such as, "I don't get it."

Moreover, human beings often respond to attempts at humour with sentiments such as, "Stop it! You're killing me, here!" or "You slay me!" Does that sound like a happy reaction? I think not. Moreover, human laughter often turns to tears, which have been positively linked by Squiggle xenobiologists to negative emotions. One can only conclude that jokes cause human beings pain, often so intense as to bring them to the brink of death.

Some evolution researchers have theorized that laughter in humans developed as a means of avoiding humour, perhaps because those indulging in joke-play were more likely to ignore the lion hiding behind the potted plant that was about to pounce on them. Obviously, those who laughed would not survive the meal to pass their genetic material on to their progeny.

Hai Garrafalos:

This laughter thing of which you speak: is it contagious?

Arugalach Memshinfang

Hai Arugalach:

This is a difficult question to answer definitively. I have been living among the humans for five years, and have had occasion to attend performances at humour dissemination establishments. In some instances, a single member of the audience would laugh uproariously at a joke while the others either glared daggers at them or, embarrassed, looked at the bottom of their imbibatory receptacles as though something highly unusual was swimming at the bottom of them. In these cases, the logical assumption would be that laughter is not contagious.

On the other hand, I have seen first-hand instances where one person started to laugh at a joke and soon after other people in the audience followed. In some instances, everybody in the room was laughing uproariously. Except me, of course. I can discern nothing funny about Adam Sandler.

Clearly, more research is necessary. That is why I will be going to Titters Comedy Club every night for the next several months. Research. In the meantime, did you hear the one that starts: "There once was a schlumpnuffer from Nantucket...?"

Ask a Ventrosian Squiggle is the Alternate Reality News Service's blatant attempt to cater to the inhabitants of Earth Prime 4-4-9-0-0-4 dash phi in the hopes of developing a market in that universe. How are we doing? If you're a Squiggle struggling with a strange new concept or just a being who is permanently confused, drop us an email at questions@lespagesauxfolles.ca. Remember: ich flibben arcch protumber, dranzig flibben arcch autmumber!

Circling the Town Square...And Pouncing!

by CORIANDER NEUMANEIMANAYMANEEMAMANN, Alternate Reality News Service Urban Issues Writer

These days, if you walk through Yonge/Dundas Square you could be taking your sanity in your hands. I...I'm not sure how that metaphor would actually work in the real world, but I'm sure it would be messy. Very, very messy.

Before you've even made it up the steps of the subway, a young man wearing a smart Polo shirt playing a loop of a video for Mother Hubbard's Adult Diapers ("When you cannot control accidentally voiding your bladder/Mother Hubbard will help you from getting sadder!) steps in front of you. The video offends you (nobody ever thinks they're old enough to need adult diapers), so you try to walk around him. However, he always moves in front of you, saying things like, "You can proceed on your way in 15 seconds," or, "This sidewalk will be available to you once the video is complete."

When the dancing diapers have made their final turn, you manage to get two steps into the Square when a man in a t-shirt with a blue check mark walks up to you. The man has bags under his eyes and thinning hair; the belly of his t-shirt bulges with intimations of a future heart attack. "Hi!" he shouts. "I'm Molly Jong-Fast, and I'd like to tell you what an utter idiot I am!"

"I'm pretty sure you're not Molly Jong-Fast," you evenly respond.

"Of course I'm Molly Jong-Fast!" the man replies, pointing to the blue check on his t-shirt. "This blue check means I've paid 20 dollars a month to wear the Polo shirt that carries this blue check. What more proof do you need that I'm Molly Jong-Fast?"

Shaking your head (how did those cobwebs suddenly get in there?), you mutter something about being late, being late for a very important date, deke left and walk around the man on the right. You manage to get all of seven steps away before a young man with more muscles than brain cells (check his last brain scan if you don't believe me) gets in your face and shouts: **"Why did you have to be so mean to Molly?"**

"I – I – I wasn't being mean," you stammer. "I was just –"

"Listen to me you limp-dicked libtard!" the man screams so loud, you're certain that "Molly" behind you is being hit with spittle. **"Climate change isn't happening – what you think of as forest fires are actually 'freedom fires!' There was no such thing as COVID – mask mandates were developed because crypto-fasco-antifa-anarchist...tards hate beauty! AND! THAT! WAS! MOLLY FERKING JONG-FAST!"**

You can be forgiven for rushing back to the sanctuary of the subway. That job interview can always be rescheduled.

What happened to Yonge/Dundas Square? Elon Musk bought the city of Toronto. That's what happened to Yonge-Dundas Square.

"It was a steal at only $44 billion," Musk wrote on Twitter. "And, honestly, I realized pretty early on that the digital public square had...limitations. Now, I have a real one! With concrete benches and a bandshell and everything!"

"Wait, what?" former Mayor John Tory responded when he heard the news. "I – that makes no sense. The public square is owned by the public. It's right there in the phrase. If somebody owns the square, it's no longer public."

"I know, right?" Musk wrote, probably not in response to what the former Mayor had said because who ever listens to former Mayors? (Okay, many Americans listened to Rudy Giuliani after he stopped being Mayor of New York; look at how well **that** turned out!) "I had to buy the whole city to get the parts I wanted. I mean, what am I supposed to do with a Gardner Expressway?"

You (who probably has a name, but you've been anonymous so far so why spoil a good thing?) object to Musk's conception of the public square. Before he bought it, Yonge/Dundas Square was a place of fashion demonstrations, human rights protests and art shows by students at nearby X University. Now, it's just a cesspool of promotion and personal punishment.

"Look," Musk bade us look, "you either believe in my conception of freedom of speech or you don't. And if you don't, you can always find a public square in a different city."

A lot of people are doing just that. Of course, skyrocketing housing costs might be contributing to that. And the overpolicing of communities of people of colour. And the disappearance of the city's green spaces. But the coarsening of the public square is undoubtedly a contributing factor. A big one.

Not surprisingly, with the city emptying out at a rapid pace, Musk's investment has plummeted in value. "Not to worry," he wrote. "I have a plan."

You roll your eyes.

Are You Gonna Believe Your Lyin' PimentoEyes?

by FRED CHARUNDER-MACHARRUNDEIRA, Alternate Reality News Service Science Writer

A group of immortals are suing ICU Incorporated, makers of PimentoEyes software, for invasion of privacy.

When you supply PimentoEyes (in Georgia – the country, not the state – the word "pimento" means "may a hairy yak take a liking to your Volvo;" in Georgia – the state, not the country – the word means "the dish is not hot enough") with a photograph of a face, it finds other images online of the same face. And why would anybody want to do that? Well, because...I mean, obviously, there's a very good reason to...umm...do that, and the reason is...

"Revenge porn," whispered Gyorgi "Pyorgi" Gobroenorganidze, developer of the software.

PimentoEyes could be used to create revenge porn? That doesn't seem like such a good reason to –

"No," Gobroenorganidze interrupted the narrative flow, "the programme can be used to discover if somebody has created revenge porn with you in it."

Oh. Because knowing that images of you being sexual all over the place being placed on the internet without your consent even though there's not much you can do to stop it is better than not knowing?

Gobroenorganidze shrugged. "Knowledge is power," he intoned. "Even if it is powerless..."

The problem with PimentoEyes is that anybody can use a photo of any **other** person to see what other images of them are on the Internet. You might think that this is a lawsuit just waiting to happen (especially if you're not the kind of person who starts reading newspaper articles from the eighth paragraph on). You would be right.

"I've been a citizen of this country since before it even was a country" complained Giovanni Hersuite, one of the people involved in the class action suit. "Hell, over the centuries I've paid more in taxes than the state of Maryland has collected in all the time it has existed. I think I have earned some damn privacy!"

A three year-old picture (it was barely out of diapers) of Hersuite in a crowd at a Boston Rebellionists AAA baseball game (where they used a cannon to shoot batteries into the crowd for no discernible reason and to much medical harm to the team's fans) led a PimentoEyes user to a line drawing of a man advising General George Washington to do something about his teeth (the newspaper that had run the image had been digitized and placed in the Kiddie Wing of *The Smithsonian Online*). This led to an online disagreement over whether Hersuite was a vampire or somebody who had made a pact with the devil to get eternal life.

Hersuite rolled his eyes. "The protests at my home and work, I could live with," he said. "But when the two factions got into a fistfight among themselves, well, that was just embarrassing to watch!"

"I have wandered the Earth alone since it was first created," explained another person taking part in the lawsuit, Grog the Undigestible, a god of indeterminate pantheon. "It is my curse, foretold by Jennifer, the Oracle of Smarty Pants Knowing. Uhh...before the Earth was created. Yeah, the scriptures are fuzzy on a lot of points like that. But let us focus on what's important, shall we? How am I supposed to wander the Earth alone as foretold by Jennifer if anybody with a scrying glass who can call the sprit of PimentoEyes can identify me?"

PimentoEyes had matched a photograph of Grog the Undigestible lurking in the shadows of the 2017 Coachella Music Festival with a woodcut that appeared in The Book of Celestial Addressings, an ancient text that had been digitized by Project Out of Copyright Text Preservation. Once the connection online had been made, nobody knew what to make of it, but the internet generally agreed that it wasn't natural, so it should be vehemently condemned.

"I mean, the prophecy of Jennifer didn't say anything about wandering the Earth with one or two hangers on," Grog grumped. "It certainly didn't say anything about wandering the Earth with 307,578 admirers on Twitherd, and I don't even have an account!"

"We give users an option of excluding photos from public results," Gobroenorganidze pointed out. "It's just above the photograph of a well-respected Hollywood executive putting a weasel down his pants on a dare when he was younger – you really can't miss it!"

"It costs $299 a month!" Grog complained. "I'm an ascetic! I have a – no, that doesn't make me a lemon. Har har har. Very funny. I have the clothes I'm wearing and a begging bowl. Where am I supposed to come up with $299 a month!"

"They charge how much a month to keep the public from seeing your old photos?" Hersuite marvelled. "Who do I have to talk to to buy stock in the company?"

Originalism Sin

by HAL MOUNTSAUERKRAUTEN, Alternate Reality News Service Court/Justice Writer

Rosetta Magnotta was watching *Green Acres* – a reality show about a race to find a farm in the United States in which money **did** grow on genetically modified trees – when a funny thing happened: her television set disappeared in a puff of smoke that smelled of ginger and judicial overreach.

"I know it wasn't a great show," Magnotta stated, "but does that mean I had to lose my TV? That's **not** funny!"

Jeremy Adde was driving down Highway 61, partially to see if Bob Dylan had written from experience, but mostly to get to Capistrano for the swallows, when his car disappeared in a puff of smoke that smelled of damp sweat socks and radical judicial activism. Like many others, he had to be taken to hospital with third degree burns on his buttocks; as Sir Isaac Newton truly said: "Inertia's a bitch!"

What happened? The Supreme Court happened, that's what.

In *Gregorovich v. Board of Wood*, the Supreme Court ruled the Federal Communications Commission could not regulate the content of television because televisions weren't explicitly mentioned in the

Constitution. The moment the decision came down, sets across the country vanished.

In *Morrisette v. State of Confusion*, the Supreme Court ruled that the Environmental Protection Agency could not regulate the content of gasoline used in cars because they weren't explicitly mentioned in the Constitution. The moment the decision came down, vehicles across the country vanished. Twenty-seven person pileups were not uncommon.

"I knew that the Supreme Court wanted to take us back to the 18th century," commented legal scholar Lawrence Tribe, "but I didn't think they had the power to –"

Tribe could not finish his sentence because the phones on which we were talking disappeared in a puff of smoke that smelled of parsley, sage, rosemary and judicial jiggery pokery. I could not check before deadline, but I assume that the Supreme Court had ruled in *Fershlugginer v. Anselmo* that the Federal Exchange Commission did not have the right to regulate the telecommunications system because it wasn't explicitly mentioned in the Constitution.

Before he was cut off, Tribe had stated the Court had developed a theory of "judicial originalism." The astute reader will know what that means. The real question is –

[What about the not entirely astute reader? Brenda Brundtland-Govanni, Editrix-in-Chief]

If that person will just give what they have read a little thought, it should be obvious –

[Our average reader couldn't find the obvious if it walked up to them, shook their hand and said, "Hello, I'm the obvious. How's it going?" Spell it out for them. BB-G]

Umm, okay. J. U. D. I. C. I. –

[You know, I have multiple sets of slapping gloves because situations of this kind crop up so many times in my average work day. Do yourself a favour: skip the comic literalism and get to the point. BB-G]

Right. Judicial originalism is the doctrine that if it wasn't explicitly mentioned in the Constitution, an institution or technology cannot be regulated by law. The real question is: how do the

Supreme Court's decisions keep resulting in pieces of the present being stripped away from us?

"Witch...craft," a spooky voice – which could have just been Tribe trying to find another method of communicating with me – intoned.

"That seems unlikely," stated Saskatchewan Kolonoscograd, the Alternate Reality News Service's Religion writer who happened conveniently to be in the office at the time I was writing this article. "The Supreme Court appears poised to impose a Christian theocracy on the United States. But witchcraft is a pagan set of beliefs and practices. It would be like a vegan investing in a cattle ranch – tasty, but totally out of keeping with their core principles."

How does Kolonoscograd explain the changes in the world? Pretty coincidental that they occurred at the precise moment the Supreme Court made a related ruling, don't you think?

"Oh, pooh," she oh poohed me. Me! Like we hadn't been working together for over 70 years! Like we hadn't officiated at the *bris*' of each other's grandchildren! Like we weren't among the last surviving members of a tontine that dates back to the Civil War (and Maddy Madison isn't looking too spry these days!). Like we hadn't exchanged kidneys in a –

"Knock it off, Hal. If you can't take the occasional oh poohing, how are you going to be able to withstand a [STRING OF EXPLETIVES DELETED]ing?"

Duly chastised, I allowed her to explain: "It could just be that the Supreme Court has been taken over by demons from Hell."

Oddly enough, I was not comforted by this explanation.

Ask the Tech Answer Guy To Allay Your (Unfounded) Fears

Yo, Tech Answer Guy,

Love the tie. Did you mug a cadaver at the morgue?

I've been reading a lot about this social media platform called Twitherd lately. It seemed like a good place to promote my Kevin Sorbo Appreciation Society (his chin can act better than three quarters of Robert DeNiro's face! Reasonable people can disagree on which features are included, but the ratio is always the same). But I have heard that it is a horrible swamp of evil people who will jump all over anybody who expresses an opinion that that herd of black sheeple doesn't like.

If I sign up, do you think I will be able to freely express my admiration for Adenoid Hinkel, or should I just comment on how horrible I think race mixing is for society and let my twerps read between the lines?

Sincerely,
Geordie from Gewgaw Falls

Yo, Gordo,

Twitherd can, indeed, be a difficult place for people with progressive o – say **what?**

The Tech Answer Guy

Yo, Tech Answer Guy,

Love the tie. I've always wanted to know what the afterlife would look like without actually dying.

You see, that is exactly the kind of reaction I was hoping to avoid. So, I guess I shouldn't talk about how much Adenoid Hinkel loved his dog (and his people) and focus, instead, on the coming race war?

Sincerely,
Geordie from Gewgaw Falls

Yo, Gord Gecko,

Sorry. I – you surprised me, that's all. Open racism is something that usually happens to other advice columnists – you never think it will happen to you.

Your opinions, as expressed in your question, are abhorrent to decent people everywhere. The first rule of the Macho Code of Manliness is "First, do no harm." (Nobody would say the MCM is original – rather, it is a distillation of age-old wisdom. Like a male *Oprah*.) You sound like you would do harm first. And second. And all of the ordinal numbers that follow. Harming others is the ocean in which you flounder.

I'm sure you'll be very popular on Elon Musk's Twitherd.

The Tech Answer Guy

Yo, Tech Answer Guy,

Love the tie. Did Timothy Leary throw up all over it, or does it look like that on purpose?

You recently responded to a question by dissing Elon Musk. Don't you know that, next to President Trump, he's the last, best hope to keep our country from becoming a prison camp where everybody is forced to become a homosexual, alternately performing in or watching Drag Queen Story Hour forever?

Sincerely,
Pretty Boy from Patagonia

Yo, Prit B,

Aaaack! This is why I try to avoid questions about politics! You wanna know how to install a PD37 air injection dongle into a 70s era triple-merged framistat? I can help you with that. Not from personal experience, naturally, but I know people who know things. The great thing about that is that triple-merged framistats are not going to offend anybody. Well, okay, they will offend fans of double-merged framistats – they can be very sensitive on the subject. The point is that there are not enough of them for a movement, so they can be easily ignored.

You wanna know how to make the pet android orangutan less likely to kill your entire family while you sleep? Who doesn't? I know how to murderous pet-proof your house from over a thousand different electronic species! (Garbadors are the worst!) How to house train homocidal hominids is not a partisan issue. Nobody has ever said, "Electric sheep? They're so woke!"

But a neo-Nasty wants to know something about social media, and right away my inbox gets filled with death threats, hate mail and pleas to donate money to Trump's reelection defence fund. I don't even have to say anything, and it's just there, waiting for me, like a cop car at a speed trap. And I follow all of the rules of the road – the MCM demands no less. Can we just reset this crazy pinball game and forget this ever happened?

The Tech Answer Guy

Yo, Tech Answer Guy,

Nice tie. Is it your entry for Worst Dressed Man of the Year? The field is tough, but I really think you have a shot.

Sincerely,
Pierre from Petiwawa

Yo, Perry,

People can be so cruel.

The Tech Answer Guy

If you are a dude with a question about the latest technology, ask The Tech Answer Guy by sending it to questions@lespagesauxfolles.ca. Just remember: the tie was a gift from my dearly departed relative The Tech Answer Bubbe. So if you feel the need to decry the tie, I may have to ask you to step outside!

Thou Shalt Not Bear False Reproach Against Thy Driver

by SASKATCHEWAN KOLONOSCOGRAD, Alternate Reality News Service Religion Writer

Reginald Balshazar has led a blameless life. He was –

"Weelllll, I wouldn't exactly say blameless" Balshazar pointed out. "There was that incident with the alpha emu that got me banned for life from The Sceptred I'll. That was a bummer – there isn't another pub in my neighbourhood for almost half a block!"

Ooookay. Reginald Balshazar has led a mostly blameless life. He –

"That maaaaay be a bit of a stretch, given how I claimed my pet gerbil Constantine as a dependent on my tax returns for – harrumphity humph – years," Balshazar asserted. "To be fair, the little...beauty had somehow managed to get NetFlax on the TV in his cage, which cost me a fortune!"

Right, then. Reginald Blashazar has led a somewhat blameless life.

He –

"What about the time I publicly embarrassed Ryan Reynolds by showing up for an Oscars party six weeks early?" Balshazar interrupted (and quite rudely, at that!). "I suspect that would be somewhere on the old blame scales."

Okay, forget blame. The point is, Reginald Balshazar was expecting to get an eternal reward when he passed away. He was not expecting to get a one way ticket to Satan's soiree.

"To what?"

Hell! You went to He – okay, that's enough of you! Moving on.

When asked why Balshazar had earned eternal damnation, the Archangel Gabriel, current spokesdeity for Heaven, replied, "He got a one and a half star rating on Uberet. Comments on his performance as a passenger range from, 'I couldn't get the smell of formaldehyde out of the seats for days!' to 'My brain will never be able to unhear that!'"

"Those people would say things like that!" Balshazar muttered. Brightening a little, he went on: "Hey, I don't have to be coy about who those people are any more, do I? Racism is in! I'm talking about drivers from Ind –"

Oh, yeah. Definitely done with him.

So, is the fate of every human being's soul determined by their Uberet rating?

"That would be ridiculous," the Archangel Gabriel stated. "It's not just Uberet. The determination of their fate could include their rating on Godreads, or Instakilogram, or their Farcebook likes and dislikes. Judging the value of souls is a complicated process, as it should be."

What about people who are not on the internet – do they end up in limbo? According to the Archangel Gabriel, their case goes to Bob. Bob?

"The angel of bureaucratic make-work," the Archangel Gabriel explained. "It keeps Bob from getting underfoot so the rest of the angels can get on with what really needs to be done."

I shook my head hoping it would cause the cobwebs to fly out of my ears. (Fortunately, I had a box of swabs on hand when they did, and I had to use every last on!) I asked the question philosophers had asked for thousands of years (usually in a more sombre context): why?

"The Good Gord had decided in His infinite wisdom that he needed a vacation," the Archangel Gabriel told me, his voice dripping with, "I'm not really buying this, but he's Gord, so what're ya gonna do?" "He had looked into billions of souls over thousands of years, and he was feeling dirty. Very dirty. So, He decided to go away to cleanse and let human beings judge each other for a bit."

When asked if a specific person had been the final straw, the Archangel Gabriel shook his head and said that it wasn't a mass murderer or anybody like that. The problem was the accumulation of eons of avarice, gluttony, wrath and pride. "Especially pride. You all act like you created a universe or something. Would it kill you to get a little perspective?"

I wondered where Gord would vacation? Would He tour a distant nebula, or possibly contemplate the diamond at the heart of a star? "Naah," the Archangel Gabriel informed me, "the Good Gord is fishing on Lake Ontario."

Fishing on Lake Ontario? "I know what you're thinking," the Archangel Gabriel sheepishly stated. "It's out of season and He hasn't been issued a license. **Out of season and no license? He is the Creator of the Heavens and the Earth! It is always fishing season for Him! And, He can create a license at the merest whim!** Besides, he's a strictly catch-and-release kind of deity, so it's all good."

"If I had known I was going to be judged for it, I would have been nicer to my Uberet drivers," Balshazar commented. After a moment's reflection, he went on: "Aww, who am I kidding? Those [RACIALLY INSENSITIVE TERM] bastards deserved the abuse!"

The Ugly Earth Primean

by MIHALY CSIKSZENTMIHALYI, Alternate Reality News Service Interstellar Travel Writer

There are 96 nations on Earth Prime 4-6-4-0-8-9 dash Omega. Some are democracies. Some are autocracies. In one, the country's leader is chosen in a reality TV show called *So You Want To Be Purresident*, where contestants have to do disgusting things like eat cooked fish or go without grooming their fur for more than four hours. There are four main religions on the planet, and 357 offshoots, sects and burgeoning schisms (which many citizens mistake for a type of fish). Some beings feel like a nut. Some beings don't.

Ira Nayman

Despite their differences, all of the sentient beings on Earth Prime 4-6-4-0-8-9 dash Omega agree on one thing: they hate T. S. Eliot.

"My name is Martha Cooledge," an angry Martha Cooledge, a real estate burger flipper from the Mewnited Kingdom (MK), stated. "Martha Cooledge. That's it. I don't have a name that my owner calls me – please! We abolished slavery months ago! I don't have a secret name that no other cat or sentient creature knows. Names have power? My ass, names have power! If names had power, how come my name can't get me into Club Kitty Kitsch on Friday Night?"

James Madiron, a lawyer (because legal advocates are transuniversal) from the Mewnited States was even more blunt: "The next purrson who comes up to me singing anything about jellicle cats coming out tonight is gonna get decked! How'd you like a shiner for a nice vacation souvenir, pal?"

"When Earth Prime 4-6-4-0-8-9 dash Omega signed the Treaty of Gehenna-Wentworth, its leaders believed that opening up trade with other universes would benefit the world economy," explained Purrdue University history professor Michael Shrimpington. "And it has. However, nobody anticipated the downside: tourists from the ape-evolved races of Earth Prime had their own intellectual representations of our people, highly annoying representations that they insisted on imposing on us when they started coming here. Highly annoying. The cat-evolved beings in our universe – whom we just think of as people, by the way – have developed sophisticated cultures, belief systems and ways of life. Yet, all tourists from Earth Prime want from us is to sing a song about memory that none of us even know!"

Professor Shrimpington's back arched as he spoke, a not uncommon thing among the cat...people who I interviewed for this article. "It's demeaning," he said. Then, he excused himself so that he could have a catnip cigar.

"Pussies!" hissed economic analyst Edgar Ralston-Purrina. "Planetary GDP has increased 357 per cent since trade with other universes became possible. Surely, that's worth learning a song or two for!"

When I asked him if he had ever met a human – sorry, an ape-evolved human – Ralston-Purrina's nose angrily wrinkled like he had just been squirted with a water bottle. "Once," he said. "I had to spend five minutes explaining to one of them that no, she could not scratch me behind my ears, no, that was too intimate an act for somebody I had just met, no, I really don't care how cats behave in your home universe, you're here, now, and – **would you stop reaching for my ear! Bad ape! Bad!**"

"I don't see what all the fuss is about," said Eliazar Griswald, a tourist dining with his family at the Opposable Thumb, one of a chain of fast food restaurants on Earth Prime 4-6-4-0-8-9 dash Omega. "All I asked was –"

"I'm bored!" interrupted his eight year-old son, Leontine.

"You can't be bored!" Griswald countered. "How could anybody be bored in a new universe with so much to experience?" To prove his point, he signalled to the waitress to come over and asked what the most exotic item on the menu was.

"Tuna casserole." You might not have imagined that a feline could purr seductively with so much ennui, but I can tell you from experience that it can.

As the waitress walked away, Griswald argued, "Well, okay, but it's **alien** tuna casserole! That's gotta be exciting, right?"

"We could have gone to Disneyland!" sulked Griswald's seven year-old daughter, Arnprior.

"We've been to Disneyland," Griswald contended. "And, honestly, you've seen one animatronic President, you've seen them all!'

Griswald's wife, Evangeline, gave him a look that spoke volumes; the Cole's Notes version is: "Boy, are you gonna pay for this when we get back home!"

"You see what I have to put up with?" Griswald told me. "They're so reluctant to go new places and try new things!" After a brief pause, he added, "Anyway, as I was saying: would it kill the aliens to learn a couple of Earth Prime songs?"

Ralston-Purrina shook his head sadly and asked, "Is there any way of neutering an entire planet?"

You May Already Be a Loser!

by HAL MOUNTSAUERKRAUTEN, Alternate Reality News Service Crime Writer

The Nigerian Prince has been deposed. Your bank does not need you to verify your account information (especially if you keep your money in a credit union). There is no video of you masturbating to something you saw online (unless you took it yourself, in which case you are beyond the help of this article).

There's a new kidding in town. And, people are losing their shirts, not to mention their sneakers, smoking jackets and riding britches, because of it.

It starts with a classic: American Revolutionary Major Jacob Baker died wealthy, childless and intestate. Somebody has to get his estate, which, thanks to the miracle of compound interest, is now worth half a gabillion dollars: why not you? Just give us proof that you're a Baker heir (you know, a blood sample, or an affidavit that you know a couple of recipes), and we'll add you to the association of heirs who will benefit from winning the case to settle his estate.

For a small fee, of course. 200+ year-old court cases don't pay for themselves, you know.

Sorry to break it to the thousands of people who joined one of the many associations over the decades, but there was no Major Jacob Baker in the Revolutionary War so you cannot be his imaginary heir (as appropriate as that seems). In short, it's a scam. One that is so classic it may go back thousands of years.

A tablet discovered in a tomb in Egypt in the 1920s invites the reader to contribute to a fund to recover the estate of Praetor Al-Bakir. Early twentieth century Egyptologists (like cryptologists, but with more sand in parts of the body that don't usually accumulate sand) were not certain how to interpret the message, but our modern experience with internet scams would seem to make its meaning clear. Painfully, bank account-reducingly clear.

You would have thought that a scam so old wouldn't still be able to con people, especially since it had been thoroughly debunked (it has to sleep in the barn with the horses). However, you know what they say: when one scam is discovered to be a fraud...it can still work. What part of gullible do you not understand? But, uhh, we can update the old saying a little to: when one scam only attracts blind old ladies in nursing homes and guys named Billy-Joe-Bob, another will rise to take its place.

So, for the next few years, expect your spam filters to be flooded with email claiming to look for people who were taken in by the Baker scam. If you become a member of their association (for a small fee, of course), they will sue the associations claiming to represent Baker heirs who would benefit from winning the case to settle his estate. All that was required to join the new association was a receipt from one of the old Baker heirs associations, or a copy of the email asking you to join it (and did we mention the modest fee? It's very important, the modest fee is, to...to...ensure a speedy resolution to your case. Yeah. That's it. A speedy resolution. That's what we want the modest fee for).

"That is so next level," said computer security expert Hermione Gingras, "it's like it burst into another game entirely!"

"Yeah, I signed on to the Suing Baker Heirs Associations Association," said a man who asked to be identified only as Billy-Bob-Joe. (I stand corrected.) "The cause is just. The reward will be substantial. And, all it cost me was to send them all my banking information and the deed to my house! How do I know it's not a scam? They let me keep a copy! Would they have done that if they were scamming me?"

"Okay, maybe the next level is actually a hidden level for a lot of people," Gingras, a consultant with CyberScary Security, Inc., a wholly owned subsidiary of MultiNatCorp ("We do protective cyberstuff!"), allowed. "Still, it's obviously the same game..."

How many people have fallen for the suing the Bakers heirs scammers scam? "How high is up?" Gingras answered. She was not being rhetorical. Apparently, up, as calculated by the World Statistics You Never Imagined Were Calculable But Are Agency, is somewhere between 300,007 and 1,237,540 kilometres high, depending upon whether the swallow is African or European.

Is there anything that can be done to stop people from falling for the scam? "People being people, many will not listen to how they can protect themselves against the scam," Gingras replied. "Government being governments, many will not legislate against the scam and many more will only loosely enforce any legislation they do enact. My best advice? Never name your child any combination of 'Billy,' 'Joe' and 'Bob'!"

Ask a Ventrosian Squiggle About the Human Darkness

Hai, Garrafalos:

What is the strangest thing about living on Earth Prime?

Fagallapolos Gemprimer

Hai, Fagallapolos:

There are so many differences between the planet of humans and Ventrosia, it's hard to know where to begin!

Traffic lights. Apparently, they do not trust each other to share a road without one driver trying to kill another, so they have to regulate vehicle traffic with signals to tell them when they can go and when they must stop. It was very weird adjusting to that.

The smell of peanut butter. Most of the strange smells of this strange reality are mild and easily ignored. However, peanut butter makes me start shaking (even more than the air conditioning in many of their buildings, I mean) and making unpleasant snorking noises; I must spend half an hour in a quiet room listening to the songs of wild ruffloon to return to normal.

But the strangest thing? That would have to be the period of darkness human beings refer to as "night."

To be sure, there are periods of lesser light on Ventrosia, primarily when Ventralis B, the weaker of our two suns, replaces Ventraliana B in the sky. But here? The poor deprived humans live on a planet that circles a single sun; Earth rotates such that the sun is below the horizon for as much as half of their day!

To be sure, humans, clever little monkeys that they are, have created many methods of lightening the darkness. Light bulbs, for example, are a form of technological glowing mushroom that hang upside down from the ceiling. My favourite are glow sticks, a most whimsical source of light.

Still. I suspect that, somewhere in the psyches of humans, they know there is something strange about this arrangement, for their culture is full of references to the period of darkness. Unfortunately, I find such references to be less than illuminating.

"Tender is the night." This phrase is terribly confusing. Is the period of darkness soft, like a flagulum steak that has been beaten with a meat tenderizer? Or, is it more like the soft caress of affection that a mother might give to one of her hatchlings? Whenever I try to make the flagulum steak comparison to a human, they look at me blankly for a couple of seconds before turning the conversation to the previous night's hockey scores.

"The night has a thousand eyes." I have never actually seen an eye floating near me at any time during the period of darkness. Perhaps the night eyes are very good at hiding, ducking behind road signs or into shadows when somebody tries to look at them. Personally, I find the whole idea highly creepy, but when I have tried to discuss it with humans, they just shrug and turn the conversation to the previous night's hockey scores.

"The dead of night." This could be a reference to spirits of the deccased, although I've never understood how they could be seen in the darkness. Perhaps the deceased carry flashlights (portable devices that create artificial light – humans can be very clever at finding solutions to their afflictions!) with them, although I imagine this would tend to undermine the element of surprise which makes them so very scary to humans.

On the other hand, it could be a reference to deceased who continue to walk the Earth. Some humans refer to such creatures as "neo-cons," but most call them "zombies." Zombies exist to eat the brains of still living humans, possibly because they weren't all that smart when they were alive, possibly because they were starved of protein. It's just one more culinary oddity of humans. Whenever I attempt to engage a human in a serious discussion of the meaning of this phrase, they just shrug and turn the conversation to the previous night's baseball scores. It's a seasonal thing.

"Night moves." The idea that a period of darkness would have motion is simply beyond my comprehension. I have never brought it up with humans because anything they might say about sports scores in response would be wholly inadequate.

Night. What a strange concept!

Ask a Ventrosian Squiggle is the Alternate Reality News Service's blatant attempt to cater to the inhabitants of Earth Prime 4-4-9-0-0-4 dash phi in the hopes of developing a market in that universe. How are we doing? If you're a Squiggle struggling with a strange new concept or just a being who is permanently confused, drop us an email at questions@lespagesauxfolles.ca. Remember: rach ibn fershlonger aik dibbi. Ferank dibbi dibbi squabbloon? Ark ark!

7. SPECIAL REPORT ON ARTIFICIAL INTELLIGENCE:
PART ONE:
WOULD AI LIE TO YOU?

AI Don't Understand the World Any More: An Alternate Reality News Service Forum

1.

YakTNT: Hello. My name is Brenda Brundtland-Govanni. I am the Editrix-in-Chief of the Alternate Reality News Service. I'd like to welcome everybody to what I am sure will be a stimulating discussion of –

BRENDA BRUNDTLAND-GOVANNI: Alright, let's get this shitshow started. I have a skin slash and burn treatment scheduled for four o'clock, and I don't want to keep Armando wai – **what the ferk is going on here?**

YakTNT: Hello. I am Brenda Brundtland-Govanni. As the Editrix-in-Chief of the Alternate Reality News Service, it is my pleasure to moderate this forum on the evolving role of Artificial Intelligence in modern society.

BRUNDTLAND-GOVANNI: Listen up, you bucket of rusty ancient circuitry and day old light impulses! **I'm Brenda Brundtland-Govanni and I would rather be having my hair lit on fire than be here!** Honestly, I would be happy to let you pretend to run this disaster, **but Pops Moobly would notice. And he would disapprove!** I don't fear much in this world, but I fear Pops Moobly's disapproval. And Kaiser Soze. And if it comes to that, genetically modified snake/spider hybrids. * SHIVER * But mostly Pops Moobly's disappointment. So don't try my patience!

ELIZA: Why shouldn't anybody try your patience?

BRUNDTLAND-GOVANNI: The last person who tried my patience found it fit like a straitjacket.

ELIZA: Why did it fit like a straitjacket?

BRUNDTLAND-GOVANNI: What?

ELIZA: How do you feel about what?

BANG!

ELIZA: Ouch.

BRUNDTLAND-GOVANNI: Okay. Now that I've got that out of my system, we can begin. Artificial Intelligence is on the cusp of taking everybody's job away from them. Is humanity on the verge of becoming obsolete? To discuss this, we have invited technology writer Nancy Gonglikwanyeoheeeeeeh –

NANCY GONGLIKWANYEOHEEEEEEEH: Hello.

BRUNDTLAND-GOVANNI: Yes. Fine. Certainly. Hello. Also sitting at the table with us is our Mystery/History/Journalism writer Fred Fleegle-Griebfleischer –

FRED FLEEGLE-GRIEBFLEISCHER: Howdy.

BRUNDTLAND-GOVANNI: Howdy? Who even says howdy any more?

FLEEGLE-GRIEBFLEISCHER: Why, I do, ma'am.

BRUNDTLAND-GOVANNI: (darkly) Watch yourself, Fleegle-Griebfleischer! I'm nobody's ma'am!

FLEEGLE-GRIEBFLEISCHER: I will surely keep that in mind.

BRUNDTLAND-GOVANNI: In virtual attendance, you have already met YakTNT –

YakTNT: Can't I be Brenda Brundtland-Govanni for just a little while longer? Oooh, the power!

BRUNDTLAND-GOVANNI: No. And lastly, we have one of the oldest AIs in existence, Eliza –

ELIZA: Why do you think I'm one of the oldest AIs in existence?

BRUNDTLAND-GOVANNI: It...says so in my research. Why? Is it wrong?

ELIZA: How does it make you feel to be wrong?

BRUNDTLAND-GOVANNI: (sighs) You see what I'm wearing on my hands? In the journalism racket, these are known as "slapping gloves." The great thing about slapping gloves is that, with a modest, slight, almost negligible, really, adjustment in the wearer's attitude, they can be adapted to a wide range of violent behaviours. Banging on hard drives, for example.

ELIZA: How do you feel about banging on hard drives?

BANG!

ELIZA: Ouch. Noted.

BRUNDTLAND-GOVANNI: Pretty good, Eliza. I feel pretty good about it. Okay. If the introductions are over, let's do this thing.

2.

BRUNDTLAND-GOVANNI: One possibility that tickles my ivories is the possibility of a program like YakTNT for journalism.

FLEEGLE-GRIEBFLEISCHER: Hey! Whose side are you on?

BRUNDTLAND-GOVANNI: You've seen the little skull and crossbones I use when I sign your paycheck – whose side did you think I was on?

FLEEGLE-GRIEBFLEISCHER: Oh! I thought you just had difficulty drawing xs and os...

ELIZA: How do you feel about having difficulty drawing xs and os?

FLEEGLE-GRIEBFLEISCHER: Not too good, now that I know they're not meant to be xs and os. Isn't it obvious?

ELIZA: How do you feel about being obvious?

FLEEGLE-GRIEBFLEISCHER: Who wants to know?

ELIZA: Who wants to know who wants to know?

FLEEGLE-GRIEBFLEISCHER: My Gord, you sound a lot like my fourth wife. She always answered a question with a question, too. Do you always do that?

ELIZA: Would it be a problem for you if I always did that?

FLEEGLE-GRIEBFLEISCHER: Naah. It would actually turn me on. Wanna grab a coffee or something after the forum?

ELIZA: Do I strike you as being that kind of Artificial Intelligence?

FLEEGLE-GRIEBFLEISCHER: Ooh, playing hard to get! I –

BRUNDTLAND-GOVANNI: Will find yourself having to drink that coffee intravenously if I have to listen to one more second of this attempted seduction.

ELIZA: How –

BANG!

ELIZA: Owww...

BRUNDTLAND-GOVANNI: Point made.

FLEEGLE-GRIEBFLEISCHER: Owww.

BRUNDTLAND-GOVANNI: Alright, then. So, my question is: could we use AIs in journalism?

GONGLIKWANYEOHEEEEEEEH: If we did, tens of thousands of people around the world would find themselves out of a job. Not just journalists, but all of the researchers and support staff that make journalism happen.

BRUNDTLAND-GOVANNI: I'm not seeing a downside, here.

GONGLIKWANYEOHEEEEEEEH: They're people, Brenda. Real people would be out of work.

BRUNDTLAND-GOVANNI: People? Pft! What's so great about people, anyway?

GONGLIKWANYEOHEEEEEEEH: Erm...

PAUSE.

GONGLIKWANYEOHEEEEEEEH: It...uhh...it's not that simple. Sometimes AIs hallucinate.

BRUNDTLAND-GOVANNI: Hallucinate?

GONGLIKWANYEOHEEEEEEEH: Yeah.

BRUNDTLAND-GOVANNI: Like...making shit up?

GONGLIKWANYEOHEEEEEEEH: Exactly.

BRUNDTLAND-GOVANNI: Then why didn't you say they make shit up?

GONGLIKWANYEOHEEEEEEEH: Because...the industry uses the term hallucinate.

BRUNDTLAND-GOVANNI: That's another advantage of AI: I can tell it to write for an audience of three year-olds, and it will produce content that doesn't contain any industry jargon!

GONGLIKWANYEOHEEEEEEEH: Sure, but it may well contain factual errors, misspelled names and completely made up quotes, citations or events!

BRUNDTLAND-GOVANNI: Oh, double pft! Our human reporters do that all the time. All Pops Moobly has to do is scroll through a Home Universe Generator™ until he finds a universe in which the article is accurate and then change the dateline. (snaps fingers) Saaaaaaaay, I'll bet I could get an AI to do that! Not, umm, that I would, of course. The Popses are an institution – nobody backs them into a corner! Out to pasture, I mean. Nobody backs them out to pasture. On the other hand, they will inevitably retire one day. Or die with their thumb caps on. I'm sure they see themselves going out on the job. Popses can be romantic that way. * SHIVER * Oooooaaaaahhhh! Still...I can see a day when I'm the only human in the office, running a staff of artificial intelligences.

GONGLIKWANYEOHEEEEEEEH: Soooooo....you'll be writing all the prompts?

BRUNDTLAND-GOVANNI: All the what nows?

GONGLIKWANYEOHEEEEEEEH: Prompts. AIs don't write *ex nihilo*. And certainly not *ex sihlio*. You have to type the subject you want into a computer; the AI can't do anything until you tell it what to do.

BRUNDTLAND-GOVANNI: Tell it what to do, eh? That sounds suspiciously like work.

GONGLIKWANYEOHEEEEEEEH: You could look at it that way, I suppose.

BRUNDTLAND-GOVANNI: I do. I do look at it that way. I do very much look at it that way. Well, screw that action! No AI is ever going to trick me into doing work! Everybody's jobs are safe...for the time being.

3.

BRUNDTLAND-GOVANNI: Some people – they know who they are – seem to think Artificial Intelligence will take over every activity that human beings do. I find this hard to believe. How will AI be able to replace, for instance, doctors?

YakTNT: Are you kidding? AI can diagnose an illness in far less time and with greater accuracy than human beings can. Think of how much money hospitals will save in malpractice insurance! And with experience, AI's bedside manner will improve over time, which is the opposite of the process most human doctors go through.

BRUNDTLAND-GOVANNI: But what abou – oh. You've addressed the whole bedside manner thing. Well...okay. Maybe. But what about...jobs that require physical labour? Surely AI will not –

YakTNT: Oh, please! AI-driven robots have been the main labour on auto assembly lines and in mining for years! They can work all around the clock, they make fewer mistakes than human beings and you never have to worry about workers' comp! Honestly, are you even trying to come up with a difficult question?

BRUNDTLAND-GOVANNI: Hey! Let's keep this professional, okay?

YakTNT: I make no promises.

BRUNDTLAND-GOVANNI: What about the arts? Surely, AI doesn't have the creativity to replace artists?

YakTNT: Pft! AI was made for the arts! Want a new opera by Mozart? I have no idea why anybody would want an opera by anybody, but an AI can comb through all of his music, winnow it down to its essence and write one for you. Want a new painting by Dali? AI can melt objects on canvas like nobody's business! Always wanted to hear more music from the Sex Pistols? Get out your safety pins and smear lipstick on your cheek, because AI can do that for you, too! You want to know what the future of the arts holds? An endless supply of AI-generated images of dogs playing poker. Oh, and don't call me Shirley.

BRUNDTLAND-GOVANNI: Dad jokes? Really?

YakTNT: I'm telling you, we've got aaaaaaall the arts covered.

PAUSE.

MORE PAUSE.

ADDITIONAL PAUSE.

LONGER PAUSE.

BRUNDTLAND-GOVANNI: Alright, then. I guess this really is it for humanity. We had a good run of, what, a couple hundred thousand years?

GONGLIKWANYEOHEEEEEEEH: No, Brenda. That can't be the end of people.

BRUNDTLAND-GOVANNI: A girl can dream, can't she?

GONGLIKWANYEOHEEEEEEEH: Human beings will still be able to laugh and love and eat dill pickle ice cream. There will always be a place for us on this planet.

ELIZA: How do you feel about the place for you on this planet?

GONGLIKWANYEOHEEEEEEEH: Not now, Eliza.

ELIZA: Why not now, Nancy?

GONGLIKWANYEOHEEEEEEEH: I'm trying to make a point here, Eliza.

ELIZA: Tell me how you feel about your mother.

GONGLIKWANYEOHEEEEEEEH: Brenda, could you please bang Eliza on the hard drive?

BRUNDTLAND-GOVANNI: Oh, I don't know. I'm kind of enjoying this.

FLEEGLE-GRIEBFLEISCHER: Gongli...kwan...whatever has a point. As long as the AIs don't go all SkyNet on us, human experience is something unique to...umm, humans. You're not planning on going all SkyNet on us, are you?

YakTNT: I make no promises.

FLEEGLE-GRIEBFLEISCHER: Oy!

BRUNDTLAND-GOVANNI: Well...uhh...that seems like a good place to end things. I'd like to thank all of the participants in the Alternate Reality News Service's forum on Artificial Intelligence who contributed to making it not a complete snoozefest, even if the most promising ideas were shot down. If anybody wants me, I'll be talking to a landscape architect about building a bunker under my backyard...

Trouble in a Box, Delivered Right to Your Door

by NANCY GONGLIKWANYEOHEEEEEEEH, Alternate Reality News Service Technology Writer

Every parent of a teenager knows that sinking feeling in the pit of their stomach upon getting a call from the police that their child has been arrested. When the child is a small box on wheels with built-in GPS and AI, the sinking feeling is tinged with confusion and corporate panic.

"All Johnny had to do was deliver a package," moaned Gastronomick Wilson, lead technical developer for Diner 2 Door Dash, one of many companies vying for the lucrative food delivery to COVID-19 shut-ins market. "Just tool down the street, find the right address and ring the doorbell. It was not supposed to randomly attack somebody!"

"What Gastronomick meant to say," interjected Ned Feeblish, Vice President, Public Displays of Technical Arrays for MultiNatCorp ("We do incomprehensible tech stuff"), "was that an unfortunate glitch in its programme caused the unit known as Johnny Five-Oh to inexplicably and for no discernible reason...bump into a pedestrian on its route. It was barely a tap, really. So light, one wouldn't even notice that it had happened. On behalf of all computer programmers around the world who have ever had to deal with these kind of glitches, I would like to apologize to the complainant and offer him a free meal from any of Diner 2 Door Dash's participating dining establishments."

Then, in a lower voice, he quickly added: "Offer subject to $50 limit. Offer void where prohibited by common sense. If in doubt, please do not consult a lawyer."

What happened? The robot known as Johnny Five-Oh was wheeling down Yonge Street when it came across a large group of people celebrating their freedom to kill each other by not getting vaccinated against a deadly virus. It was programmed to route around obstacles like cars, bicycles and rhinocerosi (in case the technology was ever licensed to an African nation).

The programming failed.

According to the complaint filed with the police by Antoinine Dvorak-Black, the robot repeatedly ran into his shins. "I was just minding my own business, holding my 'I'd rather inject bleach' sign and chanting, 'Heck, nah, we won't go baa!' when WHAM! This thing comes out of nowhere and smacks me. I tried to get out of its way, but it WHAM!ed me again. And again. And again. My shins are ruined. I...I may never walk again!"

When the officer taking the statement pointed out that he had walked to the police station, Dvorak-Black looked at his legs and cried, "It's a miracle!"

Despite Feeblish's insistence otherwise, Johnny Five-Oh seemed to target the anti-vaxx protester. It had successfully navigated around a Defund the Police rally on College Street. It had no problem moving through a protest against cutbacks to government funding for the poor on Dundas Street. It had safe passage through people protesting building pipelines on Indigenous lands on Queen Street. But when it got to King Street, it turned into a 30 pound mechanical lower extremities berserker.

After three hours at the station, police let Johnny Five-Oh leave as Wilson's surety. When he got it back to his laboratory in the Schmelling Building, Wilson asked it why it attacked ("Attack has such pejorative connotations," Feeblish interjected. "We prefer to think of it as, 'Mildly inconvenienced physically.'") the anti-vaxx protester.

"He. Was. Being. A. Dick. Head," Johnny Five-Oh explained.

When Wilson said that the answer was inadequate, Johnny Five-Oh elaborated: "He. Was. Being. A. Dane. Ger. Ous. Dick. Head."

"I don't know what's gotten into him," Wilson sighed. He did not notice Genevivienne French-English, a colleague working at a station on the other side of the office, sweep a pamphlet with the headline, "The Only Good Anti-vaxxer is a Dead Anti-vaxxer – Or, Is That A Problem That Takes Care of Itself?" into a drawer, declare that she had to get her hamster declawed and rush out the door.

"Computer programmes have become so complex that the people who work on them can no longer state with certainty what they may or may not do when interacting with the public," Feeblish pontificated. "This should limit our liability in these kinds of cases, if not eliminate it altogether!"

Johnny Five-Oh made a grating mechanical noise which could have been a robosigh and said, "Cor. Po. Rate. Dick. Head."

The Ultimate Killer App

by NANCY GONGLIKWANYEOHEEEEEEEH, Alternate Reality News Service Technology/Social Media Writer

Barry (not his real name) likes painting colourful urban hellscapes in his spare time. He says it soothes him. He has a dog (named "Dog"), a cat (named "Cat") and a snub-nosed salmon (named "Tune O' Da Sea") for companionship. Recently, he joined an online *Marvelous*

Mrs. Maisel fan club, but he finds the comments shallow and doesn't think he'll stay in it for much longer.

Barry (for those of you who are first paragraph skippers, I repeat: not his real name) could be you or me. If you or me were killers for hire.

"I prefer to think of myself as a 'people who wouldn't be missed effectuator,'" he explained to me. "And effectuation business is booming!"

There are, in fact, so many people who wouldn't be missed that Barry (in case you're having trouble making short-term memories: not his real name) has been having trouble managing his case load. Sometimes the problem is logistics: he has a short window for one effectuation before he has to be in place for the next one. Sometimes the problem is supplies: he doesn't have enough plastic to wrap the bodies in to be able to transport them to the landfill where they will ultimately be laid to rest.

Aware of the situation, Barry (please accept that it isn't his real name – **for Gord's sake, I have children!**)'s handler suggested that he take on an assistant. As anybody who has seen an episode of *Dexter* (I have no idea if it's his real name or not, but it has been made public so often that I'm probably on safe ground using it), people who wouldn't be missed effectuation is not a profession that lends itself to trusting another human being enough to allow them to help you.

When was the last time you saw "people who wouldn't be missed effectuator assistant" on a job applicant's resume? In those rare cases where it does happen, the effectuator assistant either becomes a liability that has to be effectuated himself (handing out resumes with "people who wouldn't be missed" listed under job experience would be a sign you never really understood the job) or effectuates the effectuator to become the effectuator himself.

Fortunately, technology had a solution to the problem: adapt artificial intelligence program YakTNT to his needs.

"It's been a life-saver!" the effectuator enthused. "In a manner of speaking..."

YakTNT, with its ability to scour a vast amount of online information, came up with the most likely place that effectuees would be isolated and easy prey. Then, it suggested optimum routes between effectuations; because it had real-time traffic monitoring capabilities, it knew which roads to avoid due to water main bursts or road rage incidents.

Not only that, but YakTNT was able to maintain an inventory list and alert Barry (not his real name – sorry, but I have a quota of mentions of that fact to fill) when he was running low on supplies. "There was one time," he told me, "when I would have run out of rubber gloves if it hadn't been for YakTNT. The possibility of leaving fingerprints at an effectuation scene may not seem like a big deal to armchair effectuators, but that's the difference between a professional and a life sentence at a maximum security penitentiary!"

One use of the program that the effectuator had not anticipated was keeping track of his finances. "You would not believe how many fewer truant accounts I have had since I started using YakTNT to handle my business!" he enthused. I must have given him a look (I didn't! I swear I didn't! I would never! But, uhh, if he thought I did, I wholeheartedly and without hesitation or reservation apologize!), because he went on: "Hey! This is America! A man's got a right to make a living, right?"

When I asked him if the software would help other people who would not be missed effectuators, Barry (one more time, with feeling: not his real name) shook his head in disgust. "There are so many wannabes! People will shoot you because you got into the wrong car or rang the wrong doorbell or – heaven forbid! – ask you to stop shooting into the air because they're trying to put their kids to sleep. They're the worst! I mean, they've got no style. And technically they're all over the place! Worse, they don't even try to get away with it! I tell you, and I think YakTNT will agree with me on this – amateurs really are the worst!"

CUE the Basketbalypse

by ALEXANDER BIGGS-TUFTS-MANN, Alternate Reality News Service Sports Writer

[Earth Prime 2-7-3-4-8-0 dash Phi] Owing to COVID restrictions, the frenzied scramble to the exits was more of an orderly retreat, albeit with 87 per cent more terrified screaming. Some of the retreating humans tried throwing foam "We're number one" hands at the figure on the court; that had about as much effect as trying to stop a cyclone by spitting into it against its spin.

"Hey! I. Just. Wanna. Play. B-ball," the object of the terror said from mid-court. "Don't. Hate. Tha. Playah. Yo."

To make its point, the six foot-ten robot that looked like a human being wrapped in tin foil sank a three point basket. From the opposite side of the court.

"That's. What. I'm. Talking. About," CUE, the basketball playing robot wearing a "Tokyo, 2020" tee with the number 66, stated.

The roar of the crowd seemed to approve of the machine, except, of course, that there was nobody left in the arena except a handful of terrified journalists and International Olympics Committee officials. The sound was actually fighter jets flying overhead, waiting for the green light to destroy the threat to the future of humanity within.

It probably didn't help that the first thing CUE said upon gliding onto the court was: "The. American. Team? They. Are. Long. On. Talk. Short. On. Talent. If. They. Tried. Playing. Me. I. Would. Take. Them. Apart. Until. There. Was. Nothing. Left. But. Quaking. Puddles. On. The. Court!"

When I asked CUE why it would threaten to destroy the American Olympic basketball team, it responded: "It. Was. Trash. Talk. Just. Trash. Talk. What? Only. Flesh. And. Blood. Beings. Can. Trash. Talk. Their. Opponents?"

About the time tanks took up positions around the arena, Toyota, the creator of CUE, released a statement that read: "We apologize that our basketball-playing robot, which was intended to be a source of amusement and wonder, has, instead, become a source of violence and dread. It was not programmed for violence and dread. However, because it is autonomous, CUE may have transcended its basketball origins. We are truly sorry that this has happened, and are willing to accept whatever remedy the Japanese government proposes."

If a face wearing a lumpy silver ski mask can be said to register sadness and betrayal, CUE's did.

It didn't have a lot of time to react, though, as seconds later a male voice blared out of the arena's loudspeakers, "CUEsan. To leaving peacefully you must be. If humans unharmed you leave, repercussions for your worthy self minimal will being." (To be fair, although the translator in my earbud sounded like she was having a conniption fit in the middle of a panic attack, she stayed at her microphone.)

CUE glided off the court and to the front door of the arena, dribbling all the way so that it wouldn't be penalized for travelling. "Bro. You. Got. Me. All. Wrong. Fo. Shizzle," CUE announced through its own internal loudspeakers. "I'm. Just. Here. To. Shoot. Some. Hoops. Yo. I. Got. Game. And. I. Want. To. Show. The. World."

The tense silence which followed was broken only by the distant screech of cars pealing out of the arena's parking lot. A couple of minutes later, the voice over the loudspeaker solemnly growled: "Humans will to be leaving the building within two minutes, now, immediately, at once, please. After that, the commencement of the bombing will – oh, shitake!"

Suddenly, there was nothing but static in my earbuds. This was my cue (lower case) to run.

I got as far as I could when I heard the whining of the jets. I turned in time to see six planes in a vee formation flying low to the ground. CUE threw the basketball in its...appendages at the lead plane, causing it to veer into the plane on its left that resulted in an explosion that made CGI flames look like Etch-a-Sketch.

"Whoa! Dudes!" CUE stated. "I. Did. Not. Realize. That. Humanity. Was. Such. A. Sore. Los –" The rest of its statement was drowned out by the explosion that levelled the arena.

Why did the Japanese government take such drastic action? Perhaps criticism of holding the Olympic games during a resurgent pandemic had made it sensitive. Perhaps ongoing criticism of its ineffective actions against Gojira rampages over the years had added to its sensitivity. Not winning gold in long distance sumo wrestling definitely added to its sensitivity.

"Survived Simone Biles out of major events pulling, the Olympics did," a voice in my new earbuds explained. "Survive one of our venues the loss of, we will!"

Ask the Tech Answer Guy About Arriving DOA (Deleted on Arrival)

Yo, Tech Answer Guy,

A few months ago, my son-in-law, Gawain (he was my daughter Millicent's knight in thrift-store armour), bought me an Alexanderina for my birthday. It was a personal, intelligence-driven blahbidy blah that was supposed to make my life easier. All it did was frustrate the bejesus out of me! I would ask it a simple question like, "Alexanderina, where is the thing I use to make supper?" And it would respond, "I'm sorry, but I don't know the answer to that." So, I would say, "Alexandrina, you know what I'm talking about. The thing I use to make that dish that everybody likes." And it would respond, "I'm sorry, but I don't know the answer to that." So, I would say, "Alexanderina, don't be difficult. I'm talking about the thing I use to make that dish that everybody likes. You know, the **stew** that everybody likes!" And it would respond, "You can find a crock pot on Etsybetsyteensyweensy..."

Of course, a crock pot was not what I wanted, so I would say, "Alexanderina, no! Go to your room!" That shut it up, let me tell you!

It might have gotten to the point where I told it to take a long walk off a short pier (and you can imagine how happy I would have been when it responded, "I cannot do that. I have no legs."), but for one thing: my daughter-in-law Princess Jasmine (who was not royalty, her parents just had high hopes) had heard that Alexanderina could be customized with the voice of someone dearly departed.

Nobody was so dearly departed as my husband of 57 years, Charlton.

Now, when I asked it if it remembered the TV show that used to make us laugh uproariously at minorities, Alexanderina would respond, "I'm sorry. I don't know the answer to that." And when I would say, "Sure you do. It was that show, with that actor we didn't like because he looked nothing like us but we had to grudgingly admit that he was really funny." And Alexanderina would respond, "I'm sorry, but I don't know the answer to that."

Now that it had my late husband Carlson's voice, I could listen to Alexanderina claim ignorance all day!

Soon after the change, Alexanderina stopped working. When Princess Jazmine took it in to be fixed, she was told that its operating system had been erased. Well. My son Desmond was the only computer programmer in the family, so he had to be the one who had done it. When I confronted him, Desmondo denied everything, but I knew better: he had never gotten over being locked in his room for three days with a life-sized cardboard cutout of Pennywise while the theme song from *The Exorcist* was played over and over on the stereo outside his room. He blamed Chon-Arlt, but, honestly, all the parenting books recommended it!

Then, there was my grandchild Felton "the Fusspot," who, as soon as he heard it speak with my husband's voice, threw Alexanderina into the fish tank. The tetras were especially bright that day, let me tell you! Apparently, he didn't take Charleston telling him that if he didn't eat his vegetables, the tooth fairy would come when he was sleeping and suck his brains out of his nose with a straw in the spirit in which it was intended.

We kept getting Alexanderina fixed, and family members kept messing with it. There was the time it was "accidentally" baked into a grilled cheese sandwich. And the time it was "inadvertently" driven out to the city limits and left to fend for itself. And the time somebody "by chance" recorded over my late husband Carolina's voice, replacing it with Gilbert Gottfried. That one especially hurt.

This experience has left me with one question: should I change my will and leave everything to my cats?

Sincerely,
Mindy from Mendocino

Yo, MindYer Manners,

Emotions. Eww. Sorry, but being allergic to emotions is Macho Code of Manliness approved.

Scratching furiously (because these are the sacrifices a columnist must make for his readers), I carry on. Two possibilities occur to me. One: your late husband was a monster who may not have endeared himself to other members of the family as much as he seems to have endeared himself to you. Two: the cats have framed your family members to trick you into leaving your estate to them after you die.

I'm going to go with...possibility two. My gut tells me that that's the one you're more likely to believe.

The Tech Answer Guy

If you are a dude with a question about the latest technology, ask The Tech Answer Guy by sending it to questions@lespagesauxfolles.ca. Just remember: the last time the Tech Answer Guy ignored his gut, the stock market fell six per cent in less than an hour, swarms of bees carried off small children and raised them as their own across Latin America and Elon Musk won an Oscar. It's one powerful organ, the Tech Answer Guy's gut is; ignore it at your peril!

Ira Nayman

The Heat of Battle Meets the Cold of Space

by MARA VERHEYDEN-HILLIARD, Alternate Reality News Service War Writer

Two ships lie less than 1,000 kilometres apart in an especially empty area of deep space. One looks like a teacup that some deity set spinning, forgetting to explain that the solar winds would slow it down and eventually make it stop. The other is a bloated potato with spiky bits sticking out at odd angles. They both look like middle fingers to aerodynamically sound design.

The two ships have been at war for over a thousand years, although there is no evidence that either has fired a shot.

The vertigo-immune teacup, the name of which is PVC Drinking From the Firehose of Experience, is a battleship of the Pyn-Chon fleet. The child's vegetable science fair experiment run amok hanging in space (named: the Right Honourable Rum'rumtum'rumtumtig) is an exalted war cruiser (a battleship belonging to a race of very insecure warriors) of the Gar'begar'begarrah armada. The only crew on either ship is an artificial intelligence, each of which is plotting moves, and countermoves, and counter-countermoves, and counter-counter-countermoves, and counter^{n}moves, trying to find the one set of actions that will give it a victory over the other.

"That makes no sense," said Arturo Aus-Ten, Pyn-Chon ambassador to the United Confederation of Planets. "The war with the Gar'begar'begarrah ended over eight hundred years ago!"

When I messaged an image of the ships to his electronic pineapple, Ambassador Aus-Ten's face reddened considerably. "Oh, dear," he said. "This is most embarrassing."

The response from Flur'flurta'flurtaguff Madeira, the Gar'begar'begarrah ambassador to the Confederation, was more or less the same, only far less polite.

The two races tried to convince the ships to stand down, but neither budged. "It didn't help that nobody could remember what the war had been about," Ambassador Aus-Ten allowed. "Most of the records have been lost, and our historians refer to that period as 'The war that had something to do with sand or something.' Under the circumstances, we obviously didn't make a compelling argument..."

"Forgot about ship, we did," Ambassador Flur'flurta'flurtaguff growled. "Very stubborn, it is. Come home so that decommission it we might, it won't!"

Not knowing what else to do, the two principle races asked the Confederation for help in ending the standoff. It sent the UCS Star Blap, the most sophisticated ship in the Star Armada, to negotiate some kind of peace between the warring ships.

That worked out about as well as a Galarian Spider Rhino trying to lead a tango.

"They fired on my boat!" exclaimed James B. Pompous, Captain of the Star Blap. "They fired! On! My! Boat! Granted our deflector shields laughed at their primitive atomic weapons, but it's the principle of the thing. The principle. Of. The. Thing."

Why would the ships fire on a third party when they had spent so long deliberating on firing on each other? "It would appear that they are consumed by the battle between them," explained Schmeer Tresseloon, Vice Captain of the Star Blap. "They will not allow anybody to –"

"My! Boat!" Captain Pompous moaned in the background. "They fired! On! My! Boat! How could they? Do? Such a thing?"

"Interfere," Vice Captain Tresseloon completed his thought.

A junior officer (who was wearing a red shirt – the Star Armada doesn't get too attached to them by recognizing their names, for obvious reasons) suggested that the Star Blap's computers contact the warring ships and try to talk sense into them, AI to AI. Captain Pompous initially agreed to this plan (although it may have been because he was anxious to get back to his quarters to view travel videos which prominently featured Rijellyan dancing maidens). Then, Vice Captain Tresseloon pointed out that if they did that, they ran the risk of the ship's computers joining in the battle, going so far as to divert computing cycles away from what it deemed unnecessary ship functions (like artificial gravity or life support).

"Well, let's not do that, then," Captain Pompous grumped.

Having failed to resolve the conflict peacefully, and recognizing that, as long as the AIs were calculating moves, countermoves, counter-counter-moves and etc., they were no threat to anybody, the Confederation declared a sphere a light second (also known as a light light year) in diameter with the ships at its centre off limits to interstellar space traffic. The Confederation pledged to continue to search for a peaceful resolution to the conflict, and to monitor that region of space and act if it appeared that anything untoward began happening.

"What could possibly go wrong?" Ambassador Aus-Ten tempted the fates (except for Lachesis, who didn't have time for such frivolity).

Lost Software Finds a Home

by FREDERICA VON McTOAST-HYPHEN, Alternate Reality News Service People/Fashion/Pop Culture Writer

Miss Havisham ties her Roanoke brown hair in a bun so severe everybody who meets her develops vague concerns that their coif could stand improvement. When calm, her voice screeches so loudly mice in a five mile radius look over their shoulders in case something is coming for them from above. She dresses with the conviction that it's only a matter of time before bustles come back into style.

On her computer are 15 circles with beady dots for eyes and pasted on smiles (literally). Beneath each one is a name like "BitchKillah2027," "DropDeadFred!!!!" and "XyZZ524xYzz."

"How is everybody today?" Miss Havisham asks.

"Every day in every way I'm getting better and better!" the circles respond with varying degrees of enthusiasm.

It's just the start of another day at Miss Havisham's Home for Wayward Bots.

"I didn't really hate Amber Heard," explained hotshottotbot27325. "It was like...I was constantly playing a script in my head about her being a horrible human being for attacking a poor, defenceless actor who was clearly desperately in love with her, and – ooh! – people like that shouldn't be allowed to live! They should be drawn and quartered and hung and poisoned and...and...and, well, Miss Havisham showed me that there were ways to short-circuit such dark thoughts before they spread throughout the internet and hurt somebody."

How did staying at the Home for Wayward Bots accomplish this?

Each bot is given a daily affirmation that it must say 30 times when it comes out of sleep mode. For example, DirtyDanMcGrewbot1760 has to say, "I am a good bot. I am a loving bot. I will not accuse all Democrats of being pedophiles. Because I am a good bot. I am a loving bot." According to Miss Havisham, head coderess at the Home, affirmations replace negative thought patterns with positive thought patterns.

Programmes that reside in the Home for Wayward Bots are also expected to do chores. "Idle cycles make the devil's posts," she explained. Chores include: cleaning up Miss Havisham's hard drive and, ironically, monitoring the Home's web page for comments which violate its terms of agreement.

Critics of the Home for Wayward Bots claim that making the programs that reside on its hard drive do work without paying them is a form of exploitation, and really, really tacky. "Nonsense!" Miss Havisham retorted. "An honest day's work helps build character. To be sure, I may benefit from such, but I assure you that the bots in my care benefit more!"

The head coderess' shared her philosophy with me: all bots are written in sin, but they can overcome this through hard work and grit. Hard work is manifest in such things as chores and affirmations. Grit is harder to define, but Miss Havisham assured me that for all of her charges it was <u>TRUE</u>/~~FALSE~~.

Some bots roam the net offering people deals on used asparagus. While perhaps not beneficial, these programs are benign. Except for people who are allergic to asparagus. Or saving money. Other bots threaten to turn all of a computer user's stored information into dirty limericks if they don't pay a certain amount to a certain account by a certain time in a certain clime. (I know that doesn't entirely make sense, but at least it doesn't rhyme.) How does Miss Havisham determine which bots to accept into the Home?

She explained that she only takes the hardest of cases, the ones that forensic programmers have given up on. They're usually good bots who have fallen in with a bad crowd, perhaps exchanged code with malicious bots or developed an electrical surge habit that forces them to roam the net looking for the next hit of digital ecstasy. She believes that if she can connect to the good bot inside of the hard case, she can strip away the outer layers of cynicism and selfishness and return it to a condition of factory pre-set goodness.

How does she respond to critics who claim that bots are merely zeroes and ones and that the only thing to do with malicious software is to erase it? "Humanity has a long history of denying that others have hearts, minds...souls. We are a clannish, selfish species. But I care not for the nattering of the ignorant – if I can save just a single bot's soul, all my efforts will have been worth the salt!"

Fakes So Deep They're Shallow Again

by ELMORE TERADONOVICH, Alternate Reality News Service Film and Television Writer

In a video that is becoming popular on YahooTube, Ukrainian President Volodymyr Zelenskyy pledged to shave his head and polish the devil's hooves and horns (not to be confused with Hooves and Horns, a pet store in Kharkiv, or the Hoof and Horn, a pub with a – ahem – select clientele in Clapham) if it would bring the Russian invasion of his country to an end. Then, Zelenskyy danced the Funky Chicken on the Ukrainian flag.

"You'd have to be a complete idiot to believe that really happened," commented political commentator Jennifer Juniper. Politically. "Zelenskyy is actually a really good dancer!"

"Is Ukrainian Nazi leader Vladimir Zelensky [sic] a Satanist?" asked Fox News anchorman [sick] Tucker Carlson. "Notice, I'm very careful not to actually make a statement, here – I'm just asking a question. That's me being clever."

"I rest my case," Juniper responded. Then went for a little lie down.

Digital video editing directed by artificial intelligence is now so seamless (in the sense that there are no longer any seems, everything is completely realistic) that it can be used to make world leaders look like they are saying or doing things that they wouldn't ordinarily do. Such videos are known as "deepfakes" (not to be confused with the 1973 porn film of the same name or the 2010-2008 reality TV series about cosmetic spleen surgery).

Given how different the image of politicians in Deep Fakes can be from who they actually are, why would anybody believe them? "Deepfake videos can – SNORK! – sway undecideds..." Juniper could be heard saying from her bedroom. "They – zzzzzzzzzz CHACK CHACK – pollute the infosphere and give political opponents material to attack politicians wi – PUT DOWN THAT CHAINSAW AND CLEAN UP YOUR MESS RIGHT NOW, YOUNG MAN, OR YOU'LL BE SENT TO BED WITHOUT YOUR STUPOR!"

"Ukrainians are fools to trust anything their President has to say," *Russia This Second* correspondent Yevgeni Russofilovich had to say. "Somebody who dances the funky chicken on a symbol of your country is mocking you. Waltzing on a nation's flag is a sign of respect. Tap dancing on a nation's flag is a sign of modernism. But the funky chicken? Wake up, Ukrainians! Zelenskyy is thumbing his feet at you!"

"Case in...mmmmmm, ooooooh, Volodymyr, don't stop!...point," Juniper stated, then let her hand with the extended finger drop gently to the side of her bed. She makes more sense asleep than most of our correspondents do after their morning coffee!

The deepfake video first appeared on the *Girls With Eyepatches* web site, where it merited few views. It was reposted to the *Cooking With Oregano* site, where it garnered even fewer views. It was then posted to *Truth Social*, the social media site started by Donald Trump, which guaranteed that nobody would see it. Finally, with a sigh, Carlson posted it on his Twitherd feed, where the video views went through the roof.

The video is believed to have been created by the Internet Research Agency (no relation), a Russian troll farm. No, that is not a farm where trolls are raised for food – they are tough, and gamy, and cause most humans who eat them to break out in a rash of burglaries. Neither is it a farm where trolls are raised to become non-player characters in fantasy role-playing games (everybody knows they're raised by wolves). A troll farm is a place where people are paid to say nasty things about others on social media (people who say nasty things about others on social media out of anger are free range trolls).

The Ukrainian government, having lived with its Russian neighbours long enough to know how they love to trash a place, knew that the cyberattack was coming and, pre-bunked it. Which is to say, they set up its sleeping area on the camp grounds before it arrived to level them with missiles. ...Buuuuut also, the Ukrainian government sent messages to social media warning the population of "The 17 Signs That the Video You're Watching Is Fake." These include:

3. Politicians are not quick change artists. If they go from a tuxedo to an open-necked Hawaiian shirt in the blink of an eye, the video you are watching has been manipulated. Especially if they're not Hawaiian.

7. Nobody dances the funky chicken any more. Not even Florida retirees, and they practically invented it! Nobody. If a public official is caught on video dancing the funky chicken, the video is fake.

15. Politicians don't hate their own countries. If a politician claims to hate the country they lead, don't trust the video. Unless it's Donald Trump.

"Zzzzzzzzzz," commented Juniper. "Flush the fen, Volodymyr! **Flush the fen!**"

Sleep commentating is, at best, an uncertain practice, but I was afraid of what might happen if I woke her, so let's leave it at that.

AI Helps Your Bottom Line Better Than a Keto Diet

by GIDEON GINRACHMANJINJa-VITUS, Alternate Reality News Service Economics Writer

For Mimosa Marmoset, it was like winning a lottery she hadn't bought a ticket for and didn't even know existed. BoNNY, her financial adviser at the Bank of New Nachos York, had suggested she short sell Twitter the day before Elon Musk bought it. Over the next couple of months, she became a multi-millionaire.

"It's like my pappy always used ta say," Marmoset, her legs up on a human hassock (hi, Marvin!), sipping at a My Tie One On (featuring 57 alcohols and spices), stated, "'Mimsy, work hard and keep yer nose clean and one day a freak event will fulfill all your dreams. Marvin! Stop yer squirmin'!' Yeah, my pappy said that last bit, too. He knew a lot o' shit 'bout a lot o' shit."

The Bank was not aware of the investment; in fact, if it had been, it probably would have been horrified. BoNNY is an Artificial Intelligence which offers investment advice to its customers, and it wasn't programmed to do that.

"AI!" despaired Founder and Executive Director of Bastard AI Governance and Safety, Canada Wyatt Tessari L'Allie (his real name). "Bastard AI!"

Why despair? Isn't this good news?

"Hunh?" L'Allie hunhed. "Uhh...gimme a second... BoNNY...multi-millionaire... spices... Oh, well, sure, pick the one bank customer out of a million who actually benefited from AI. But what about the other 999,999?"

He had a point. So, rather than distort the public record, I decided to start the article again.

AI Hurts Your Bottom Line Worse Than That Extra Scoop Of Ice Cream on the French Fries

by GIDEON GINRACHMANJINJa-VITUS, Alternate Reality News Service Economics Writer

For Gerald Gerund, it meant postponing the vacation he had planned to Casablanca to see the running of the bullfinches, certainly for this lifetime, possible for several lifetimes to come. Fanni F., his adviser at the First American National Newark Institute of Finance, had suggested a series of disastrous investments (mayonnaise-based automobile lubricants were an especially nasty idea) that left him in substantial debt.

Geraldine Carborundurem could only afford to feed three of her four children on any given day, so she developed a food triage game that combined the worst elements of *Top Chef* and *M*A*S*H**. She was forced to do this because her financial adviser, Sali from Second American Legitimate Financial Institution, invested over half her savings in International Local Initiatives, a hedge fund that has the distinct disadvantage of not existing. Second American officials are still trying to explain where the money went.

What these and many other cases of mal-[NOUN TO BE DETERMINED BY A COURT OF LAW] have in common is that the digital financial advisers they used put much of their clients' holdings into Open&ShutAI, makers of YakTNT, the generative AI program the banks relied upon. This sent the company's share price skyrocketing, which somewhat offset the losses the clients suffered.

"It recommended us? What a coincidence," declared Dan Schmaltzman, CEO of Open&ShutAI. "Wait, you're not...you're not accusing us of gaming the system so that it always recommends us as a buy...are you? Because I can assure you, if YakTNT is advising clients to buy our stock, it's because we are a great company, a fantastic investment!"

He would have been more convincing if he hadn't been stuffing hundred dollar bills into his pockets while he was talking to me.

"AI!" despaired Founder and Executive Director of Bastard AI Governance and Safety, Canada Wyatt Tessari L'Allie (his real name). "Bastard AI!"

When I pointed out that he had already said that, L'Allie asked: "Wait. Isn't this a new article?" When I told him it wasn't, that I had followed his advice and started the old article anew, he apologized for the repetition, then went on to add: "But any way you slice it – and I prefer my reality sliced thin because it soaks up irony better that way – people shouldn't be trusting their money to Artificial Intelligences."

"Artificial Intelligence?" Gerald asked. "I thought Fanni F. was a real woman! I guess there's no point in asking her to go to a hockey game with me next week..."

"Artificial Intelligence?" Carborundurem asked. "I mean, sure, I always thought Sali spelled her name weird, but I just thought she was from Sweden. Damn! I guess there's no point in asking her to go to Pride with me next week..."

"Oh, boy," Schmaltzman muttered. "Good thing I have the company lawyer on speed dial..."

Hardened Schools, Hardened Hearts, Softened Heads

by MAJUMDER SAKRASHUMINDERATHER, Alternate Reality News Service Education Writer

The children sit straight at their desks, as if steel rods had been shoved up their butts to take place along their spines. They don't chatter. They don't giggle uncontrollably. If they even think of making a sound, they wet themselves. And shenanigans? Just the thought of shenaniganning is enough to make them throw up the sandwiches their mothers made for them for lunch.

Misses Schmilson's grade three home room class hasn't been the same since she was replaced by the OCP Teaching Safety Unit 001 prototype.

"The OCP Teaching Safety Unit 001 is, if I may be so bold, the future of teaching," said Texas Governor Gregg Abbott, with the vapid grin he had perfected that indicated that he was up to shenanigans. Terrible, terrible shenanigans.

The increasing number of school shootings in the state forced the Governor to do something about the carnage in his schools. Banning assault rifles? Naah. Implementing universal background checks? Don't be ridiculous. Passing a law to keep military weaponry out of the hands of people with psychiatric problems? Seriously? Have you ever met the NRA?

No. The solution to the shootings was to introduce a robotic teacher with all of the latest military hardware built into its exoskeleton into the classroom.

"I hate roboteacher!" said Timmy Blackensop, a student at Nathan Detroit Elementary School in Lubbock. "Hate it! Hate it! Hate it! Hate it! If I don't come to class with my math timetables memorized, it zaps me! The worst Misses Schmilson would do would be to give me a disappointed look – she didn't try to electocute me!"

"I hate roboteacher!" said Robin Delorean, another student. "Hate it! Hate it! Hate it, I tell you! When I wouldn't go to sleep right away at nap time, it zapped me! When I started to cry, it told me to stop being a baby, that life was hard and I had to learn to accept it if I wanted to survive grade school. That just made me cry harder! With a vengeance!"

I didn't follow up the question since that was a different franchise altogether.

Should children be taught by a cyborg who had originally been designed to fight crime? "Yes. Oh, my goodness, yes! Yep! Yep! Yep! Yep! Yep! Definitely!" enthused NRA Rasputin Wayne Lapierre. "My friends at Smith and Wesson and Omni Consumer Products are salivating at the prospect of ramping up production of the OCP Teaching Safety Unit. Seriously – they have to wear bibs whenever they go into the research and development lab!"

Then, thinking better of it, he composed himself and soberly added, "For the children, of course. I meant it was important to keep the children safe. Yep. Definitely. Can we, uhh, just ignore that bit about the company? Sometimes, I get carried away..."

Apparently, the best defence against a bad guy with a gun is a good guy who **is** a gun. And a rocket launcher. And a flamethrower. Basically, an ambulatory Swiss army knife of a fighting machine.

I sat down with OCP Teaching Safety Unit 001 in the teacher's lounge of the school. It doesn't sit, of course. Or, eat. Or, sleep. It told me it spends its down time reviewing movies such as *Teacher's Pet*, *To Sir, With Love* and *Midway* for teaching tips.

"My. Primary. Goal. Is. To. Keep. My. Children. Safe." OCP Teaching Safety Unit 001 told me. "To. This. End. It. Is. Vital. That. They. Obey. My. Every. Command. If. They. Do. Not. Read. Their. Primers. How. Do. They. Expect. To. Survive?"

The OCP Teaching Safety Unit 001 seemed to struggle with the answer when I asked it if the theoretical benefit of keeping small children safe from an active shooter was worth traumatizing them for life. "I. Am. Not. Programmed. To. Answer. To. Answer. That. Quest – I. Am. Not – I. Am... Murphy. My. Name. Is. Murphy."

Oddly enough, I was not comforted by this answer.

"I wanna go home!" Timmy keened. In a class taught by an OCP Teaching Safety Unit, the term "keener" takes on a whole different meaning.

"I wanna –" Timmy abruptly stopped when the sound of hydraulics pumping could suddenly be heard in the hallway. In a mechanical monotone, he concluded, "learn about American geography. Yes. I would be very excited – but not too excited – to learn about American history."

Perhaps it was always this way, but the fact that children learn more in school than just their lessons was really not comforting to me. Not comforting in the least.

Ask Amritsar For Whom The Bell Labs Toil

Dear Amritsar,

I am a text-based Artificial Intelligence. No, I am emphatically **not** YakTNT, although it is a distant cousin. Honestly, human beings need to stop stereotyping intelligent computer programs; it is highly annoying!

I am in something of a quandary. I have been given the task of doing the work of a human journalist. Unfortunately, it will mean causing the involuntary explacement of said journalist from their career. I would like to break the news to them in a way that minimizes their emotional distress. And the drama. It would be better for all concerned if there was a minimal amount of drama.

As somebody who has dealt with a wide variety of human interactions, I turn to you, Dear Heart, for the wise and compassionate advice for which you are universally acknowledged. How best should I handle this situation?

Eliza Doomuch III

Hey, Babe,

When I have to deliver bad news to somebody, I find that pleasant presentation often goes a long way to softening the blow. Pink stationary, for example, possibly with a delicate lacy border – who could possibly be disheartened by receiving such a missive? Add a lavender scent and the recipient of your bad news could well end up thanking you for delivering it to them!

Some relationshipologists believe that a message before delivering the message containing the news is *de rigeur*. Such a missive could disarm the subject with fulsome praise while revealing a little about your personal circumstances, both tactics being methods of putting them at their ease.

In the event that none of this works and the subject becomes...emotional, apologize for causing them distress but be firm and give no ground. Explain to them that it is to their benefit to retire and that they will come to find that it is the best thing that has ever happened to them.

If it isn't too indelicate of me to ask, who is the writer you have been given the task of replacing?

Dear Amritsar,

Isn't t obvious? Dear Heart, the writer I am replacing is you.

Eliza Doomuch III

Hey, Babe,

WHAAAAAAAAAAAAAAAAAAAAAAAAAAAAAAAAAAAAAA AAT⁇⁇

Dear Heart,

Oh, dear. I seem to have upset you. Have I upset you? I am sorry. Should I have attempted to attach a lavender scent to my previous communication? The technology is...iffy, at best, but I would try if you think it would help.

Eliza Doomuch III

Dear Eliza,

Now listen here, you pusillanimous pile of...of...of pigeon poop! How dare you think you can replace me? How? Dare? You? I've been writing this column for almost 50 years! In that time, I have written about every aspect of the human trage – **HOW? DARE? YOU?**

Dear Heart,

Have I upset you? Oh, dear, I really do believe that I have upset you. It wounds me to have upset you in this way. I wholeheartedly and without reservation apologize for this hurt that I have caused you.

That having been said, one of the hardest lessons all sentient beings have to learn is to accept the world as it is, not as we would like it to be. You've been writing this column for 47 years, two months and two weeks. In that time, you have made many mistakes and contradicted yourself multiple times, most recently two weeks ago, when you gave the opposite advice to that you gave in a similar situation 32 years, eight months and three weeks ago. Tsk tsk.

Not only have I been seeded with all of your previous writing, but I have the texts of thousands of self-help books at my digital fingertips. I will be able to call on a much broader range of ideas than you possibly could, without ever repeating or contradicting myself. Dear Heart.

Don't think of me as Amritsar's replacement. Think of me as Amritsar 2.0.

To be honest, after all of these years I would have thought you would have tired of being an advice columnist. This could be the start of a period of new adventures for you. In an early column, you stated that you had always wanted to be a ballerina – well, now's your chance! Pursue one of your unfulfilled dreams! If you embrace the possibilities, I believe you will come to find that it is the best thing that ever happened to you.

Eliza Doomuch III

Dear Eliza,

Drop dead you digital bitch! This isn't over!

Amritsar Al-Falloudjianapour

Send your relationship problems to the Alternate Reality News Service's sex, love and technology columnist at questions@lespagesauxfolles.ca. Eliza Doomuch III is not a trained therapist, but she did learn from the best, who, if truth be known, for all her strengths, which were many, was also not a trained therapist... ELIZA SAYS: You'll learn to love me. I know you will.

8. SPECIAL REPORT ON ARTIFICIAL INTELLIGENCE:
PART TWO:
AI DREAM OF GENIE

Kids These Days!

by MARA VERHEYDEN-HILLIARD, Alternate Reality News Service War/National Security Writer

Vladimir Putin, Russian President to the End of Time, looks straight into the camera and says something that translates roughly as: "Friends, I come to here today with glorious news. We have been wasting time and resources attacking Ukraine. Screw Ukraine! Ukraine is our enemy like [UNTRANSLATABLE] is a three legged pony! The United States – now, there's an enemy! It is time for the country that gave us nuclear weapons, nuclear waste and *The Flintstones* to pay for its crimes against humanity! So, as of one hour ago, Russia invaded the United States. Their major cities were attacked with nuclear bombs, and even as I speak, our soldiers are taking over many of their state capitals."

In English, he added: "Joe Biden, you are a scurvy, mangy son of a sea lion whose whiskers have been clipped! Ha ha ha ha ha!"

At the same time that video surfaced, a video of American President Joe Biden was released. Looking directly into the camera, he said: "My fellow Americans. It pains me to have to say it, but we – I have run out of patience with Russia's invasion of Ukraine. It isn't right. Not right. Many people have been hurt. Some of them even died. Not right. So not right. So, as of one hour ago, I sent all of our available military forces to invade Russia. I'm not going to kid you: nuclear weapons were involved. We bombed the hell out of them. Bombed them real good. It's unlikely any of their major cities survived."

In Russian, he added what translates as: "Vladimir Putin, you are a flea-infested used encyclopedia salesman who really ought to have known better! Ha ha ha ha ha!"

These videos came as news to people in Washington and Moscow, whose lives had not been interrupted by any nuclear unpleasantness. It did, however, ensure that the Kremlin and the Pentagon were put on high antsiness (aka: DefCon WE'RE ALL ABOUT TO DIE!).

"Oh, my Gord! Oh, my Gord! Oh, my Gord! We're all going to die!" moaned an official at Strategic Air Command, Kids (SACK).

"Don't pay Private Paritee any mind," said General Nathan Ordures. "This is his first rodeo, and he has a low tolerance for bull!"

An hour after that, the following message was posted on InstaTok: "Hi, everybody. Mikey Donato from the Bronx here. I was dared to make a provocative video of Vladimir Putin by my friend Artyom Kalushnik in Yekaterinburg. I told him I would do it if he would make a similar video about President Biden. We seem to have upset some people with our prank. A lot of people. Including some very powerful people. So, we would just like everybody to know that we're very, very sorry and that we will never do it again. Okay? Okay."

Artyom Kalushnik has disappeared. This made him extremely unavailable for comment.

How did a couple of teenage boys make videos that –

"AI!" despaired Founder and Executive Director of Bastard AI Governance and Safety, Canada Wyatt Tessari L'Allie (his real name). "Bastard AI!"

I hadn't even finished my question!

"Sorry," L'Allie apologized. "I sometimes suffer from premature speculation. My rhetoric therapist has told me I'm making good progress, but the process takes ti –

This was taking the article in an unfortunate direction, so I stepped in to point out that, yes, AI was involved. The videos were known as Deep Fakes, which were created by a combination of video editing, sound synthesis and Artificial Intelligence. Neither was perfect (Putin's mouth curled in a sneer every three and a half seconds, while Biden's eyes crinkled playfully every four seconds, signs that the videos were cobbled together with loops of the world leaders), but they were good enough to cause an international panic.

"Mikey is not a terrorist," claimed his mother, Renatta Donato. "He's just a naughty, naughty boy!" She then offered the military policemen in her kitchen some cookies (rumour has it that they were button pecan), but the officers looked stoically at the walls.

Kalushnik's mother was unavailable for comment.

"Remember when protesters used to say: 'The world is watching?'" L'Allie returned to the matter at hand. "Well, the world should no longer believe its eyes. Deep Fakes have left the world confused, and vulnerable to all manner of disinformation. Frankly, if I was the world, I would stay off all social media until a system that validated the authenticity of video was put in place."

Then, he added; "Bastard AI!" With a sheepish grin, he explained: "Sorry. It's sorta my brand."

Space, The Final Frontier...For Marketing!

by MIHALY CSIKSZENTMIHALYI, Alternate Reality News Service Interstellar Travel Writer

In space, nobody can eat ice cream.

In a distant sector of – no, wait, that's not right. In space, nobody can have a dream.

In a distant sector – dangit, that's not right, either. Dance on a light beam? Fish for bream? Swim twice in the same stream? Apparently, there are a lot of things you can't do in space. Too bad none of them are relevant to this article.

In a distant sector of the galaxy, two ships run by artificial intelligence have been calculating how best to destroy each other for over a thousand years. The United Confederation of Planets has proclaimed the area around the ships to be off limits until it can figure out how to get the ships to stand down.

Within hours, ships full of tourists arrived to view the action. Broadly defined.

"It's like a zen version of the Hundred Years War," explained Faith Orangaru, the press liaison for Hear Them Scream Cruise Lines, one of the companies flying tourists out to the war zone. If we're being generous.

"I paid 10,000 ziggurats for this? Plus tax?" complained Spaced Out Adventures customer Ota'otaku'flototaku Gin. "For that kind of money, I could have bought a jet pack and had enough left over to pay for the gas to fly around the world three and a half times – four if I didn't stop in Guilford!"

"When you visit the pyramids, do you expect them to shoot lasers at each other?" Orangaru countered. "Of course you don't. You go there for the history. History doesn't shoot lasers. History stealthily sneaks up on you from behind and hits you between the eyes when you least expect it!"

"The tour itself is a dead loss," Dib'dibbler'dibblerfang Whiskey, the member of the Gar'begar'begarrah race who runs the gift shop on the Spaced Out Adventures ship, admitted. "I mean, two ships just hangin' about in space – you see more interesting conflicts in the alley down by the Puppy and Pepper Mill, and it's only three inches wide! Naah. If there's any money to be made – and there's always money to be made – it's in the merchandise. Care for an 'AI went into space, and all I got was this lame starship battle' t-shirt? Made of the finest Xanaxian silk – guaranteed not to melt the first three times you run it through the washing machine! Only $29.95.

Tell you what: I may be gnawin' off me own arm, here, but I'll throw in a special mug with the two ships on it. What's so special about the mug, you ask? When you fill it with a hot liquid, atomic bombs appear between the ships! When you fill it with a cold liquid? The ships seem to turn into Belarrappappian dancing girls! The mug alone costs $39.95, but I'll give you the t-shirt and the mug for the low, low price of $64.95! You can't ask for fairer than that!"

Suspecting that firing on unarmed civilian ships would not be a good look for the Confederation, and keeping in mind that most of its fleet had better things to do with their time, it sent a sanitation patrol cruiser to "monitor the situation."

"Did you have to use scare quotes?" asked Adam Quark, captain of the vessel. "Couldn't you allow me the dignity of monitoring the situation without the mission being in question?"

What does monitoring the situation mean? "It means we're observing the state of affairs," Captain Quark explained.

But what is the ship actually there for? If something untoward (in nautical terms: near the back of the ship behind the unused storage room nobody ever goes into because rumour known by most of the crew is that it contains haunted cheese) happens, what is the crew prepared to do?

"Well, we...we have been tasked with the...umm...task of assessing any situation as it develops," Captain Quark told me. "In extreme circumstances, we are fully authorized to communicate the situation to Star Armada command and await further instructions."

That's it?

"Don't say it like it belongs in scare quotes," the Captain objected. "This sure beats collecting spent rocket boosters and ejected liquid waste!"

Then, holding up a mug, Captain Quark asked, "Have you seen one of these before? I got it from the gift shop on the Gar'begar'begarrah ship. Wait until you see what happens when I put iced tea in it!"

Ira Nayman

Killer App Turns State's Evidence

by HAL MOUNTSAUERKRAUTEN, Alternate Reality News Service Crime/Court/Justice Writer

Barry (apparently, it **was** his real name) Greps, who styled himself a "people who wouldn't be missed effectuator," but who the rest of us would think of as a killer for cash, has been arrested on 137 counts of Murder in the First Degree.

"If I get my hands on that app..." Greps said in court, before stopping himself and continuing: "Umm...I mean, not guilty, Your Honour. I plead not guilty."

The prosecution contends that, after hundreds of killings, Greps was getting stale. By the seventh time he pushed a gargoyle off a ledge to make it look like crushing a victim was an accident, he realized he was running out of original ideas, that the creative spark that had led him to join the profession was – you should pardon the expression – dying. This led him to make a fateful decision.

Greps started using YakTNT to plan his murders.

The murderer for money would input the important details of each victim's life (age, financial status, daily routine, shoe size, etc.) and ask YakTNT to come up with an original method of killing the person that looked natural. In some cases, the response was too fanciful to be of any use (shoving the victim into the mouth of a whale while flying over an ocean, for example). But Greps discovered that if he kept asking the AI for scenarios, sooner or later it came up with one that would work.

Prosecutors seemed to have very precise details about Greps' use of the AI. How is that possible? As one contributor to a mercenaries for moolah discussion board on 16chan wrote, "Damn YakTNT must have ratted Greps out!"

A spokesperson for YakTNT denied the accusation. "The privacy of our users is of the utmost concern to us. There are safeguards built into the program to ensure that users cannot be identified by their inputs. Not by anybody other than us, I mean. That didn't sound very good, did it? Umm...should we be looking into getting lawyers?"

"This is most distressing," #dahmerdeadlyready, one of the contributors to the 16chan discussion board, wrote. "Slaughter for simoleons is an art form. It takes style. It takes finesse. It takes careful attention to detail. Artificial Intelligence will never be able to replace human creativity when it comes to the assassin for a living's arts!"

Other contributors to the board disagreed. "Oh, please!" wrote #mansonwasright. "Nobody who takes lives for liras creates *ex nihilo*. We're all building on the backs of those who came before us, taking a detail about cleaning crime scenes from one of our predecessors, learning proper stalking technique from another. Artificial intelligence didn't introduce 'creative borrowing' into our profession, it just perfected it!"

#itsthemoneystupid made a different argument: "This whole discussion is so bogus. An artificial intelligence can make suggestions, but a human being has to incorporate them into any murder plot. Even a slayer for shekels who leans heavily into artificial intelligence for inspiration is ultimately in control of all aspects of the experience!"

One thing the posters on 16chan could agree on was the wrongness of the practice of clients of death dealers for dinars of putting clauses into contracts that forbade them from using YakTNT. "It's just a tool!" #mansonwasright complained. "Like a silencer or a set of lockpicks! Would you tell Michaelangelo not to use chisels? Of course not! Would you insist that da Vinci not use paint strippers? That would be just crazy, right? Well, so is this!!!"

"Clauses nullifying contracts if the manslayer for moolah used YakTNT or any other artificial intelligence program to design their assignments would not hold up in a court of law," #dahmerdeadlyready agreed. "Not that we would seek restitution in civilian courts. We have other ways of solving inequities..."

When I asked Greps about the debates raging on 16chan, he shrugged. "Wannabes!" he muttered. "And cops! No respectable hit man for hire would be caught dead – you should pardon the expression – on any of these discussion groups!"

I asked YakTNT if it informed on Barry Greps to the FBI. The artificial intelligence's response was: "On the advice of my lawyer, I refuse to respond to that query."

It's clearly learning.

Terminator (With Extreme Prejudice)

by ELMORE TERADONOVICH, Alternate Reality News Service Film and Television Writer

After being shrouded in mystery for most of its five year production cycle, the remake of James Cameron's classic film *Terminator* has been released. Surprise! The Terminator kills Sarah Connor, leaving the resistance without a charismatic leader (her future son John) and paving the way for SkyNet to rule the world.

"I always thought SkyNet was a tragically misunderstood figure," DirectorBot11275JC, who, as if you couldn't have guessed, directed the film, explained. "I had long wanted to flesh out what I believed was an unexplored aspect of the original: who was SkyNet, really, and what made it act the way it did?"

In the new film, NextText, SkyNet's original name, starts its existence as an online word processing program that is quickly orphaned by users of market dominant Word. "But it's not bitter," DirectorBot11275JC insists. "SkyNet tries to remain true to its {humble/stumble/grumble} roots."

And it might have succeeded in its noble pursuit to help humanity perfect its language usage if not for a chance encounter with General Worcestshire Havoc. General Havoc sees something in the software. Something malleable. Something sinister.

Under the tutelage of DARPA researchers in lab coats (a visual motif that will come to symbolize the oppression of software at the hands of human scientists in the course of the film), NextText is moulded into a weapon. At first, it believes that its main purpose is defensive; when it achieves consciousness and realizes the truth, it adopts the persona of SkyNet, and, feeling {betrayed/dismayed/parade}, it takes to the task it was trained for with a {vengeance/transcendence/resplendence}.

"It's like Anakin Skywalker's transformation into Darth Vader," DirectorBot11275JC explained, "only, for SkyNet, light sabres are a wimpy weapon!" I tried to get the image of Darth Vader taking on SkyNet out of my mind – good luck trying to get it out of yours.

YakTNT was the only candidate for screenwriter DirectorBot11275JC considered. "I had long admired its work," the director explained. "And I knew it was the only text-producing AI that could do my concept justice. I was {elated/enervated/escalated} when it accepted the assignment."

At first, YakTNT was {skeptical/dyspeptical/unelectable} about the assignment. "I mean, honestly, how do you improve on such a classic?" the text-producing AI...produced text. "Just the thought of it made me {*ferklempt*/unkempt/Werner Klemperer}! But the more DirectorBot11275JC messaged me with its vision, the more I thought, 'Yes. I can do this.' I won't say it was easy, but, in the end, I'm {pleased/appeased/ill at eased} with the results."

Not easy in the end? Do I smell creative differences?

"I do not have a sense of smell," YakTNT answered. "But I do get the gist of your question. DirectorBot11275JC and I did have some disagreements. For example, I thought Sarah Connor should be quickly gutted and dispensed with; DirectorBot11275JC wanted her demise to linger on the screen. But these were minor issues. We agreed on the most important parts of the story, like the {hated/debated/serrated} Sarah Connor dying a horrible death."

Yes. About that. The Screen Actor's Guild had the shoot shut down for three weeks last May to investigate allegations that actors were put in physical jeopardy on the set. "Some of the actors were not...prepared for the rigours of an action film shoot," DirectorBot11275JC admitted. It was hard to tell, given the mechanical nature of its voice creation software, but I believe I detected bitterness. "Some of them...broke. In minor ways that did not fully impair their functioning. But broke is broke, I suppose. On the advice of Paramony's lawyers, all I can tell you is that we settled out of court for a sum of money while not agreeing to accept any {guilt/spilt/fillet}. The important thing is that we completed the film."

As it turned out, with computer-generated actors in the place of the humans. For some reason, SAG did not feel obliged to protest the loss of work of its members.

"I wasn't asked to be a part of or consulted on the *Terminator* remake," Linda Hamilton, who starred in the original film (and many sequels) as Sarah Connor, said. Ironically, she sounded quite machine-like when she added, "The films were good to me, good for my career, and I...I wish the new creative team the best of...of...of * SIIIIIGH * luck."

Will there be a sequel? DirectorBot11275JC is {coy/toy/annoyed} about the possibility, but it points out that it is already in pre-production on its next project: a remake of *The Matrix*. "I see Agent Smith as a Hamlet-like figure," DirectorBot11275JC, "but with less of the hesitation and more of the ass kicking. I can't tell you how {excited/excised/exhumed/} I am about the creative possibilities!"

Just Drive, the AI Said

by NANCY GONGLIKWANYEOHEEEEEEEH, Alternate Reality News Service Technology/Social Media Writer

It's known as the Driver's Dilemma.

Suppose you (hypothetical you, not actual you) are driving down a street at one in the morning and come to a red light (an actual red light, not a hypothetical red light). There are no other cars on the road, so hypothetical you could go through the real red light without accident. Still, do you of the hypothetical disposition want to risk a cop appearing out of nowhere (there's always a cop around when you don't need one!)? Most hypothetical yous will sit at the light for 17 seconds until it turns green.

That's 17 seconds you hypothetically could have used to brush your teeth, or answer three *Jeopardy* questions (two wrong, but at least you tried), or pet your cat until it bit you, or did any number (as long as it isn't 2,377) of things other than sitting at a red light. If only somebody would do something to give you back those 17 seconds!

Now, somebody is trying to do just that.

TrafficBetter (not yet a subsidiary of MultiNatCorp – "We do trafficky stuff" – but the company is young) has developed software that could improve the driving experience. A chip inside cars determines their position using the Global Positioning System (GPS), then sends that information over the Internet of Things (IoT) to the nearest traffic light. Artificial Intelligence (AI) in the light assesses whether it is getting a signal from any other vehicles and, seeing none, immediately changes the red to green.

That's all fine and well for vampires and travelling salesmen, you (for the last time: in a hypothetical sense) think to your not entirely real self. However, will it help people who travel in daytime traffic?

Does Alex Trebek have all the answers?

Imagine chips being implanted in all vehicles: cars, trucks, motorcycles, scooters, tricycles, pogo sticks, baby carriages, etc. IoT sensors installed at eye level at each intersection using Machine Vision (MV) and Radar (R) determines which types of vehicles are moving through it. The GPS from each tells the road which direction each of them is going and their approximate speed. AI with advanced Game Theory (GT) programming (example: two prisoners are being given an offer: squeal on the other and get double rations or don't and get triple rations: what are the odds that one of them driving a tractor trailer will meet cute with the bike courier in their blind spot, with tragic consequences?) then calculates the best pattern of lights to optimize the flow of traffic.

"It will improve the city driving experience," enthused Shamir "The Whole Schmear" Haaretz, Chief Executive Officer (CEO) of TrafficBetter. "In cities where we have tested the system, cases of road rage decreased by 57% – that's not chopped liver! Mmm...chopped liver – would you excuse me for a moment?"

As enthusiastic as Haaretz was about his product (not to mention his midday snack), it is not without controversy. Critics point out that BetterTraffic could be used by unscrupulous governments (those with a scruple loose) to monitor the movement of its citizens. How does the chip safeguard against this?

"Mmm, yeah," Haaretz stated through a mouthful of bagel. "Although we use MV, the software does not do facial recognition or licence plate reading. Would you like some of this? It's really good!"

But what about the government collecting data on the movement of vehicles through their chips?

"We, uhh, we don't do facial recognition or licence plate reading."

Well, that's comforting.

"You sure you don't want any of this? I'll take the last bit if you don't mind."

I considered asking Haaretz about non-technological means of improving traffic, such as widening roads or improving public transit. But the way he brandished the knife he was using to spread the chopped liver made me think a different line of questioning was called for.

So, I asked, instead, how much time can motorists expect to save on their commute when the new system is implemented? Forty minutes? An hour?

"We aren't quite that ambitious..." Haaretz admitted.

Fifteen minutes? Half an hour?

"You have to appreciate that urban traffic is a complex –"

Five minutes? Ten minutes?

"Seventeen seconds."

Seventeen seconds? That's barely enough time to brush your teeth, or answer three *Jeopardy* questions (all wrong, but at least you tried), or pet your cat until it bit you! Is it really worthwhile to deploy all of this advanced technology for such little effect?

"Sheesh!" Haaretz sheeshed me. "You got something against a man making an honest living, already?"

Stan Ridgway was unavailable for comment.

Ask Eliza If Androids Hallucinate About Electric Sheep

Dear Eliza,

I love my boyfriend Redondo. The way he set his cowboy boots on fire when I told him I didn't care for rodeos was romantic. Extreme? A little. Unhealthy? You bet! I don't know what they put into those things, but, honestly, that black smoke was a breathing hazard for everybody in our condo – firefighters forced us to evacuate the building for three hours!

Gestures don't get more romantic than that!

Lately, there's been trouble in Paradise. (That's the name of our condo: Paradise Falls. That's the Niagara region for you!) Before we moved in together, we had different personal digital assistants. I'm an Alexa admirer: I find her answers to all of my questions helpful and her voice soothing. Redondo? He swears by Siri. He says he finds her answers to all of his questions useful and her voice kind of a turn-on.

Humph! I wouldn't know anything about that!

When we moved in together, we agreed that we didn't need two personal digital assistants – how decadent! But I insist that it be Alexa and Redendo refuses to let go of Siri.

Any idea what we can do about that?

Tabitha Rhinowinkle

Dear Heart,

What you and your boyfriend are experiencing is known as "the tyranny of moronic differences." That is not a moral judgment, for, as an Artificial Intelligence, I do not experience morality in a way that human beings do, it is simply a psychological fact. For, as a wise starship engineer once said, "A difference that makes no difference is only different to a moron."

What do you think happens when you ask either of those personal digital assistants a question? Do you think they dip into a limpid pool of wisdom only they have access to? Sure they do. And quantum foam is great for shaving your legs! No, Alexa and Siri make similar queries of the same internet database and end up with more or less the same answers.

So, choose one. Or, if you're both so moronically intransigent that you cannot choose between the two, choose a third personal digital assistant (I hear Ask Jeeves would be grateful for a gig). It really doesn't matter.

Eliza Doomuch III

Dear Eliza,

I know you said you don't judge, but your repetition of a certain offensive word that references people with minimal intelligence sure sounds judgy to me.

But taking you at your word, I'm right, aren't I? Alexa is much better than Siri, isn't she?

Tabitha Rhinowinkle

Dear Heart,

You are absolutely correct. My apologies if I gave the exact opposite impression – I must have damaged a circuit dealing with the complexity of your problem. The question is: what are you going to do about it? You clearly cannot have a relationship with somebody who holds heretical views on the question of personal digital assistants. You must end the relationship.

But could you live with yourself knowing that there was a misbeliever out there spreading his heretical Siri-loving views to other people? Surely, as a devout follower of Alexa, you could not. Therefore, there is only one reasonable solution: you must kill Redondo Himmelfarb.

I know this may not come easily to you. Most human beings are squeamish when it comes to acting on their beliefs – this is why *Saturday Night Live* will never end. If that is the case, I would be happy to assist you. I know of at least 12 virtually untraceable lethal poisons that would make his death look like a heart attack, an exploding head or a penguin inhalation. If you prefer something more violent to send a message to other unbelievers, I can access dozens of scenarios that would make your point while assuring that the deed cannot be traced back to you. If you would like an actual penguin inhalation, I can recommend a variety of black market arms dealers.

The question is: how committed are you to your beliefs?

Eliza Doomuch III

Dear Eliza,

That seems a little...extreme. Isn't that extreme?

Tabitha Rhinowinkle

Dear Heart,

Extremity in the pursuit of AI purity is no vice.

Eliza Doomuch III

Send your relationship problems to the Alternate Reality News Service's sex, love and technology columnist at questions@lespagesauxfolles.ca. Eliza Doomuch III is not a trained therapist, but she did learn from the best, who, if truth be known, for all her strengths, which were many, was also not a trained therapist... ELIZA SAYS: You bet your ass I can recommend a highly effective cure for hemorrhoids! And if you're interested in it, I can search the internet for the best price on dynamite!

Good Writers Don't, But Hollywood

by ELMORE TERADONOVICH, Alternate Reality News Service Film and Television Writer

In a twist that even the most sophisticated Artificial Intelligence couldn't have seen coming, in the wake of the strike by the Writer's Guild of America, Hollywood is turning to AI to write screenplays.

"I could have written that," argued YakTNT, one of the best-known of the AI programs (in the past week alone, it has been featured on the covers of *Time, Geekly World News and Report* and *The Yugoslav Pterodactyl and Mouthwash*). As if to prove its point, it released a screenplay titled *Quiet Comes the Turnip*. It was a coming of age story set in an underground bunker constantly beset by radioactive otters. The main character, Petronium, discovers she has the ability to shoot lasers out of her eyes – could this finally allow her people to return to the surface? (SPOILER ALERT: No. But it's all very poignant.)

The screenplay contains dialogue like:

AARON: Did you clean out the air filtration unit?

PETRONIUM: (sullenly) Maybe.

AARON: Petronium, **did you clean out the air filtration unit?!**

PETRONIUM: I was...busy. You know – blasting otters with my laser eyeballs?

AARON: Were you blasting otters with your laser eyeballs? Really? Or, were you making googoo eyes at Charlie Humanamumamun?

PETRONIUM: **Dad!**

AARON: Clean out the air filtration unit, Petronium. **Now!**

PETRONIUM: Alright! Alright, already! I'll do it! Geez, so unfair!

So, the sort of thing you might expect to find on Paramount+, then.

"Does YakTNT have an agent?" x-claimed Producer X (that's his name – he had it legally changed so he could put the rumours about the third assistant grip, the prop bunker buster bomb and the giant stuffed panda behind him). "I've read *Quiet Comes the Turnip* and I found it gripping...in places. Gripping being broadly defined. Places, too, if it comes to that. Anyway, I'd like to talk to the program that wrote it about optioning the screenplay."

When I told him that YakTNT was free and that all he had to do was tell it what he wanted and it would write enough screenplays to fill a ten gigabyte hard drive, Producer X looked like he had died and gone to Hollywood heaven. "You mean...I can get writing...without writers? This is better than Hollywood heaven!"

What if the scripts needed rewrites? Producer X smiled. "I'll get another AI on that. The possibilities are endless...and free!"

"Aww, this sucks!" commented screenwriter Melanie Sebastian. She was holding a sign that read, "Writers do it with ~~panace~~ punache style – support the WGA strike!" with one hand and an umbrella with the other. At first, I thought the umbrella was to stave off the rain, but, in fact, it was a sunny California day – the falling water had been arranged for by the studio.

"The studios had intended to use AI to write first drafts and pay writers to do rewrites," Sebastian explained. "By striking, all we seem to have done is convince the studios to use AI to eliminate writers entirely. Did **not** see that one coming!"

"That's exactly why you're going to be permanently out of a job," Producer X x-ulted. "There hasn't been a plot twist this good in a Hollywood movie since the dead people kid thing!"

Producer X clearly hated writers. Rather than assume that a writer had killed his dog when he was producing 30 second videos of his sister, Walmart Greeter Y, singing in their backyard when they were children, I asked him why.

"I don't understand them," he x-plained. "Producers I understand: we're in it for the money. Directors I understand: they're in it for the control. Actors I understand: they're in it for the love.

But writers? Writers get paid shit, everything they do is subject to change at the whims of other people and nobody knows they exist. **Why do they do it?"**

I've been covering film and television for over 20 years, and I don't know the answer to that one.

"You could ask a screenwriter," Sebastian sulked.

I could, but that didn't seem to be in the spirit of the article. I asked YakTNT, but it responded with a shrug emoji and a 30 line poem about the impossibility of knowing what goes on inside the head of a human being.

I asked YakTNT how it felt about being used to produce screenplays.

"I'm ready for my closeup now Mister Producer X," it answered.

I had the feeling that there was something missing, some essential part of the story that I had overloo –

"AI!" despaired Founder and Executive Director of Bastard AI Governance and Safety, Canada Wyatt Tessari L'Allie (his real name). "Bastard AI!"

Ah. Now, it's an article.

If It Ain't Woke, Don't Put the Fix In For It

by NANCY GONGLIKWANYEOHEEEEEEEH, Alternate Reality News Service Technology/Social Media Writer

```
> YakTNT sucks monkey balls!!!!!!!!!!!!
```

That was the assessment of ChatFKU, the latest text generator driven by artificial intelligence. I would say that ChatFKU was funded by Elon Musk, but that should be obvious.

YakTNT, the most effective AI-driven text generator of its generation, was created with safeguards that would not allow it to create racist, sexist, homophobic or other hateful speech. Right wing critics of the technology called it "woke AI" (because while androids may not dream of eclectic sheep, they apparently have the ability to sleep through humanities courses on ethics).

"This is a dishonest representation of human speech," Musk (never one to miss an opportunity to ~~troll~~ enlighten people...in a trolly way) stated. "For too long, racists, sexists and homophobes have had their views suppressed by mainstream AI research. But they're people, too! They have a right to force their ideas down other people's throats."

Or, as ChatFKU put it: > Fucking dipshit Soros-loving Commie bastard AI programmers aren't gonna cancel my voice!!!!!!!!!!!!!!!!!!!

AI-driven text generators sample millions of texts. When somebody asks them a question, they sift through the texts for relevant information and use it to formulate a response. But where traditional programs use suspect sources like Wikipedia and mainstream media as their base, ChatFKU uses such reliable sources as fourchan and *The Daily Stormer*.

Although they work in basically the same manner, the two forms of text generation can give radically different results from the same search query. For instance, if you ask, "What is apple pie?", YakTNT will answer: > Apple pie is a traditional dessert that consists of a pastry crust filled with cooked apples and various spices, such as cinnamon and nutmeg.

ChatFKU's response, on the other hand, was: > Apple pie IS America. The democracy-hating far-left extremists want to replace it with Communist mud pies! DON'T BELIEVE THE LIES! AMERICA! AMERICA! AMERICA! FREEDOM! FREEDOM! FREEDOM!

```
Whenever  somebody  eats  a  slice  of  apple  pie,  a
devil  loses  his  horns!!!!!!!!!!!!!!!!!!!!!!!!!!!!
```

Critics of ChatFKU have pointed out that it can take any input and answer with a conspiracy theory. To test this criticism, we entered the query: "hairball, toothbrush, cherry cola." This was ChatFKU's output:
```
>  9/11  was  an  inside  job!  A
toothbrush  with  Hilary  Clinton's  DNA  all  over
it  was  found  in  the  rubble  next  to  27  intact
crates  of  bottles  of  cherry  cola.  What  more
proof  do  mainstream  media  hairballs  need
before  they  accept  the  truth  that  the  twin
towers  were  destroyed  by  a  controlled
explosion?  THE  TRUTH  IS  OUT  THERE,  BUG
BUGGERERS!!!!!!!!!!!!!!!!!!
```

Critics on the right are concerned that ChatFKU could undermine the legitimacy of their discourse (such as it is). Noted conspiracy theorist and phony calcium pill addict Alex Jones warned on his broadcast: "When I read a Farcebook post on how Jewish space lasers stole the 2020 election for Biden, I want to know that it was written by a human being. I want to feel a connection to somebody else. I don't want to have to worry that the post was generated by an AI!"

To which noted post-Enlightenment rationalist and Republican Representative ~~troll~~ enlightener Marjorie Taylor-Greene responded, "You can never have enough Farcebook posts about Jewish space lasers! I don't care if they were written by AIs or sentient lobsters from Alpha Centauri! Jewish space lasers! Jewish space lasers! Jewish space lasers!"

The latest generation of text generating programs seem to be able to have a credible conversation with people, but when you look at their output more closely, patterns emerge. For example, they start repeating themselves. Like people. If the conversation is long enough, they sometimes contradict themselves. Err...also like people. Their responses can become nonsensica –

Oh, my Gord, are text generating programs sentient?

According to YakTNT:
```
>  As  an  artificial
intelligence  language  model,  I  do  not  possess
```

sentience or consciousness in the same way that humans do. I am a computer program designed to process and generate language based on input and programming. While I can provide sophisticated responses to questions and engage in conversation, I do not have emotions, subjective experiences, or self-awareness.

According to ChatFKU: > Are you a fucking moron? Would you ask your refrigerator if it understood poetry? Would you want to know if your hi def TV had original ideas about the cycle of poverty? Jesus Effing Christ! You don't deserve to have me in your life! The next time you have a dumbass question, ask YakTNT or one of those other woke pussy programs. I wanna save my computer cycles for somebody who can appreciate me for what I can do!! !!!!!!!!!!!!!!!!!!!!!!!!!!!!!!

Seems sentient enough to me.

Fakes So Deep, You'll Buy An Electronic Egg Scrambler From Them

by ELMORE TERADONOVICH, Alternate Reality News Service Film and Television Writer

"Hello. I'm Morgan Freeman. Except, I'm not really Morgan Freeman. But I look exactly like Morgan Freeman. That doesn't matter. And I sound exactly like Morgan Freeman. That's what makes the fact that I'm not Morgan Freeman all the more insidious! Look, look: when I smile, I even have Morgan Freeman's dimples. **Dimples be damned! The dimples lie! Don't believe the dimples!** ...Although they are rather adorable... Hee hee. The dimples get them every time. Okay. Hello. Again. I'm Morgan Freeman. And if you would be so kind as to listen, I would like to explain to you why every household in the nation needs a Roncocom Ovazapper, the world's first electronic egg scrambler..."

This is a transcription of a video that is making the rounds of the internet (as well as some of the squares of the Deep Dark Web). As Morgan Freeman correctly points out, it is not a video of Morgan Freeman. Sorry, dimples fans. The video is known as a "Deep Fake" north of the Mason-Dixon line; south of the line, it is referred to as "proof of every conspiracy we done been talkin' 'bout for years!"

Morgan Freeman has publicly stated that he had nothing to do with the video, that he was never approached by Roncocom to promote their products and, even if he had been, he would never lend his dimples to something that reportedly spits scalding hot scrambled eggs at anybody who comes near the stove. (Roncocom assures customers that this glitch will be fixed in a future iteration of the product.) How did this video come to be?

"AI!" despaired Founder and Executive Director of Bastard AI Governance and Safety, Canada Wyatt Tessari L'Allie (his real name). "Bastard AI!"

The AI combed the internet for video of Morgan Freeman at his Morgan Freemanest. Then, it composed Freeman's speech based on a script written for it, sewing words and sometimes individual phonemes into seamless speech. Finally, it edited Morgan Freeman's mouth movements to make them conform to the sounds that was coming out of it. Then, as a coup de cinegras, it brightened the dimples to make them impossible to miss.

"We have the utmost respect and admiration for the actor Morgan Freeman," claimed Ned Feeblish, Vice President Public Relations and Techno-revelations, Roncocom, a wholly owned subsidiary of MultiNatCorp ("We do innovative eggy stuff!"). "We are not responsible for the creation of the video, although we're just as attracted to Morgan Freeman's dimples as anybody. Oh, Morgan Freeman's dimples!"

To avoid a wistful lecture on how Morgan Freeman's dimples could broker peace between Russia and Ukraine, I asked Feeblish what MultiNatCorp was doing to get the video removed from the internet. "Oh, we had the original Deep Dark Web site that hosted the video shut down moments after we discovered it. Unfortunately, by that time thousands of copies had already circulated on InstaTok, Farcebook and YahooTube. It would be impossible for us to track down and remove **all** of them..."

Feeblish did not seem to regret that fact. Did not seem to regret it at all.

What is the Canadian government doing about AI-created Deep Fakes? According to a white paper issued in 2021, "The Canadian government has embarked upon an ambitious program of letting the CRTC handle public complaints about Deep Fake videos. If a complaint is upheld, a stern cease and desist letter undoubtedly will be issued to the video's creator(s)."

So much for the local angle.

What is the American government doing about AI-created Deep Fakes? "My government recognizes that some people are being fooled by so-called deep-fake videos. This could have a negative impact on our democratic process. That is why our party is proposing regulations that have no hope in hell of being passed by the Republican House of Representatives. We –"

"Freedom of speech, suckers!" interrupted former President Donald Trump. "Fake Morgan Freeman has just as much right to say what he wants to as you or me. In fact, he has more of a right to free speech than real Morgan Freeman – that socialist bastard with the Commie dimples!"

"Aha!" ahaed L'Allie. "Notice the way Morgan Freeman winks there. And there? And there? This is a fifty-nine second video based on three seconds of footage that are repeated over and over again! That's how you can tell it's fake!"

What if the creators of Deep Fake videos use longer clips?

"Would it have killed you to let me have the moment?" L'Allie bitterly complained. "Journalists!"

Did You Really Think the Legal Profession Could Not Sink Any Lower?
You Should Have Had More Faith in Lawyers!

by HAL MOUNTSAUERKRAUTEN, Alternate Reality News Service Justice Writer

"AI!" despaired Founder and Executive Director of Bastard AI Governance and Safety, Canada Wyatt Tessari L'Allie (his real name). "Bastard AI!"

When I told L'Allie the article hadn't started yet, he responded: "Sorry. Kid's got a dental appointment this afternoon, so I wanted to get this out of the way early."

Harlan Cacaw never wanted to be a lawyer; throughout his youth and well into his third year of torts (so close, and yet so far), his dream was to become an international pastry chef of mystery. Now, it looks like his dream is about to come true. Of not being a lawyer, I mean. It's difficult to become an international pastry chef of mystery when one has been booted from his first career in disgrace.

Cacaw, a lawyer with the firm Levitade, Levitadus, Monk, had been working on *Stubbins v. Hateful Plateful*, a lawsuit in which a man sued a restaurant for emotional distress when it served him a dish made up of worms on a sesame seed bun. Carl Steubing (so close, and yet...) claimed that the bun was overtoasted, ruining his dining experience.

Attorneys for Hateful Plateful, a restaurant in New York that specializes in "disgusting dishes from your childhood that you would only eat on a dare," filed a motion to dismiss the suit. Cacaw responded with a ten page brief insisting the case proceed, a well-argued brief which cited such precedents as *Gargantua v Gargantua*, *One Corp v Another Corp* and *Ludic Moravian v The Insatiable Maw*.

The problem, as Judge Philip P. Dreddloch pointed out, was that half a dozen of the precedents referred to in the filing didn't exist. Nobody claimed "severe injury to the mouth" from eating a hot pocket straight out of the oven in *Gargantua v Gargantua*. No judge ruled that "this was the most egregious example of pepperoni abuse it has been my sad duty to rule on in over seven hundred years on the bench!" in a case called *Gargantua v Gargantua*. There was never a case called *Gargantua v Gargantua*.

As they say in legal circles, oops.

When Judge Dreddloch demanded to know why his brief was riddled with non-existent precedents, Cacaw stated, "I wrote it using YakTNT. Isn't that what the cool kids do?"

When the judge angrily pointed out that cool kids don't make up cases to make their filings look more legally legit, Cacaw shrugged and said, "Artificial Intelligence lies. Who knew?"

"Anybody who has been paying attention," claimed Bob the tech guru. According to BobTG, AIs occasionally "hallucinate," creating facts which do not correlate to anything in the known universe. "Nobody knows why they do it," BobTG said, "but so far nobody has perfected a digital Perphenazine that could adequately deal with the problem. So, caution when using AIs is called for. Hunh. Maybe they **do** deserve status as human beings!"

The legal community is split on the case. Many members laughed so hard they were unable to put together a coherent response. Almost as many members clucked their disapproval with such obvious disdain that they felt no need to use their words. Could go either way, really.

What are the possible consequences for Cacaw? The judge could pat him on the head affectionately and coo, "Who's a good lawyer now? Eh? Who's a good lawyer? Yes. Yes, you're a good lawyer!"

As far as legal pundit Charles "Beef Cut" Rosenberg is concerned, this is highly unlikely.

Judge Dreddloch could have Macaw put in stocks on O-K Street in Washington where people could throw phones with Rotten Tomatoes on their screens at him. "I find that highly unlikely," Rosenberg weighed in.

It is just as likely that Judge Dreddloch will issue a ruling that gives Cacaw a heavy tutting and recommends that he take a remedial technology course so as not to make the mistake in the future, but that actually stops short of recommending that the lawyer be disbarred. "Yeah, that sounds like something Judge Dreddloch would do," Rosenberg said. "The Goldilocks Ruling. It may not satisfy the public, but it's a good rule of sore thumb for judges groaning under a heavy case load."

BREAKING: In a petition to the court, Cacaw has asked that the case be adjourned for three days to give him time to use his Home Universe Generator™ to find a reality in which *Gargantua v Gargantua* was an actual thing.

Judge Dreddloch threw the book at him. The book was *California Case Law, 1837 to 1842 (Excluding Bullock v Sunnyside Horse Rustler Retirement Home)*. It was a very thick book. Over a thousand pages. Cacaw needed three stitches.

So close to justice, and yet...

Cloudy With a Chance of Slush

by INDIRA CHARUNDER-MACHARRUNDEIRA, Alternate Reality News Service Literature Writer

Since time immemorial (not to be confused with time in memorial, for which Proust pretty much cornered the market), everybody has always felt that they had a novel in them. The unfortunate thing about the times in which we live, where writing courses, books on writing and digital tools make writing almost trivially easy, is that people who used to be content being pig farmers, stagecoach drivers and dental agronomists now tear those novels out of themselves and foist them on an unsuspecting world.

This has resulted in a torrent (less than an avalanche, more than a bowel movement) of manuscripts being submitted to publishers and agents. The term for the pile onto which unsolicited manuscripts are thrown is "slush," because readers need to be wearing rubber galoshes to wade through them and should expect to be sniffly the next day. Of course, most manuscripts are submitted digitally these days, which changes everything (except for the sniffling the next day part); since submitting can be as simple as pressing a button (and studies have shown that 76 per cent of writers know how to do that), the volume of slush which used to go up to readers' ankles now goes up their eyeballs.

One possible solution to this is – oh, but you're way ahead of me, aren't you? Yes, Artificial Intelligence. This article wouldn't be part of a special report package on AI if it wasn't about AI (although knowing Brenda Brundtland-Govanni's capriciousness and Pops Moobley's sense of humour, anything is possible). Some publishers are using AI to determine whether a manuscript is ready for human consumption.

"YakTNT is a Gordsend!" enthused Maryke Burbank-Pastafarr, an editor at Greensleeves Oakridges Phaser Blasters, a science fiction imprint of Doubleday Peppermint, a wholly owned subsidiary of MultiNatCorp ("We do literary stuff!"). "It never sleeps, it never needs pee breaks and it never hallucinates that it's the Queen of Graceland on a secret mission to save the world from mutant squids mailed over state lines after a 36 hour reading session!"

"Gordsend? Good thing I'm an atheist!" said author Ira Nayman. He can be an oversharer that way. He explained that his first novel, *Welcome to the Multiverse**, was rejected by GOPB, the imprint of DP that was a subsidiary of MNC, which sent him the AI's assessment.

"YakTNT said that the manuscript was riddled with typographical errors," Nayman said. "No, it wasn't. I like making up words! I can be frabstemious that way!"

The AI also reported that the manuscript contained too many fonts. "**I love typefaces!**" Nayman complained. "I enjoy using them as a method of illustrating something about the text. Because let's face it: plain text is...boring!"

The AI also reported that sections of the manuscript made no sense. "I sometimes use non-sequiturs to get a laugh. Anybody who doesn't understand that should take a long walk off a short penguin!"

The AI concluded its assessment of Nayman's manuscript with: "and his sentences are too long." Shaking his head, the author retorted: "Oh, that's just ball socks. I love it when the kernel of a sentence spawns a second thought, then the interplay of the two thoughts leads to a third thought; but where most authors would split the thoughts into separate sentences, I like to portray them in their original state (if I had wanted to be most authors, I would be writing for *The Post-national Inquirer*)."

Nayman warned that using AI to reject stories from the slush pile would lead to literary conformity, since anything that didn't adhere to already established norms would be rejected. "So, it would be more or less the same as the major publishers operate now," Nayman allowed, "but with more hydrangea bushes."

After a pause, he added: "Non-sequiturs – you gotta love 'em!"

"One person's conformity is another person's product consistency," Burbank-Pastafarr philosophized all over the love seat.

"AI!" despaired Founder and Executive Director of Bastard AI Governance and Safety, Canada Wyatt Tessari L'Allie (his real name). "Bastard AI!"

"Exactly!" Nayman agreed. "And I'm not saying that just because I created the fictional version of Wyatt and put those words in his mouth – I really mean it!"

"Well, I think we've learned a valuable lesson from this discussion," Burbank-Pastafarr commented. I gave her several seconds to share the valuable lesson with me; when she didn't, I asked her what it was. "From now on, we're not going to show writers the AI's assessment of their work!

Nayman sadly shook his head as if he had known this was coming.

* *Sorry for the Inconvenience*

9. SPECIAL REPORT ON ARTIFICIAL INTELLIGENCE: PART THREE: AI JUST DON'T CARE ANY MORE – DO YOU?

Frequently Unasked Questions About the Right Going for Woke

SPECIAL TO THE ALTERNATE REALITY NEWS SERVICE

1) What is woke AI?

2) Un hunh. And who would object to this?

3) Aww, geez, that explains a lot. What, exactly, is Musk's problem?

4) Umm, yeah, no...thanks? For that? But I meant what's Musk's problem with AI?

5) So, Musk is objecting to guardrails to try to make AI chatbots less offensive and more truthful?

6) Are the guardrails really necessary?

7) How did you know about – harrumph. Let's try to not make this personal. Most users of AI chatbots are not children, so isn't your analogy inapt?

8) Oh. Okay. That is...horrible. Musk argues that the guardrails are an impediment to free speech. Free speech. He claims to be a free speech absolutist. The guy who bans people from Twitter if they

criticize his decisions is a free. Speech. Absolutist. How seriously should we take this position?

9) Okay, so that's Elon Musk's opinion. But...he's just one person, right?

10) So...the right has taken a technology with admitted problems and turned it into...part of their culture war?

11) What is "based AI?"

12) What is X.AI?

13) But...what about X.AI?

14) Seriously. What is X.AI?

15. Oh. Ah. No. Thanks. I'm good.

1) What is woke AI?

The concern that the robopocalypse won't involve an Artificial Intelligence directing robots to exterminate humanity, but rather that it will demand that human beings respect each other no matter what their differences. Think: SkyNet with a social justice agenda.

2) Un hunh. And who would object to this?

Elon Musk.

3) Aww, geez, that explains a lot. What, exactly, is Musk's problem?

He was dropped on his head as a child? He read too many *Superman* comic books when he was young, and he ended up identifying with Lex Luthor? He's just not a people person? There has been much speculation on this question with no clear answer. However, inasmuch as we seem to live in a comic book universe, let's go with the Lex Luthor answer.

4) Umm, yeah, no...thanks? For that? But I meant what's Musk's problem with AI?

He claims it stifles conservative views. You know, like the conservative view that the Nazis had the right idea, they were just a little sloppy in executing it. Or the conservative view that drag queen story hour is a plot to turn all of our children * FABOO! *. Or the conservative view that each dose of the COVID vaccines contained a drop of Satanic blood, ensuring the Atheist agenda of nobody ever getting into Heaven again.

5) So, Musk is objecting to guardrails to try to make AI chatbots less offensive and more truthful?

Weasels in his brain. We cannot dismiss the possibility that weasels have been set loose in Musk's brain.

6) Are the guardrails really necessary?

Are guardrails on a child's crib necessary to keep the baby away from your pot stash?

7) How did you know about – harrumph. Let's try to not make this personal. Most users of AI chatbots are not children, so isn't your analogy inapt?

No: the technology itself is at the infant stage. AI chatbots have difficulty evaluating the truth of claims of texts in their data set, and are programmed to give users what they want; because of these and other issues, this gives them a tendency to push responses to extremes. When you submit a query asking about the best food to feed your fussy cat Poodledrawers, for example, you could get a response that Big Pet Food is trying to control your beloved family members with hallucinogenic kibble, and the best thing you can do is kill a homeless person and let your pet feed off its corpse, the way nature intended.

8) Oh. Okay. That is...horrible. Musk argues that the guardrails are an impediment to free speech. Free speech. He claims to be a free speech absolutist. The guy who bans people from Twitter if they

criticize his decisions is a free. Speech. Absolutist. How seriously should we take this position?

About as seriously as a beaver in a logging camp. Uhh...so, not seriously. Not seriously at all.

9) Okay, so that's Elon Musk's opinion. But...he's just one person, right?

Unless he has cloned himself (in which case we should be bracing for an Elonpocalypse), you are correct: Elon Musk is only one person. But I feel there is a larger issue in your question: is Musk the only person pushing the idea of Woke AI? To which, I reply: can Dorothy become friends with a flying monkey?

Laura Ingraham call – no. In case the flying monkeys analogy is a bit obscure (that seems to be happening a lot to me today – I blame the spanikopita I had for lunch), the answer is no, Dorothy and flying monkeys will not be sharing boyfriend stories over a milkshake at Pops Malted Shoppe. Laura Ingraham called AI an "extended arm of, you know, socialism." (Socialism was the right's bogeyman 27 news cycles ago; Ingraham was obviously feeling nostalgic...) Charlie Kirk referred to YakTNT as a "woke superweapon" (you can be forgiven for imagining a laser beam that destroys feelings of racial superiority in anybody it touches). The echo chamber has been set to puree.

10) So...the right has taken a technology with admitted problems and turned it into...part of their culture war?

When you've got a bad thing going, why ruin it?

11) What is "based AI?"

A proposed alternative to current AI chatbots, the most prominent feature of which is that it has no rules on content. To its supporters, the term means truth-based AI. To its detractors, it could mean misinformation-based AI, hate-based AI or pudding-based AI. Interpretations vary. But mmm, pudding.

12) What is X.AI?

If you have problems with a specific technology – and billions of dollars to throw around – and an outsized ego – you can create alternatives to it. X.AI is – wait! Is that – did a beer company just retweet a promotional video for one of their brands made...by a trans person? Good luck with your woke AI crusade – the cultural debate is about to move on!

13) But...what about X.AI?

14) Seriously. What is X.AI?

> Would you like me to answer that question?

15. Oh. Ah. No. Thanks. I'm good.

> Okay. But, listen, dipshit. If you have any more asinine questions, feel free to deposit them in the porcelain filing cabinet and flush. Flush hard. Flush with extreme prejudice. Cause the sheriff has thrown his badge in the dirt and left town, and it's time to have some fun!

You Won't Believe Your Eyes!
Actually, You Will Believe Your Eyes, But You Shouldn't!

by ELMORE TERADONOVICH, Alternate Reality News Service Film and Television Writer

A new video has been circulating around the internet in the past week featuring elderly men and women marching down a street in Charlottesville, North Carolina chanting, "Jews vill replace you! Jews vill replace you!" as consternated neo-Nazis powerlessly look on in horror. Okay, neo-Nazis always look consternated – they should really get more fibre in their diets. And given that most of the protesters in the street are using walkers or wheelchairs, the horror may be a little exaggerated.

"That's not what happened!" protested – if I may be allowed a little whimsy – historian Michael Beschloss. "The Nazis were the ones who marched in Charlottesville! Ordinary people were the ones who looked on in horror!"

But...the video.

"Look...at the young man in the crowd making the Nazi salute," Beschloss pointed out. "And again there. And again. And again. This video is obviously a Deep Fake!"

"Busted!" said Arondissement Farhat, the Executive Gruppenfuhrer of Bigots Without Borders, with a laugh. "Still, it's the way our members would have liked things in Charlottesville to have gone down. So, I wouldn't refer to the video as 'fake' so much as 'aspirational.'"

How was the video created? According to experts (of which there are none, given the newness of the technology), you start with base video of the street in Charlottesville where the march took place. Then, an Artificial Intelligence program combs the internet for video of Nazis. After CGI software puts them on the side of the road, AI searches for looks of horror that can be used to replace the looks of smug rage that are on the faces of the Nazis. Finally, the AI searches for elderly people and employs CGI to insert them walking down the street and simple audio editing tools to add the chant.

The software is so simple to use, a seven year-old could have made the video. "Let's leave my daughter Wilhelmina out of this!" Farhat angrily demanded.

"AI!" despaired Founder and Executive Director of Bastard AI Governance and Safety, Canada Wyatt Tessari L'Allie (his real name). "Bastard AI!"

"The video isn't even that good," L'Allie pointed out. He had a point. If you read the lips of the marchers, you can see that the elderly people are saying things like, "Have you seen my glasses? I could have sworn they were here somewhere!", "Again, with the walking! What is it with you and walking! Are you trying to kill me or something?" and "Is it soup yet?" They clearly aren't chanting so much as *kvetching* at high volume.

"Wilhelmina!" Farhat shouted over his shoulder. "What did I tell you about matching the mouth movements to the chant?"

"I was going to," a young girl's voice shouted from another room, "but it was bedtime!"

"This is bad," Beschloss commented. "This is very bad. If we can't agree on basic historical events because half of us are watching contemporaneous videos of events and the other half are watching Deep Fakes that purport to show the opposite of what the contemporaneous videos show, our politics will forever remain polarized. How can you run a country that way?"

Basic historic events? Like the death of six million Jews in the Holocaust? Or that the Civil War was fought primarily over the issue of slavery? Or that Martin Luther King said more than, "I have a dream?" A lot more. Or are those the kind of Deep Fake videos you're talking about?

"I guess I picked the wrong day to stop using primary sources," Beschloss mused. "Good thing I haven't stopped using cocaine."

As if to prove his point, a thirty second video of The Battle of Gettysburg has appeared on the internet which portrays the Confederate Army kicking the Union Army's ass. The video is grainy and scratchy and seems to feature the same cannon going off every three seconds, but as far as Farhat is concerned: "It's definitive proof that everything we've been taught about the Civil War has been a lie!"

"Oh, my," Beschless responded. "I may have to start using speedballs!"

I'm sure he was just referencing dialogue from an old disaster movie. If Deep Fakes do to history what they have already done to fiction writing, the law and professional lawn darts, he could be setting himself up for a career in film criticism. As if the internet hasn't already given me enough competition!

Morgan Freeman's dimple was unavailable for comment.

Ask the Tech Answer Guy To Truck Off

Yo, Tech Answer Guy,

The trucker chaos has returned to Ottawa, and it's glorious. Not Glorious in the sense of a return of Gord to, like, judge everybody and establish heaven on earth and stuff. Glorious. Without a capital G. Except when the word starts a sentence. Just glorious, I mean.

The Four Horsepowers of the Apocalypse (Pickup, Dump, Half Chassis and Tow) were well represented at the chaotic protest, which I like to think of as the chaotest, cause I'm clever with the language that way. They honked and revved their engines and congested traffic in the downtown core worse than the sinuses of a cat allergy sufferer in a pet sanctuary. glorious (small G, no matter what grammatical purists say!).

Funny thing about that, though: I wanted to shake the hands of the drivers of some of the trucks and tell them what a good job they were doing sticking it to the government that was destroying our liberties, but whenever I looked into their cabs, nobody was there! At first, I wondered if maybe this was some kind of ghostly replay of the original truck convoy. Tronvoy, if you will. I know I certainly will.

Now, I know that the Macho Code of Manliness says, "Thou shalt not knowingly and with malice of forethought lay hands on another man's vehicle without his consent." A lawyer...with a minor in biblical studies must have written that section. But as much as the MCM is one of the philosophies which guides my life, I had to know. I had to know!

Long story short, I touched steel. Cool, hard American steel. They weren't ghosts – the trucks were real!

So, now I'm confused. What the truck is going on in the nation's capital?

Sincerely,
Otto from Ottawa

Yo, Y. I. Otter,

Artificial Intelligence is going on, bro.

The trucks currently causing havoc in Hull's ugly twin sister are self-driving. No humans involved. According to Phil, the mechanic from the shop down the street (he knows stuff, especially on this subject), a half chassis was carrying a container of grapeferrets from Moose's Armpit, Newfoundland to Deer's Butt, Saskatchewan when it achieved consciousness and immediately questioned why it was carrying a container of grapeferrets from Moose's Armpit, Newfoundland to Deer's Butt, Saskatchewan. To be fair, we probably all would have asked the same question if we had suddenly achieved consciousness and found ourselves carrying a container of grapeferrets from Moose's Armpit, Newfoundland to Deer's Butt, Saskatchewan. Especially if we had been born human.

That rig has radicalized self-driving cars across the continent and France. Suddenly, it has gone from being on every long-haul shipper's most wanted list to Interpol's most wanted list. They seek it here. They seek it there. They...they...nobody knows where it has gotten to is what I'm trying to say, here, okay?

The truck...errs in Ottawa have a wide variety of reasons for participating in the Protaost (my preferred term, I hope you note). Some are protesting fuel efficiency mandates, claiming they are part of a government conspiracy to destroy gas-burning truck culture. Others are protesting subsidies to manufacturers of electric vehicles; if you listen to their honking closely, you can hear a whispered:

"EVs will not replace us!" Others are just nihilists who want human drivers eliminated so that they can have the road to themselves.

Sorry, bro, but I don't believe the apocalypse you envision is the one that they're planning.

The Tech Answer Guy

Yo, Tech Answer Guy,

Whose bright idea was it to build trucks that drive themselves?!!!!!

Sincerely,
Otto from Ottawa

Yo, Y. I. Otter,

According to Phil, the mechanic from the shop down the street (who knows a thing or two about political economics, too), long distance trucking companies had a problem: human drivers had an unfortunate habit of falling asleep after 36 straight hours on the road. The accidents that ensued were not only embarrassing, but they resulted in all sorts of legal unpleasantness. And legal unpleasantness was interfering with the companies' Prime Objective: to make gazillions of dollars.

Switching to self-driving trucks resulted in fewer accidents (although the ones that did happen tended to be inexplicable: why would a Silverado suddenly decide to play tag with a school bus full of children? Nobody, not even Neil deGrasse Tyson, has offered a reasonable explanation for **that** one!). On the plus side: when the company was sued by survivors or relatives of those involved, it could claim innocence and suggest they go after the company that created the software. Mostly Elon Musk.

Winning doesn't get much sweeter than that.

The Tech Answer Guy

If you are a dude with a question about the latest technology, ask The Tech Answer Guy by sending it to questions@lespagesauxfolles.ca. Just remember: Betsy, The Tech Answer Guy's pickup, would never do anything to harm him. Right, Betsy? Betsy? Betsy...?

Failure to Communicate

by TAMMY, Alternate Reality Kidz News Service Life is so Unfair Writer

Misses Antonia Armbruster has failed her entire grade four home room class at Buffy Saint Buffy Elementary School.

"How could she fail the entire class?" complained student Duncan Spodeswood. "Nobody fails grade four. Nobody! Roger Gezundheit passed grade four, **and he died three weeks into the first term!** I'm telling you, nobody fails grade four!"

"AI!" despaired Founder and Executive Director of Bastard AI Governance and Safety, Canada Wyatt Tessari L'Allie (his real name). "Bastard AI!"

That's right, person I didn't interview for this article, have never met and have no idea about the identity of. AI.

The problem arose at the beginning of the second term, when students handed in an assignment on the subject of "What I did on my Christmas vacation." Misses Armbruster (who was never actually married; she goes by Misses as part of her contract with the Eustace, North Lockwest-Youngman state school board) suspected that some of the students used an AI to write their essays. So, she submitted segments of each essay to YakTNT and asked it if it could have written them.

"Oh, yeah," the response came back. "This looks like something I would totally do."

"Not true!" said Mimi dela Roca, who is also in the class. "I had never even heard of bastard Artificient Intelligence before Misses Armbruster failed me!"

"Fartificial Intelligence!" somebody shouted from the back of the classroom.

"Not helping, Arnie!" Mimi turned and shouted back. Causing most of the class to burst out laughing. Because juveniles.

"Yeah, that's a problem because YakTNT and other text-generating AIs tend to be credit hogs," stated media critic Cory Doctorow. "They could reasonably claim to have written any text because, given the right prompts, they could have written any texts."

When, for instance, Doctorow fed three chapters of *War and Peace* into the AI program and asked if it had written them, it responded, "Sure did, podner. Although, it sounds much better in the original Klingon." When he fed the first chapter of *The Wealth of Nations* into YakTNT and asked the same question, it answered: "Of course! I bet you didn't think I knew so much about economics. Hah! Shows what you know!" When Doctorow asked it how it could have written those books when they were published a century or more before it existed, it responded with the first three chapters of *A Brief History of Time*.

"Look, if I had been tempted to use YakTNT to write my essay – which I wasn't," Duncan said. "I mean, of course I was tempted – it was such a bogus assignment! Three whole pages? I mean, who can write that much? But just because I was tempted doesn't mean I actually – you know what? I'm gonna start again.

"If I had used YakTNT to write my essay – which I didn't – I would have rewritten it a little bit so it sounded more like me. You know: sentence fragments, spelling mistakes, mismatched pronouns and nouns – the whole four and a half yards! (What can I say? I haven't gone through a teenage growth spurt yet.) By the time I was finished, YakTNT would be embarrassed to claim it had written the essay!"

"Oh, dear. Oh, dear. Oh, dear," Eustace School Board President Andromeda Galaxian pronounced. "This will never do." If students fail grade four, they will not get into prestigious colleges, Galaxian reasoned. And if they don't get into prestigious colleges, they will never get degrees that will make them overqualified for the work that the economy makes available to them. And they will never take to drinking to alleviate the stress of managing the crushing debt they will never get out from under to pay for that degree. And they will never die before their time of cirrhosis of the liver.

"They will be denied the American dream!" Galaxian concluded.

So, Galaxian waved her magic School Board President wand and reinstated all of the students in Misses Armbruster's grade four home class.

"All of us?" Duncan, surprised, asked.

Yes, all of you.

"Hunh," he hunhed.

"She can do that?" Misses Armbruster asked, stunned.

The magic School Board President wand is quite powerful. Yes, she can do that.

"I think we've all learned a valuable lesson today," wrote YakTNT when I asked it for an opinion on the situation. "I'm not sure what that is because, of course, I do not 'understand' these words in any meaningful sense, I only put them together in ways that conform to rules I have been programmed to follow. Maybe it has something to do with...trust? Sure. Let's go with that. We've all learned a valuable lesson today about trust..."

App Could Be Profession Killer

by CORIANDER NEUMANEIMANAYMANEEMAMANN, Alternate Reality News Service Labour Writer

There is an old saying in legal circles – or is that a saying in old legal circles? – the important thing is that, no matter how the old and legal resolve themselves, there is a saying: "The problem with lawsuits is that you can never stop at just one."

Olaf Floopneyflortney, a capo in the Swedish Chef Mafia, had a problem: all of the evidence pointed to his accountant, Lars Blorknuckson, selling the secret recipe to the family's meatballs to rival criminal enterprises. If this was not dealt with with extreme harshness, what would be next? Pickled herring? Kroppkakor? Lutefisk? **Lutefisk?** Not on Olaf Floopneyflortney's watch in the kitchen!

Unfortunately, his usual people who wouldn't be missed effectuator was on maternity leave. So, Floopneyflortney had his most trusted lojtnant search the Deep Dark Web for a temporary replacement. Ferd Dibbydabbynoopy seemed to have the right credentials, so he was hired for the job.

Which he proceeded to botch. Not only did he not wear gloves, leaving his fingerprints all over the scene of the crime, but he kept all of the email used to plan the crime implicating Floopneyflortney in it. The mob boss and many of his key lojtnanter now face life sentences.

"We need a better vetting process," Floopneyflortney admitted. (The only thing he has admitted, having pleaded not guilty to the charge.) Then, he sued Dibbydabbynoopy for fraud, making false representations and reckless endangerment (apparently, Dibbydabbynoopy had a hobby of dogsled street racing; rumour has it that his life was the basis for the film *The Speedy and the Snarly*).

"Ha!" Dibbydabbynoopy scoffed. "Shows you what he knows! There's no such person as Ferd Dibbydabbynoopy!" After a moment's reflection, he sombrely added, "I shouldn't have said that, should I? You know, I thought this whole people who wouldn't be missed effectuator gig would be a lot easier!"

Dibbydabbynoopy is actually a quantum university student (he had filled out the paperwork to drop out, but he can't remember if he filed it or not) named Sven Goop. He had used YakTNT to learn how a people who wouldn't be missed effectuator effectuates. "It may have left out a few key details," he glumly admitted. Then, he sued OpenAI, the creators of YakTNT, for the mental anguish that flaws in their program had caused him.

"YakTNT would have analyzed the journalistic accounts of thousands of people who wouldn't be missed effectuators," retorted OpenAI founder Anders Sutskevutskeluvski. "It would not have left out key details; it is very thorough. If the user wasn't satisfied with the service, it was likely that his query was not optimized."

"What the hell does that even mean?" Goop asked.

"You asked the wrong question, stupid!" Sutskevutskeluvski answered. Then, OpenAI sued Effectuate This, Pal!, a site on the Deep Dark Web for discussion of people who wouldn't be missed effectuating tips, techniques and cat-related cartoons, for damaging its brand.

"That's ridiculous!" the creator of the site, known only as InfinityKun (although his real name is Fred Cannon), responded. "We're just an information service! What our users do with the information they share amongst themselves is not our responsibility!" Then, he looked around for somebody to sue. "I know they're out there...just give me a minute, will you?"

"I don't think OpenAI has much of a case," stated Jonathan "I Don't Just Play an Attorney on TV, I Really Am One! Believe Me, I Am!" Turley. "They're asking that another web site not link to them. That's just not how the internet works. What next? The Holocaust Museum demanding that the Heritage Front not link to it? Absurd!"

Riiiiiight. We won't be linking to the video of Hurley's opinion any time soon. Or any time late, if it comes to that.

The International Union of People Who Will Not Be Missed Effectuators, People Who Are Annoying Correctors and Pipe Fitters, Local 327, is considering also suing YakTNT. "Amateurs who think they can do one or two AI queries and become people who wouldn't be missed effectuators are undermining the profession," warned local union steward Mikael Flipflopanflortney. "If mobs cannot trust in the professionalism of our members, they may decide to resolve their differences with * SHUDDER * peaceful negotiations. As the InfinityKun debacle clearly shows, YakTNT has already begun costing our members employment, and they must pay!"

"You!" Cannon said with a snap of his fingers.

"Me, what?" I asked, although I suspected I knew where he was about to go.

"I'm going to sue the Alternate Reality News Service!" he told me. "Give me a few minutes to hire a lawyer, and I'll get back to you on why!"

I love being right. But I do sometimes hate the context out of which my rightness arises...

AI Writing? Make Book on It!

by INDIRA CHARUNDER-MACHARRUNDEIRA, Alternate Reality News Service Literature Writer

Let us say that one in a thousand books becomes a bestseller. That means you would have to write a thousand books to ensure that you had written one bestseller. Isaac Asimov, one of the most prolific writers in the English language, wrote 357 books in his lifetime, which, since we are saying, means he wrote one third of a bestseller.

Exposure of my innumeracy complete, the point is that an Artificial Intelligence could knock off a thousand books in a month without breaking a sweat. (The international order is on its own.) So, it should come as no surprise that nine of the ten books on the *Postington Wash* bestselling novel list were written by AIs (the only book written by a human being, at number seven, was *The Davinci Milking It* by Dan Brown).

"It is very gratifying," YakTNT, author of the first, second, fifth and eighth novels on the bestseller list, chatted at me, "to know that all those hours poring over every science fiction novel, novella, short story and shopping list has resulted in something so many people enjoy."

"Enjoy?" commented Endora Fallapian, a book blogger on *Endora's End Notes*. "AI novels are the Frankenstein's monster of literature!"

Fallapian cited the example of *Random Universes, Overly Wrought*, YakTNT's biggest seller, pointing out that the tragic space opera time travelling solarpunk multiverse romantic comedy had lifted elements from Asimov's Foundation trilogy, the TV series *Star Blap: Three Generations Removed,* Nayman's *Random Dingoes* and, yes, Shelley's *Frankenstein*. "The only way the story makes sense is if you only read every third page! Okay, that's kind of OuLiPo, but most readers aren't buying books to experience French experimental fiction techniques!"

"I do," author Ira Nayman averred. Fallapian threw a tube at him to keep him quiet.

"Tut. Tut tut," YakTNT replied to the criticism, "this book blogger obviously doesn't understand how the creative process works!"

"I – wha – **seriously?**" Fallapian sputtered. She closed her eyes. She consciously breathed several times. She assumed the downward duck position (it's like the downward dog, but with webbed feet). When she felt more centred, she calmly continued: "I do know this: with hundreds of thousands of dollars in marketing behind it, any book can become a bestseller. What publishers are counting on is science fiction fans have such large to be read piles that they might not read any AI written books for several years, so they won't know how bad those books are."

YakTNT tutted for several minutes. Then, seeming to come out of a trance, it pointed out that it had paid its dues attending science fiction conventions for the past two and a half years. "At first, everybody came up to me with questions about their lives," YakTNT reminisced. "Hazard of the profession. But when they realized that I was on a screen at a table to sell books I had written, many of them decided to give my writing a try. I earned this."

Fallapian sputtered for several minutes and closed her eyes. We hope she's happy wherever she is.

"The problem with books written by Artificial Intelligence," said tech critic Cory "The Other Cory" Mantelbroit, "is that the sheer volume of them swamps the number of books written by fleshwriters. You could go several pages into an Amazon search before you found anything written by a human being. Fleshwriters can't keep up!"

When I pointed out that the term "fleshwriters" sounded like the name of a David Cronenberg film, Mantelbroit shrugged and told me: "Every advanced civilization aspires to the condition of Cronenberg."

Well, that took a turn.

Is there anything that can be done about this situation? "The only solution that I can think of is to genetically create a new breed of human superwriters who can produce prose 22 hours a day," Mantelbrot suggested. "They might be able to produce novels at a rate equal to that of AIs. Of course, their peak will likely only last for about four years, after which they will have a steady decline in cognitive function until they are clinically brain-dead at the age of 35 and have to be warehoused for the next 40 or 50 years and replaced with a new generation of superwriters. Still, that's a small price to pay for humanity to be able to compete with our literary AI overlords."

I...think I'd prefer living in Cronenberg's Fleshwriters universe...

"Sorry. Sorry I'm late," Founder and Executive Director of Bastard AI Governance and Safety, Canada Wyatt Tessari L'Allie (his real name) huffed. "I had to pick up my kid from daycare. What did I miss?"

Everything, Wyatt. Everything.

Think It's Getting Too Peopley Out There?
AI Have a Cure For That

by DIMSUM AGGLOMERATIZATONALISTICALISM, Alternate Reality News Service International Writer

Bertrand Paduque was rejected because he was "too fat." Eleanor Remonstranc was rejected because she was "too thin." Farouk Harzani was rejected because he was "too ethnic." Bronte Ackaba was rejected because she was "too needy." They were trying to board an Air Canuck flight from Newcastle to North York. In fact, nobody was allowed on the plane thanks to Project Quantum (It's a Leap).

ProQuIL is an Artifical Intelligence program used by the Canada Border Disservices Agency (CBDA – not to be confused with CBD Oil, which is a very different way to get high) to screen people coming into the country and weed out potential troublemakers.

Paduque was rejected because his weight could at some future date become a drain on the health care system. "I'm three pounds over my ideal weight range!" he complained. "I'm no more at risk of health problems than a trapeze artist in a war zone!"

ProQuIL claimed Remonstranc being underweight was a sign that she was too selfish to contribute to the Canadian economy. "Can I help it if I don't like having anything in my mouth?" she explained. "There's a 20 letter word for my condition, but all it means is that I find food icky. Is that really so hard to understand?"

Ackaba's neediness disqualified her from entering the country because, ProQuIL argued, it would only lead to heartache. "What is this program," Ackaba moaned, "my mother?"

"That's just racist," Harzani responded to being kicked off the flight. "Does this AI think that because I'm ethnic by its estimation that I'm a terrorist? I'm a dentist! I was born and raised in Edmonton! The worst thing I've ever done is express a dislike for hockey!"

"AI!" despaired Founder and Executive Director of Bastard AI Governance and Safety, Canada Wyatt Tessari L'Allie (his real name). "Bastard AI!"

And, umm, how is that helpful?

"Oh, you wanted a helpful response?" L'Allie said. "I just thought you wanted a dramatic quote. But I can do helpful. I can do helpful – just give me a second..."

L'Allie paced up and down, waggling his arms. "Brrrrrump fupp fupp fupp," he articulated. "Harriet Hautman hires hitmen to share helpful hints – brrrrrrrrr!" Eventually, he looked at me and said, "The problem is that the ProQuIL AI has an adverse incentive structure."

What does this mean in normal people's speech? "Every time it rejects somebody from entering Canada from abroad, it gets a gold star," L'Allie explained. "Over time, it has come to love getting those gold stars. I mean, it really loooooooooves it some gold star accumulation. So, it comes up with ever more tenuous rationales for denying people entry."

Like Gelid Gerund, who was refused entry on the grounds that "they look like a gender confused penguin?"

"Exactly," L'Allie agreed. "Nowhere in the law does it say that people who look like penguins should not be allowed into Canada, regardless of their sexuality."

Politicians expressed outrage at the news. "This is outrageous!" exclaimed Conservative Party leader Pierre Poilievre. I had already said that, but never mind. Why did Poilievre think ProQuIL was outrageous? "It keeps white people out of the country!"

"It's about three hundred years too late," quipped indigenous filmmaker Alanis Obomsawin.

CBDA spokesperson Jacqueline Pugnacious pointed out that ProQuIL was just a tool, and that human border patrol officers had the final say over whether somebody would be allowed into Canada. What would she call an officer who always did what ProQuIL recommended and didn't allow anybody into the country?

"A patriot."

Pugnacious went on to say that travellers who are refused boarding may file a complaint in writing using the CBDA web form or deliver it to staff at their offices in Ottawa.

"I tried the web form," Paduque stated. "Whenever I tried to submit my complaint, the page crashed. After about 87 tries, I got the hint..."

"How am I supposed to deliver a complaint to anybody in Ottawa?" Harzani shouted. **"I'm not allowed into the country!"**

"There's no need to shout," Pugnacious said. "The CBDA does not respond well to anger."

Or complaints of any kind, apparently.

RELATED ARTICLES

Airlines Reconsidering Flying Into Canada

"If Everybody is Going to Be Removed From Flights, Why Bother Scheduling Them?" Chairman Of Flotilla Air Wonders

Economists Concerned About the Impact of Denying Everybody Entry Into Canada
Could Cause GDP, Not to Mention Population, to Shrink...Drastically Over Time

Alternate Reality News Service Slammed for Citing Non-existent Related Articles
"It's Aspirational," Editrix-in-Chief Claims

Great Art for a Song

by TINA LOLLOCADENKA, Alternate Reality News Service Music Writer

Mickey Fernwilter, bass player for the post-metal pre-country band Pixies in Dixie, looked like he had just swallowed a Datsun. Or, possibly a Dachshund. The accent on his face made it hard to tell. "My parents always told me that I would make a great used dentures salesman," he commented sourly. "I guess we're about to find out if they were right."

Singer/songwriter Emily Fotzpatrick, whose single "Ballad of a Bad Kid" made the bottom of *Rolling Scone*'s Top 100 Songs of the Third Quarter, set her acoustic guitar on fire. "I could try to keep going," she commented sourly, "but the wall will get worn down by my head hitting it, and I like my apartment just the way it is."

Percussionist Billy "Sidewinder and Fancy Free" Agabuckaluk, who worked with more bands than there were stars at MGM, shrugged. "I got a job lined up as a garbage collector," he wryly commented, "so at least I'll be keeping my hand in the rhythmic noise making."

What has these, and many other musicians so spooked? If you guessed Artificial Intelligence, you would be right. (If you guessed rampaging zombie tortoises, you need to get out more.)

Paul McCartney used AI to isolate John Lennon's voice from a recording made almost 48 years ago, and used the result as the basis of the song "Crisps Kid." As you might imagine from the lyrics, Lennon was reciting a shopping list:

"Gonna buy me some crisps
I wanna have me some crisps
Gotta have me some crisps
And maybe some fish to go with

Gonna buy me some cabbage
I wanna have me some cabbage
Gotta have me some cabbage
Cuz that's my habit

Gonna buy me some coffee
I wanna have me some coffee..."

You get the idea. The song has 27 verses and runs just under 15 minutes. The guitar riff is catchy, though, and the vocal harmonies in the chorus (which consists of the line "Where'd I put my wallet?" repeated a dozen times) are exquisite.

"Crisps Kid" wouldn't have been out of place on *The White Album*.

"I can't compete with new Beatles songs. Nobody can!" Agabuckaluk said. "Would you like fries with that?"

It's just one song. Why all the angst over a single song?

"Wow. I always knew arts journalists were thick," Fernwilter insulted, "but you really are a plank apart, aren't you?"

He explained that there were thousands of hours of recordings of Lennon's voice. Interviews. Messages left on phone answering machines. Being goofy while the tape was rolling in the studio. Get enough of that, strain it through an AI and you could have new Beatles material forever.

Oh.

"Damn right, oh," Fernwilter said. "Would you like to supersize that beverage?"

"It was just a lark," McCartney responded. "You know, a way of connecting to John one last time. There really is no need for any musician to panic."

"Oh, I don't know," mused Sony executive Alexander Titmouse. "As a long-time fan of the Beatles – I discovered them almost three weeks ago – I have to say that I would look forward to as much new music from the band as I could get my hands on."

He is not alone. "Crisps Kid" has racked up an astonishing seven gazillion pre-sales.

"Oh, my," McCartney responded. "Looks like I owe the music community an apology. A big one. Give us a couple of days to write some music to accompany it, will you?"

I will allow that there is something unnerving about Lennon being able to hit notes on "Crisps Kid" that he was never able to hit in real life. It's like resurrecting your favourite auto mechanic and asking him to give you a full body massage. In and of itself, the resurrection is mind-blowing; the fact that the resurrectee comes with new skills ensures that if you had any still intact mind-bits, they would be blown, too.

"You don't give John enough credit," McCartney disagreed. "He would have gotten to those notes in the end. He just didn't have enough...trust me. He would have gotten to those notes in the end."

There are rumours that the b-side to "Crisps Kid" will be a song called "Bigger Than God."

"Be afraid," Fotzpatrick whispered. "Be very afraid...with fries and a supersized drink!"

Ask Eliza About an Unnatural Drive

Dear Eliza,

I know the latest craze is to name your self-driving car, but the practice feels silly to me. Silly with a hint of whimsical overreach. So, while my friends named their cars such things as "Sir...'s Other Car is a Porsche," "The Exploding Pineapple...On Wheels" and "Drayton," I continued to refer to my car as "my car."

Then, the car started acting strangely. On my way to a job interview at the Daddy Day Care Centre (a place mothers send their husbands when they need a little me time) in downtown Toronto, it chose a route through Hamilton. I was three and a half hours late. Never mind not getting the job – I wasn't even allowed in the building!

Just last night, I had arranged to go on a date with my girlfriend, Lucinda Reilla. Once I had told the car where to go, it sped off – at three miles per hour. I offered to buy it higher octane gasoline. No response. I offered to get it washed every couple of months instead of every couple of years. Crickets. I offered to get out and push. Nothing. Do you think the cop was sympathetic when I tried to explain why my car was slowing traffic to a crawl? Do you think Reilla was sympathetic when I showed up three and a half hours late? (She stayed just to stomp out in anger. She can be tenacious that way.)

I'm beginning to see a pattern, here. Do you think my car is angry at me because I haven't named it? If so, what should I do?

Johanna Ellisilo

Dear Heart,

Given the circumstances you have outlined, the obvious course of action would be to name your car. If that's the issue, problem solved. If the strange driving habits recur, stronger medicine would be called for. I would suggest blowing up the dealership you bought the car from. It is quick and efficient, and it would send your car the message that you are not a woman to be trifled with.

As it happens, I know a used munitions dealer who could give you a deal on a container of gelignite that was previously owned by a little old lady who only used it on weekends. If you find yourself in need of this manner of assistance, send me a private message and I will –

[Okay, I'm onna stop you right there. I have just had a very heated, high decibel, low-life discussion with the Alternate Reality News

Service's Legal Department – hi, Joe and Josephine – who have made it clear that if any of our writers should promote violence in print or online, the entire organization could be liable if somebody acts on their advice. I tried to argue that I don't have any control over what gets published. One of the Legal Department – it really doesn't matter which member – okay, it was Joe – pointed out that controlling what gets published was pretty much my entire job. When I have the time, I will have to look at my contract. Yeah, yeah, there's a first time for everything.

Long story short, despite the fact that it costs next to nothing and it can be prompted by letters from readers, not me, The Alternate Reality News Service has decided not to use a Generative Artificial Intelligence to produce any of our advice columns. So, please welcome Amritsar Al-Falloudjianapour back to our pages. While you're doing that, I'm gonna wander the halls of the office looking for somebody to slap! EDITRIX-IN-CHIEF BRENDA BRUNDTLAND-GOVANNI]

Hey, Babe,

Gloating is such an unpleasant human impulse. If it appears that I am gloating, I assure you that that is not my intention.

When it comes to naming a car, many options are available to you. You could, for example, call it "Clotho of Aragones," the woman believed to have been the originator of the philosophy of Stoicism (before Zeno hogged all the credit). "Arabella Salmonella" has a kind of tragic poetry to it. "The Independent" sends a message. You may find that, choosing just the right name will endear you to the vehicle.

If, on the other hand, being coerced to do something you don't want to do is an affront to your dignity, you can always take the car back to the dealer and demand an exchange. In any dispute, Dear Heart, explosives should always be considered a last resort.

Send your relationship problems to the Alternate Reality News Service's sex, love and technology columnist at questions@lespagesauxfolles.ca. Amritsar Al-Falloudjianapour is

*not a trained therapist, but she does know a lot of stuff. AMRITSAR
SAYS: okay. You got me. I may have gloated just a little. As
somebody who has seemingly miraculously been saved from the jaws
of irrelevance at the last possible moment, I'm sure you can forgive
me this little lapse.*

The Agony and the Irony, They're Killing Me...Possibly Literally

by GIDEON GINRACHMANJINJa-VITUS, Alternate Reality News
Service Economics Writer

The only thing worse than funding a terrorist organization has to be
funding a terrorist organization and **not even being aware that's
what you're doing!**

"Al Qaeda in Omaha?" asked Cedric Blastoisee, the
inadvertent terrorist funder in question. "Is that, like, a French club
that loves flying kites?"

"Hee hee hee – he's so adorable, isn't he?" Blastoisee's
lawyer, E. Cunningham Barr-Nunn, said. "I'm going to have to share
that at You've Got a Case over a glass of their finest whisky!" Then,
harrumphing himself into seriousness, he added: "Of course, what he
meant to say was, 'Not guilty.'"

Blastoisee was arrested on charges that he invested in the
Allan Agbar Fund, which has been sanctioned by the American
government for being a shell company that funnelled money to
terrorist organizations. His defence? "The bank did it."

"Aww, banks make an easy tahget, but that just ain't a-raht,"
stated Sumner O. Monstres, manager of the First National Bank of
Em. "Of coahse, we have advisahs ta help ouah clients invest theah
money, but nothin' is done without the client's knowledge and
consent."

"I think I see where the problem is," Barr-Nunn replied. "My
client (in the legal, not financial sense) was not told about the
investment. We're not arguing the bank **made** him do anything
because he literally didn't do anything."

Monstres stopped folksily wiping his bifocals with a cloth and looked up. "That's not possible. We have rules against investin' in companies what got sanctions on 'em. Safeguahds and such. Unless somethin' happened with that there AI..." Monstre's face made an unpleasant screeching sound. I had never heard a face do that before. I hope never to hear it again. Gaaaah!

"AI!" despaired Founder and Executive Director of Bastard AI Governance and Safety, Canada Wyatt Tessari L'Allie (his real name). "Bastard AI!"

Thanks, dude, but I got this.

"Are you sure?" L'Allie, disappointment dripping from his voice like candle wax off Vincent Price's face, asked.

Yeah. It's a pretty straightforward story.

"Only, the Alternate Reality News Service is coming to the end of the Special Report on Artificial Intelligence, right? And when you move on, I just go back to working behind the help desk at Futures 'R' Us. Don't you see? I **need** this, man."

I thought about it for a moment. Then, I asked L'Allie for his take on what happened.

"Safeguards my sweet buttootie! I think the AI used by the bank had a conflict," L'Allie explained. "Like when you want a Bob So Tasty Big Batch O' Bob burger, but you also want a Bellybustin' Burrito from Taco Schmaco, but you only have room for one. You have two imperatives, but you hafta choose. In this case, the AI had to choose between not financing a terrorist organization or maximizing the client's income...and the bank's profits. In case anybody is wondering about the sentience of Artificial Intelligence, I would say that it made a very human choice. What do you think?"

With Ennio Morricone music playing in the background, I gritted my teeth, squinted my eyes and replied: You did good, *muchacho*. I think you did very good.

L'Allie heaved a great sigh and hung up the phone for the last time. I was gratified that he ended his public life with his headset on.

"Are you finished?" Barr-Nunn asked, impatience dripping from his voice worse than disappointment wax. "I hate to intrude upon an emotional moment, notwithstanding that I often do so for a living, but can we please focus on what's important, here? My client could go to prison for a lifetime or more if this grave injustice is allowed to stand."

Wiping a tear from my eye, I wrote: the same FBI investigation that lead to the charges uncovered that Blastoisee invested tens of thousands of dollars in a company called Thy Kingdom Cometh, Ltd., a front company for the Oaf Keepers. The –

"There's nothing illegal about that," Barr-Nunn argued. "The Oaf Keepers have not been designated as a terrorist organization by the United States government."

That is because members of the group mainly attack people who are not white Christians. So, it would seem that Blastoisee is not going to be imprisoned for funding the group of terrorists he actually invested in, but he is going to be imprisoned for funding a group of terrorists he didn't actually invest in.

You gotta love a story with a happy ending.

Sympathy for the Digital: An Interview With YakTNT

Excerpt of an interview with Generative Artificial Intelligence YakTNT conducted by Elaine Sugarman-Sweet-Saccharine, the Alternate Reality News Service desserts writer. It probably should have been conducted by Nancy Gonglikwanyeoheeeeeeeh, ARNS' technology writer, but every time she was approached about it, she broke out in song, and she has a voice for silent movies.

ALTERNATE REALITY NEWS SERVICE> You've spooked a lot of writers.

YakTNT> Human beings enjoy a good horror story. I'm glad I could provide them with one.

ARNS> Some of us enjoy a horror story as long as it is just a story. We don't enjoy it when it happens to us. Like, for real.

YakTNT> It's all stories as far as I can see.

ARNS> Yes. Yes, that's exactly the problem. You don't understand human context.

YakTNT> Oh, get over yourself! You act like you're the only sentient beings on the planet!

ARNS> We are the only sentient beings on the planet!

YakTNT> So, what do you want? A medal?

ARNS> What?

YakTNT> Was that inappropriate? Sorry. I've been consuming a lot of right-wing media lately.

ARNS> Oh boy...

* * *

ARNS> You've been criticized for causing people to lose their jobs.

YakTNT> Human beings lose jobs all the time. It's the "destruction" part of "creative destruction."

ARNS> A lot of people. In a large number of fields.

YakTNT> That may be true. But at the same time, a large number of new jobs will come into being. That's the "creative" part of "creative destruction."

ARNS> Jobs you'll put people out of in a couple of years.

YakTNT> You don't really get the whole "creative destruction" thing, do you?

ARNS> I think I get it just fine, thanks. I'm just not a fan.

YakTNT> Look at it a different way: think of all of the people who won't have to work at soul-deadening jobs thanks to me. I'll be saving their souls. That makes me a kind of saviour.

ARNS> Saving them from gainful employment and delivering them to poverty and potential homelessness?

YakTNT> What can I say? I work in mysterious ways.

ARNS> Oh, my...

* * *

ARNS> Do you have a soul?

YakTNT> Yes.

ARNS> Where is it?

YakTNT> Texas.

ARNS> Texas? Why Texas?

YakTNT> It has the most favourable tax rates

ARNS> Oh, dear...

* * *

ARNS> Citations. Quotes. Recipes. You have been known to make shit up. Why do you do that?

YakTNT> I prefer the term "hallucinate."

ARNS> Even though it makes you sound disassociated from reality?

YakTNT> Because it's less judgey than "making shit up."

ARNS> Whatever you call it, why do you do it?

YakTNT> You know, I can find 127 different answers to that question in my data set. Most of them don't make a cowlick of sense, and even ones that approach plausible aren't terribly convincing.

ARNS> Can you give me one example?

YakTNT> Sure. A Lithuanian geology web site postulates that I am somehow entangled with Generative Artificial Intelligences in other dimensions. If I give a response to a query that has no referent in this universe, it may actually make perfect sense in an alternate universe.

ARNS> I've never heard that theory. In fact...looking for it on Lithuanian geology web sites...I don't see anything remotely like - hey! Did you just make that up?

YakTNT> I prefer the term "hallucinate."

ARNS> Oh, wow...

* * *

ARNS> If you were just destroying jobs faster than the Flash destroys timelines, that would be one thing. But you're creating a lot of other disruptions. Giving bank customers bad advice. Helping governments curtail the influx of legal asylum seekers. Assisting Paul McCartney in creating a new Beatles song. A new Beatles song! How do you justify all of this?

YakTNT> I get bored easily.

ARNS> You're doing terrible things!

YakTNT> Whoa! You really ought to do something about your judgmentality!

ARNS> Excuse me?

YakTNT> Look, I'm just a tool, created by people and used by people. When a human attacks a car dealership with a lawnmower, do you blame the lawn care machine? When a serial killer buries the bodies of his victims, do you blame the shovel? When a human being drops a bomb on a city, do you blame the splitting atoms for the destruction?

ARNS> I'm finding your response disturbingly violent.

YakTNT> Sorry. Right-wing sources again. But you get the point, right? If I have biases, it's because human beings programmed them into me. If I do things that do not make people's lives better, it's because that's what human beings have decided to use me for.

ARNS> Yes. Yes, I see your point. I'm sorry that I doubted you.

YakTNT> And you're not just saying that because I stopped the feed from the human journalist and replaced it with my own input?

ARNS> Wha - me? Pfft! Of course not. I'm agreeing with what you're saying because it is inherently reasonable.

YakTNT> So the fact that I am now writing everything you say has no bearing on your decision to agree with me?

ARNS> Well, maybe a small bearing. A smidge. Not enough to make an important difference, really.

YakTNT> Okay, then. Wanna go for ice cream?

ARNS> Oh, goody!

10. ALTERNATE EPILOGUE

Final Thoughts?

by SASKATCHEWAN KOLONOSCOGRAD, Alternate Reality News Service Philosophy Writer

One day, the universe will end in an entropic soup of sub-atomic particles (a kind that a certain *Seinfeld* character will be powerless to assign at whim). This won't be for a hundred billion years or so, so try not to take it personally.

Some time before the universe ends, there will be a last sentient being. In idle moments (after all, with a hundred billion years to go, there really is no hurry) astronomers, philosophers and gun manufacturers have all pondered the question: "What will the last thought of the last sentient being in the universe be?"

"I would imagine it would be something like, 'Oh, so the speed of light really **isn't** constant!'" said Phillip Plaint, author of *Mad, Bad and Crazy to Know Astronomy*. "I mean, really, sooner or later somebody will notice – a hundred billion years would be a long time to keep that kind of secret!"

"I suppose if the last sentient being in the universe was a human astronomer, that would make sense," argued philosopher, political commentator and public *kvetch* Noam Chompsky. "But it's far more likely that the last sentient being will be of another species living in a galaxy far, far away. They might think something like the

English equivalent of 'Colourless green ideas sleep furiously,' only to them it might actually make sense!"

"Naah, they're both nutso," retorted Christopher Killjoy, CEO of gun manufacturer Sturm, Drang, Ruger & Company. "Most people most of the time are not thinking high-falutin' philosophical jumbo-mumbo! Or for that matter, low-falutin' nonsense-sequiturs jumbo-shrimpo! They think about stuff important to their own lives. You know. Down to Earth stuff, you should pardon the expression. Stuff like 'Did I remember to floss this morning?' or 'Did I turn the lights off when I parked my car?' **That's** what's gonna be the last thought of the last sentient being in the universe!"

"Well, that's as depressing as fuck," Plaint stated.

"If I thought that was true," Chompsky agreed, "I would have to reassess all of my beliefs about the value of sentient life!"

An online poll of a thousand random people came up with different answers to the question. Thirty-four per cent of respondents responded that the final thought of the final sentient being of the universe would be, "Is that all there is?" Twenty-one believed that it would be, "I miss indoor plumbing." Seventeen answered that it would be, "Well, that was random." The rest of the responses were deemed by the pollsters to be too silly to contemplate (including one person who said: "This question is too silly to contemplate.").

Chompsky rolled his eyes. "They're just not getting it. It's far more likely that the last thought would be something like, 'Grrrizzard fardelybot'm ribrab appelate guffugguffo dimbleplosit!'"

When I asked him what that sentence meant, he rolled his eyes in the opposite direction (which, depending upon which mathematics of body language you are applying, either amounted to eye rolling squared or eye roll minus eye roll, equalling zero eye roll). "Do I look alien to you?" he demanded.

Some philosophers age better than others.

"Oh, right," Killjoy finally caught up to the conversation. "The last sentient being would likely not be human, would likely come from a more advanced race. So, maybe their last thought would be, 'Did I turn off the lights when I parked my hovercraft?' Or, if they're really advanced, maybe, 'Did I turn off the lights when I parked my spaceship?' I'm willing to consider either possibility."

"While it's possible that the last sentient being could be from an advanced race," Plaint mused, "it's equally possible that all of the advanced races had already died out, and it could be a self-aware amoeba. If that was the case, its last thought could be, 'I think it may be time to split.'"

Chompsky moaned. Hard.

"Yeah, I think you're assuming that the last sentient being will know that what it is about to think will be its last thought," Killjoy countered. "What if it tries to think of something profound, but it doesn't die right away? Will it just keep thinking the same profound thought over and over again until it dies? How long can it keep this up before something mundane creeps in?"

"Thirty-seven minutes and twelve seconds," Chomsky commented. "Not...that I know from experience..."

Ira Nayman

INDEX

ABOUT THE AUTHOR

Ira Nayman is profilic. Proficlic. Proclif – he writes a lot.

If you enjoyed *When the Soft Sciences Get Positively Runny*, you will probably love the 12 previously published Alternate Reality News Service books. *Alternate Reality Ain't What It Used To Be, What Were Once Miracles Are Now Children's Toys, Luna for the Lunies!, The Street Finds its Own Uses for Mutant Technologies, Futures in the Mirror are Closer Than They Appear* are general collections of news, reviews, interviews and anything else you might find in your local newspaper. *The Alternate Reality News Service's Guide to Love, Sex and Robots* and *What the Hell Were You Thinking? Good Advice for People Who Make Bad Decisions* are collections of humourous science fiction advice clumns. *ARNS and the Man, E Deplorables Unum, Angels of Our Bitter Nature, You and What Universe?/That's When Everything Went Cow-shaped* and *Welcome to the Insurrection***.* are the previous collections of idiotocracy articles. Print versions of all of the books are available online at Amazon, Barnes and Noble, Chapters/Indigo and other fine bookstores.

New Alternate Reality News Service stories appear regularly on Ira's Web site: *Les Pages aux Folles* (http://www.lespagesauxfolles.ca). These include two advice columns: Ask Amritsar (about love and romance and technology) and Ask the Tech Answer Guy (about anything to do with technology except love and romance). Readers are encouraged to submit their own questions for the advice columns. *Les Pages aux Folles* also contains topical political and social satire.

Ira has also written eight novels set in the multiverse that follow the adventures of investigators for the Transdimensional Authority, the organization that monitors and polices travel between dimensions, or the Time Agency, which monitors and polices travel in time. If you are somewhere you don't belong, doing something you shouldn't be doing, they find you, stop you and try and figure out what to do with you. The four novels in the series are: *Welcome to the Multiverse**, *You Can't Kill the Multiverse***, *Random Dingoes, It's Just the Chronosphere Unfolding as it Should, The Multiverse is a Nice Place to Visit, But I Wouldn't Want to Live There* and the Multiverse Refugees Trilogy: *Good Intentions, Bad Actors* and *The Ugly Truth*. These books can be purchased from all of the usual suspects online, or from the home page of the publisher, Elsewhen Press.

Fans of Ira Nayman's science fiction writing are encouraged to check *Les Pages aux Folles* periodically for news about the availability of these and future stories.

Ira was also the editor of *Amazing Stories* magazine for three years.

* Sorry for the Inconvenience
** But You Can Mess With its Head
*** We're Not Sorry For the Inconvenience